Amelia Ford graduated from Birmingham University, UK with a degree in History and after teaching for fifteen years decided to turn her hand to writing contemporary women's fiction. She lives with her husband and three children in the heart of Kent. Tagan's Child is the first novel in the Tagan series.

For more information about Amelia and her books visit
www.amelia-ford.com
www.facebook.com/AmeliaFordAuthor

ALSO BY AMELIA FORD

Tagan's Change, Book 2

Tagan's Chase, Book 3

Tagan's Chance, Book 4

Coming Soon

Damned and Damaged

TAGAN'S CHILD

THE TAGAN SERIES - BOOK 1

AMELIA FORD

COPYRIGHT © 2018 AMELIA FORD

2nd Edition

ISBN 978-0-9929-882-7-2

Acknowledgements

Thank you to all those people who helped me on this journey. Without your help and support this book would never have reached completion. You know who you are. I would also like to thank @sirjotajota for producing such a brilliant front cover. Finally, thank you to my amazing children who have put up with a mum whose head has been in a fictional world for a significant portion of the last three and a half years.

For my husband whose encouragement and support are unstinting.

"**G**oodnight lovely boy." I stroked the side of my eight-year-old nephew's pale face, noticing the purplish smudges under his eyes caused by a day of crying. I tucked his duvet in around his shoulders. "Your mummy would be so proud of you. *I'm* so proud of you, it's been a difficult day and you've coped with it so well."

"I miss her auntie Sophie." His voice wobbled and I watched a tear roll down each cheek. My heart went out to him. There had been times today when my grief had threatened to engulf me, and yet, in spite of his tears and his own grief, he had tried to be *my* pillar of strength.

"Come here." I gathered him in my arms and he began to sob quietly into my shoulder.

It was the first anniversary of Katie's death. A year ago today her life had been snuffed out on a lane just outside our village when her car had skidded on a patch of ice causing her to lose control and nose-dive into a ditch. She suffered fatal head injuries. It was the tragic end of a young woman's life, the end of a doting mother and the end of my very special sister.

"I know you miss her, my darling, I miss her too." My throat constricted. I closed my eyes and took a deep breath willing my tears to stay put. The pain my sister's death had caused could only be matched by the pain I felt for my nephew's loss. No child should ever have to suffer the death of their mother.

Toby took a shuddering breath. "Do you think she can see us?" He wiped his eyes.

"I'm sure she can." I gave him a reassuring squeeze. I sat back and put my hands on his shoulders. "Your mummy is with you every second of every day, watching over you, watching you grow into a clever, funny, and wonderful young man."

He gave me a weak smile.

"She loves you and is counting on you to hold your head up high and be brave."

He sat up a little straighter and wiped his nose on the sleeve of his pyjamas. "I mustn't let her down must I?"

His look of fragile determination swelled my heart. "You could never let her down."

He was a handsome little boy, tall and muscular for an eight-year-old with a natural talent for sport and a distinct phobia of hairdressers.

I brushed a curl away from his right eye. I felt a desperate urge to reassure him and let him know he wasn't alone. "I want you to know that I'll always be here for you.

I may not be your mummy, but I will always look after you and keep you safe as if I were."

Toby nodded and his bottom lip trembled.

I wasn't sure I could hold it together for much longer. I got to my feet. "It's getting late and you've got school tomorrow."

I said this maybe a little too brusquely as I struggled to hold back the tears. I needed to go downstairs and bury myself in the sofa so Toby couldn't hear my sobs. But not before I had made a significant dent in the bottle of wine chilling in the fridge.

I stood up and switched the lamp off beside his bed.

"I love you Auntie Sophie."

"I love you too," I said, swallowing back the lump in my throat. I bent down and gave him a kiss on the cheek. "Sleep tight and see you in the morning."

I made my way down to the kitchen taking a deep breath and exhaling slowly in the hope that it would ease the pain lodged in my chest. It had been a tough day and I felt sad and wrung out. I knew that Toby would be asleep in a matter of minutes. I, on the other hand, would struggle to find any respite in sleep until the early hours of tomorrow morning. Insomnia had become my new best friend since Katie's death. Why was it that, as an adult, I had lost the ability to switch off? I envied that about children.

I let Toby's dog, a Weimaraner called Mungo, out for a last wee before retrieving the bottle of wine from the fridge. All I wanted to do now was curl up on the sofa and cry until I couldn't cry anymore. I made my way into the lounge and poured myself a glass. I downed it and stared into the fire roaring in the log burner. My tears began to fall. I put my glass on the coffee table and buried my face in the cushions. I sobbed for my sister and the future she would never have, for Toby who would never feel his mother's comforting arms around him again, and for myself, who felt the loss of Katie so keenly that it had been a constant weight tugging at my heart over the last twelve months.

Eventually, my tears subsided and my grief was reduced to dry, chest heaving sobs. Despite feeling exhausted, I knew if I went to bed now I would only lie there, staring at the ceiling in the dark. I scoured the sitting room for my Kindle. The days I could cope with, I could keep busy and push the shadows of grief to the background, but it was the nights I struggled with most when the house was quiet and dark. Darkness only seemed to emphasise my sadness and fear.

Mungo barked outside the back door. I suspected he hadn't barked sooner because he'd been through the rubbish bag I'd put out earlier. I opened the door and he came trotting in licking his lips confirming my suspicions. "You are a naughty dog!"

He gave me a look as if to say *'Well, if you hadn't left me out there so long I wouldn't have been forced to do it'*. An uninvited blast of cold air chased in after him and I shut the door quickly. "It's chilly out there Mung."

Disinterested in any assessment of the weather, he sat expectantly, swishing his tail across the floor waiting for his last biscuit of the day. I couldn't help but chuckle. "Mungo, all you think about is your stomach." I held out my hand. "Paw!"

He quickly obliged. I gave him a biscuit and he swallowed it whole. I smiled and bent down to give him a kiss on his wet nose. Even though he was Toby's dog and his greediness knew no bounds, I was fonder of the mutt than I cared to admit. He sauntered off to his bed and I went back into the lounge, refilled my glass and sat back down on the sofa.

Earlier this afternoon, we'd visited the place where we had scattered Katie's ashes. It was a beautiful spot and a great vantage point on the South Downs. It was one of the places where we had all loved to walk. Toby and I had spent a long time sitting on the hill, looking into the distance and reminiscing about the sweet, gentle, fun loving person we had both lost. We laughed and cried and hugged one another, and then walked down the hill to the village pub where they were holding Hatherley's annual Thanksgiving festival. It was a celebration peculiar to our village, a throwback to the area's farming roots. We stayed long enough to watch the procession leave the pub as it began the traditional candlelit walk through the high street, and then went home. Neither of us felt in the mood to take part.

I sighed. Where was my Kindle? I felt between the cushions of the sofa to see if it had slipped down between them, but there was no sign of it. I continued my search until I remembered it was on my bedside table. I checked the front and back door were locked and switched off the lights before heading upstairs, leaving the darkness of downstairs behind me.

I passed Toby's bedroom door and a sad smile crept across my face. Katie had met his father, Tagan, at a bar one night whilst she was in her first year at university. She'd quickly become besotted with him. Two months later he walked out of her life as quickly as he had walked in, leaving her pregnant and devastated. She had tried to contact him, but he hadn't return her calls. *Callous Bastard!* He was obviously a player and my poor sister had got her fingers burnt. The only good to come out of it was Toby, who quickly became the centre of her life and it was him that helped to heal her wounds. Unfortunately, the wounds ran deep and it was obvious to anyone who knew her well, that some of the sparkle had gone from her eyes.

I brushed my teeth and padded into the bedroom, my eyes settling on the Kindle on the nightstand. *Ah, there it is!* I got into my pyjamas and climbed into bed, my thoughts turning to my own love life. I had been dating Marcus Hampton one of the junior partners at the local doctor's surgery for a couple of months now. He was keen and clearly wanted to take our relationship further. I enjoyed our meals out, trips to the cinema and a kiss at the end of the evening, but after a number of failed relationships, that had been enough up until now. I liked him. He was nice looking and had a good sense of humour, even if he was a bit short. The problem was, like with most of the men I had dated, I didn't feel there was much chemistry. I remember Katie telling me that when she and Tagan had been together it was like there was a palpable electricity that charged between them. I had to take her word for it because I'd never felt anything like that. I obviously wasn't the chemical or electrical type.

When I really thought about it I had never really let anyone get too close. I preferred to keep men at a distance where they couldn't hurt me, disappoint me or *die*, just like most of the other important people in my life had done. Unfortunately, there had been a rather sad pattern to my existence. I had lost my father, my mother and now my sister and their deaths had left me with a debilitating fear of what the future might hold. I was powerless against the nasty little voice in my head, which was always ready to whisper sickening doubts about what could happen and what might be. I did my best to silence it, but it was never long before it resurfaced.

I sighed and looked over at the bedside clock. It was getting late. It was Monday tomorrow and the usual routine would begin for another week. I hadn't ironed Toby's school shirt and I had to get to the Cash and Carry first thing.

My phone bleeped with a message. I picked it up.

'Hi Gorgeous. Hope today hasn't been too traumatic for you. Just to say I'm thinking of you. I've got a busy week ahead, but can't wait to see you on Friday. Thought maybe we could catch a film and go for dinner afterwards. Give me a call and let me know what you fancy. Marcus x'

I smiled to myself. He *was* very sweet. I tapped out my reply.

'Thank you. It's been pretty tough. I'll have a look at what's on and give you a ring.' I paused. Oh what the hell! *'I'll miss you. Sophiex.'*

It was the first time I had said anything like that to him. Perhaps it was time to settle for what I had and move our relationship on. My phone bleeped back almost immediately.

'I'll miss you too! Marcusxxx'

I put the phone back on my bedside. Yes, maybe I would give Dr Marcus Hampton more of a chance.

2

The persistent buzz of the alarm clock dragged me out of my slumber. *I had slept!* I couldn't believe it. I had actually fallen asleep quickly and slept *all* night. I couldn't remember the last time that had happened. I jumped out of bed. A good night's sleep was a good omen. Yesterday had obviously been somewhat of a watershed and I had woken up feeling uncharacteristically optimistic. When I had showered and dressed I went into Toby's room. "Time to get up," I said, pulling back the curtains. There was a slight stirring, but no answer so I left him to come to on his own and went downstairs into the kitchen. Mungo was lying in his bed and barely opened his eyes to register who it was.

"You need to go outside, whether you like it or not." I held open the back door. He ignored me. "Mungo!" I said more insistently, "Out!"

He got up, stretched as if he had all the time in the world

and ambled out, not giving me a second glance. I switched the kettle on and put the breakfast things out on the table.

"Toby!" I turned the radio on and found myself humming along to it and then Mungo scratched at the back door. I let him in and he went straight back to his bed, grumbling to himself as he did two circuits of the confined space before settling back down. I made a cup of tea and Toby came into the kitchen in his pyjamas, looking half asleep.

"Morning sweetheart," I said brightly.

He mumbled something which I think was '*Morning*' and got into Mungo's bed, laying his head on the dog's shoulder. He sucked his thumb and absentmindedly stroked one of Mungo's silky ears. I had spent the last year trying to persuade him not to suck his thumb, but had failed miserably.

"Don't lie in the dog's bed you'll smell all doggy," I groaned.

"But he's nice and warm," Toby protested, making no attempt to move.

"Go and put your dressing gown on. It's cold this morning."

"I can't find it," he said around his thumb.

"It's at the bottom of your bed."

He got up reluctantly and sauntered back upstairs.

I couldn't help marvelling at my nephew's lack of urgency in the mornings. If it was up to him, he wouldn't get to school much before lunchtime, unlike me who felt the pressure in the morning, largely due to my reluctance to come to terms with the alarm. Once I was able to drag myself out of bed and stumble downstairs to make a cup of liquid first aid, I would gradually start to come round. A shower and a second cup of tea was the final passage into full consciousness. When it hit, I usually had about twenty minutes to have breakfast, chivvy Toby along and take him the eight-minute drive to his village school. We rarely got to school before the bell.

But this morning was different. I looked at the clock. This morning I was actually early. And as if to celebrate my good start, the sky was a brilliant blue and the November sun was doing its best to look less like a watery Satsuma and more like the fiery ball it was. It buoyed my spirits no end.

Toby re-joined me wrapped in his dressing gown and poured the milk onto his breakfast, slopping a glug of it over the side of his bowl.

"Toby!" I dabbed at it with the dishcloth.

"Sorry," he said sheepishly.

I could never be cross with him for long, he was always so endearingly contrite. "Have you put your homework in your bag?"

He nodded his mouth full of Cheerios.

"And your reading book?"

He nodded again. He was getting better at being more organised.

"And don't forget you're going to Adam's for tea tonight."

"I know. Can I take my army gear?" he asked.

One of Toby and his best friend's favourite games was

playing armies. It usually involved building a camp with cushions from the sofa and then hours of quiet discussion as they planned and plotted their next move. It was always more about tactics and strategy than loud, raucous attack.

I started to clear the dishes away. "Go and get dressed and I'll bring your shirt up when I've ironed it."

WE MADE it to the school gates well before the school bell. I gave Toby a kiss on the cheek. Adam joined him at the gate and they walked into school with their heads together, thick as thieves. I smiled and pulled away in my old red Land Rover that clung to life by a spark plug.

I wasn't happy about having to buy stock from the Cash and Carry, it went against all my principles of only using local produce, but I was left with no choice after being let down by one of my usual suppliers. Fortunately, my dear friend and saviour, Audrey Goodfellow was opening up the shop this morning.

The Coffee Shop was a bustling little place and I was pleased to still be doing a good trade in spite of the economic downturn. I had built on the success of my mother and sister's efforts and despite the sometimes haphazard way I went about things, I discovered I had a natural business sense which surprised nobody more than me. I'd tweaked the menu since I had taken over. The local workmen still came in religiously for a fry up, but I had also managed to attract the later commuters with a more upmarket fare.

I got what I needed at the wholesalers and drove back to the shop. The last year had been a real period of personal adjustment for me. Not only had I had my sister's death to deal with, but I was plunged into parenthood overnight, fulfilling my promise to Katie that if anything ever happened to her I would become Toby's legal guardian. Nothing had prepared me for the daunting sense of responsibility and self-doubt this new role had engendered. I sighed as I pulled into the back yard behind the shop, I refused to dampen the optimism I had felt first thing this morning and ground the gears as I shoved my poor old Land Rover into reverse. It had been a tedious three-and-a-half-hour round trip and the lunchtime rush was starting to kick in.

"Hi Sandie," I said as I heaved a box up onto the counter in the tiny kitchen. Sandie, a local girl who other than Audrey, was my only employee, was busy frying eggs.

She glanced up. "Hi Sophie, alright?"

"Yeah good thanks, you?"

She nodded in response and carried on cooking. She was a sweet girl but like most seventeen year olds was master of few words. I smiled and finished unloading the car.

The coffee shop wasn't a big place, it could seat thirty at a push, but it kept me, Audrey and Sandie busy. At that moment, Audrey came rushing into the kitchen. "Sophie love, thank goodness you are here, we are rushed off our feet."

"Don't worry, the cavalry has arrived," I said, squeezing her shoulders affectionately as she made her way back into the shop with an order.

It turned out to be a hectic couple of hours. A coach load

of American tourists had come to visit Betherlands, the local stately home, and had wandered into the village. Apparently, they'd been told by their tour guide that Hatherley was a typically quaint English village. Fine by me, that kind of talk was good for business. By four o'clock, however, the shop was empty, the sun had admitted defeat and it was getting colder by the minute.

We all sat down for a well-deserved cuppa. "Oh, I meant to tell you Sophie, a man came into the shop looking for you this morning. He was most insistent about knowing where you were," Audrey said disapprovingly.

I sipped my tea. "Really, did he say what he wanted?"

"No, but he wasn't very happy when I refused to give him your mobile number. I told him to come back at lunchtime. He didn't come back though, did he?" She turned to Sandie for confirmation, who just shrugged her shoulders and shook her head.

"He seemed very keen to find you," Audrey continued.

"What did he look like?"

"Well, he was tall with very short blonde hair and spoke with a foreign accent."

"And he was *hot*," Sandie added.

Audrey gave her a withering look.

"What? He was!"

I was puzzled by my mystery visitor. "I wonder what he wanted."

Audrey looked concerned. "I assumed you would know."

"He'd be difficult to forget if you had met him," Sandie said.

Audrey ignored her. "I don't like strangers turning up asking for your number, it's not right and I didn't like his tone at all," she said, sounding cross. "If he turns up again I shall give him a piece of my mind."

"It was probably just some salesman," I said, trying to reassure her. "If it was urgent, I'm sure he will come back."

Audrey harrumphed her disapproval. Dear Audrey, she was like my mother should have been.

"How was yesterday?" she asked, changing the subject.

"Well, pretty hard, as expected. Toby was a little trooper though," I said with a sad smile.

"He's a dear little lad and he's coped with the loss of his mother so maturely. You are doing a great job." Audrey patted my hand. Many a time I had poured out my insecurities about being Toby's guardian to her.

"I'm doing my best. He supports me as much as I support him."

"You are lucky to have one another."

"It's hard though, I miss Katie so much."

"I know you do, we all do," she said sympathetically.

I took another sip of my tea. "But, do you know what? As tough as yesterday was, I actually woke up this morning feeling optimistic about the future, probably for the first time in the last year. Toby and I have an easy relationship, he's getting on well at school and the shop is doing okay." I left out the bit about moving things forward with Marcus.

"That's the spirit my dear."

I looked into Audrey's kind face. She was an attractive older woman; she was lined, but her bone structure was delicate and her skin unblemished.

"Thanks Aude you are such a support; I don't know what I'd do without you." I squeezed her hand. "Let's shut up shop and head home early, I don't think anyone else is coming in this afternoon." I glanced outside. "It looks like it might snow." Even though it was dark the sky had taken on a heaviness in the light of the street lamps that hadn't been there before. I picked up our mugs.

"Now that's enough of that kind of talk, I'm not built for the cold," Audrey said, shaking her head and shivering as she walked past me to get her coat.

"Don't be such a spoil sport, there's nothing like a dump of snow, especially when there's sledging potential," I said, putting the mugs in the sink.

"Yeah, I love a bit of sledging," Sandie agreed, showing an uncharacteristic enthusiasm. The girl obviously had hidden depths.

Audrey shook her head. "I'm afraid I'm getting too old for that sort of thing."

"Rubbish, you're a spring chicken Aude," I teased. "I bet you could give the kids a run for their money."

She laughed. "Forty years ago maybe. I prefer a more sedentary pace of life now."

She had always been very secretive about her age but she had to be in her mid to late sixties. I smiled and shrugged on my coat. "Can you lock up at the front? I'm going out the back."

"Course love, see you tomorrow."

"Yeah, see you tomorrow," I said. "Bye Sandie."

"Bye," she replied.

I could see my breath in the glow of the security light out the back. I pulled my scarf up to my chin. My old truck started after a few throaty attempts and I patted the dashboard. "Good girl," I said gratefully and reversed out of the shop's back yard.

I drove home and thought about Audrey. She was such a good friend and support. She lived alone with two cats she adored, and it so happened that her friend and neighbour, Paul Franklin, was the love of her life, not that she had any idea I knew. Unfortunately for Audrey, Paul was his wife's loyal and totally committed full time carer. Once a week, Audrey and Paul would spend companionable time together when Eva went into respite care. They did the crossword together and discussed the news topics of the day and I knew it was these moments that Audrey secretly lived for. Poor Audes, she was such a warm, loving person, but had never been married and I would have liked nothing more than to see her settled with someone she loved.

I turned into my road and was dragged away from my thoughts by the sight of a tall shadowy figure standing by my front gate. My mind flitted to the conversation Audrey and I'd had earlier about the mysterious stranger who had come into the shop asking questions about my whereabouts. I felt a shot of adrenaline and did a quick risk assessment as I often did in situations that made me feel vulnerable. The street was quiet and there were no lights on in the house next to mine. I contemplated turning around and then thought better of it. If this was the guy who had come into the shop this morning, he was obviously persistent and would no doubt catch up with me sooner rather than later. It was about time I toughened up.

I pulled into the drive at the side of my house and glanced in the rear-view mirror. I hoped the man might have moved on, but not only was he still there, he was walking up the garden path ready to meet me at the front door. My new found bravery wavered and I grabbed my mobile phone, bringing Marcus' number up on the screen as a precaution. I got out of the car and held my phone in my pocket as I approached the man, who was now waiting for me under the porch.

He was tall and wore dark jeans and a dark jacket. His collar was turned up and his hands were pushed hard into his pockets in a gesture against the cold.

"Can I help you?" I said with a cheeriness I didn't feel.

"I'm looking for Sophie McAllister," he replied in an accent I struggled to place. He didn't look like my idea of a homicidal maniac, in fact far from it. Sandie had been right, he was spectacularly good-looking. His hair was fair and very short, he had a well-defined brow and an angular jaw. All in all, pretty breath-taking. I found myself staring at him struggling to assimilate the oxygen I was drawing into my lungs and momentarily forgetting my earlier assumption.

"Do you know where I could find Ms McAllister?" he repeated, interrupting my appraisal of his not inconsiderable good looks.

"Um yes, I'm Sophie McAllister," I replied breathlessly. *Get a grip!* He might be a fine example of a man, but that didn't mean he was any less inclined to do me harm, judging by the size of him, he could probably throttle me with one hand. "Can I help you?" I asked again.

He offered his hand for a handshake and I flinched at the sudden movement.

"My name is Ahran Elessar."

His hand was as warm as mine was cold.

"Are you the legal guardian of the boy?"

3

His terminology struck me as odd and then I realised he was talking about Toby. I snatched my hand from his. The hairs on the back of my neck stood up like the hackles on a dog and the unease I felt when I first saw him returned. I decided to play ignorant. "I'm sorry I'm not sure what you mean. Who did you say you were again?"

"Ahran Elessar," he said, enunciating it as if I was either deaf or stupid. "I need to talk with you about your nephew as a matter of urgency. Could we step inside?"

How did he know anything about Toby? My uneasiness increased. Who *was* this guy? He was clearly no salesman and the last thing I had expected was the topic of conversation to be about my nephew. Apprehension prickled across my skin.

"Can we go inside and talk?" he urged more insistently.

I stood on my doorstep weighing up whether I should let him inside or just tell him to get lost. He acknowledged my hesitation by taking a step closer and lowering his voice. He was close enough for me to smell his citrusy aftershave.

"You and your nephew are in grave danger, I have been sent to protect you." His expression was serious and fear crashed through my body causing my fingertips to tingle. "I know how this might seem," he continued, "But it's very cold out here. Can we talk about this in the warm?"

Why were our lives in grave danger? I stared at him blankly.

He didn't appear overjoyed about being here, but there was something about him that was calm and reassuring.

"Are you the police?" I asked.

"No," he replied, looking mildly amused.

"Then how do I know you don't mean us any harm?"

"Please believe me when I say I'm not here to hurt you. If I meant you any harm I could do it right here, right now."

It was true, he could attack me on my doorstep and no one would hear my screams.

"You and your nephew are not safe and I am here to protect you," he said, repeating his earlier statement. "Can we please go inside and I will explain?"

His sincerity seemed genuine, but it was the thought of Toby coming to any harm that finally forced my decision.

"Okay. Although my boyfriend will be home any minute." This of course, wasn't true.

My hand was shaking when I put the key in the lock. I opened the door and Mungo rushed out of the kitchen and charged up to my unexpected visitor wagging his tail and whimpering like an idiot. *Great! Some guard dog you are!*

Ahran had to duck as he walked through the doorway

and my hallway suddenly felt very small. *I must be mad!* I thought to myself, but instead of sending him away I found myself offering to take his coat.

He hesitated as if I had caught him off guard. "Er, yes, thank you." He shrugged out of his jacket and handed it to me.

I hung it up and got a waft of his aftershave again mixed with the kind of smell you get when your skin has been exposed to hot sun. I wondered how he could possibly smell of the sun when it had been freezing cold all day.

Mungo was going over the top with his canine welcome and I grabbed his collar. He could be so irritating. "Mungo, that's enough!" *Dogs were supposed to protect their owners, weren't they?* "Sorry," I apologised and led him into the kitchen. Fortunately, I had lit the Aga yesterday and the kitchen felt warm and inviting.

"In your bed," I commanded before Mungo could even think about resuming his overly friendly assault on my visitor. He did as he was told, but shot me a look of disappointment at having his enthusiastic greeting curbed, it wasn't often we had new people to the house for him to sniff and lick.

Jeez! In the light, the guy was even better looking than I had first thought. "Come in," I swallowed. My mind was reeling. The presence of Mr Elessar was unsettling, but I couldn't help wondering what it was we had done to make someone want to harm us? Toby was just a child and the worst I had ever done was thirty five in a thirty zone.

"Please take a seat." I congratulated myself for my calm manner when I felt anything but calm.

He pulled out one of the wooden chairs at the kitchen table and it creaked as he sat down. Without his jacket he was lean and broad. His skin was lightly tanned and his eyes were the most mesmerizing shade of blue, it was difficult not to stare at them. I cleared my throat. "Can I get you a drink? Tea…Coffee?"

"Just a glass of water, please."

I switched the kettle on, feeling like I needed the comfort of a mug of tea. I poured his glass of water and tried to still the tremor in my hand.

"Thank you," he said, taking the glass from me, his hand as steady as a rock. At least he was polite, which wasn't a quality I usually associated with serial killers.

"Where is your nephew now?" he asked, wasting no time in getting to the point.

I chose to lean up against the counter rather than take a seat opposite, for some reason it made me feel like I had more of an advantage. I held my mug with both hands seeking its reassuring warmth.

"He's at a friend's," I replied.

I eyed my unexpected visitor warily. I'd have placed him in his early thirties. He sat with an easy confidence and wore an expensive looking black sweater that clung to what must have been some seriously toned muscles underneath. He had faint laughter lines at the corners of his eyes and mouth, but other than that, his face was flawless. His long legs were muscular and clad in a pair of designer jeans and he wore a pair of brown leather Chelsea boots. All in all, expensively turned out and not what you would expect of a potential bodyguard.

"Okay so can you please tell me what this is all about?" I insisted.

Ahran leant forward on the table, his expression solemn. "The boy in your care is very…" He paused searching for the right word "…special."

I gave a humourless laugh. "You don't think I know that? He's the only family I have left."

"I understand he is important to you after the loss you have suffered, but what I mean is he is special in an…" Once again he searched for the right words, "… unusual way."

I felt confused. How did he know what loss I had suffered? And what did he mean Toby was *special* and *unusual*?

"How do you know anything about us?" I demanded.

"I know a lot more about you and the boy than even you know."

More than even I knew? He was talking in riddles.

"Do you know who the boy's father is?" he continued as if to prove his point.

"*Toby*, his name is *Toby*," I said in frustration. I was beginning to feel out of control.

He ignored me and raised his eyebrows waiting for my answer.

I sighed. "His father is called Tagan, but he doesn't have anything to do with Toby and never has had," I said bitterly.

Ahran made no comment and continued with his game of 'I Know More Than You'. "His name was Tagan Halsan and he was my cousin."

"Well you can tell Tagan Halsan to go to hell. If he thinks he's having Toby he is sorely mistaken." I put my mug down and stepped away from the counter. "If this is why you have come then you can get out of my house." I could feel hot tears prickling at my eyes. They would have to take Toby away over my dead body and not without a fight before that. A sinking feeling dragged at my stomach. I could almost feel the cracks beginning to fracture my fragile world. I was a fool this morning to think I could lead a normal and settled life. Things always turned to *shit!*

Ahran remained calm. "I don't think you heard what I said. Tagan *was* my cousin. He died over eight years ago." He paused and let me digest this information. "And I have no intention of taking the boy away from you," he said, his expression softening just a little.

"Then why have you come to see us now? As far as *Toby*," I said, emphasising his name again, "Is concerned, his father was never interested in him when he was alive, why should it matter now that he is dead?" I couldn't help feeling a small vindictive twinge of satisfaction knowing that Tagan no longer walked this earth.

"Tagan never knew he had a son," Ahran replied in a clipped tone. My vilification of his cousin was obviously beginning to annoy him.

"Yeah right, more convenient to play ignorant at least there is less chance of having to pay maintenance," I continued, unable to help myself.

He drew in a deep breath before continuing. "We had no idea Tagan had a son at first and it took me a while to find you both. If Tagan had known he had sired a son, believe me he would have come looking for him himself."

I snorted. *Sired* a son. *Hello? We are in the 21st century!* And where *was* that accent from?

Before I had a chance to question him, Ahran continued.

"The picture you paint of my cousin is not an accurate one. Tagan would have been very proud if he had known he had a son even if he is..." Ahran stopped himself. "He just would have been very proud and I'm sure he would have wanted to get to know him."

"What were you going to say? Even if he is *what?*"

"It doesn't matter." Judging by the expression that flickered across his face, it was something he found disagreeable. "What does matter is that my family has enemies and we have reason to believe that they may come after Toby."

Suddenly I felt nauseous. "What kind of enemies? Are you in the Mafia or something? Its drugs isn't it?" I said, throwing my hands in the air and shaking my head, not giving him the chance to answer any of my questions. "I knew it!" I thought about Toby's good for nothing father it wouldn't have surprised me to find out that he was some addict who had got into debt to some badass drug dealer. Whatever illegal pies Tagan and his family had their fingers in, Toby and I wanted no part of it.

Ahran laughed. I couldn't help noticing how the humour softened his face.

"No, we are not the Mafia and drugs are not important where I come from. I'm afraid the people who might come after Toby are far more dangerous than the kind of people you might have seen in some gangster movie."

This was *not* what I wanted to hear. I'd seen *The Godfather* I couldn't conceive of anyone more dangerous than a

Mafia gangster. I started to feel the room spin and my knees began to buckle at the thought of Toby being hurt. I clutched the edge of the counter behind me.

"Are you okay?"

I glared at his outstretched hand as if it was a poisonous snake. "No, I'm not okay," I spat. "You turn up out of the blue and tell me that the most important person in my life is in danger, an innocent boy who has never caused anyone any harm, his only crime that he is the son of some..." I searched for the right word, *Ooh, I could come up with some choice ones!* "Criminal!" I seethed and glared at him. His expression grew darker.

"You have the wrong impression of my cousin."

"Oh have I? Well, *your cousin,*" I said with exaggerated emphasis, "Got my sister pregnant and walked away never to be seen again. Katie never received any support. Toby has had to grow up not knowing who his father was and now, because of him, his life is in danger. I'm sorry if I seem a little bitter." I didn't sound in the least bit apologetic.

I took a deep breath and closed my eyes which caused tears to spill down my cheeks as it all began to sink in. Suddenly, I felt as if all my fight had just up sticks and left. I sobbed into my hands.

I felt Ahran's warm hand on my arm. I wasn't prepared for his sympathy. I pulled away. I didn't want to know who Toby's father was and what trouble he and his family were in. I just wanted Ahran Elessar to go away, rewind back to this morning and for Toby and I to carry on with our lives blissfully unaware of everything he had just told me.

I wiped my eyes.

"Can I get you a tissue?" He offered awkwardly. My tears were obviously making him uncomfortable.

I sat down at the kitchen table. "Could you just get me a glass of water please?" I muttered. For some reason I was finding it difficult to think straight when he was stood so close. I felt upset and confused.

"Yes of course." He looked relieved he had something to do. I got the impression he wasn't used to emotional women, although I'm not sure why, there had to be a long line of broken hearted females trailing not too far behind him.

I took a sip from the glass he handed me.

"I know it's a lot to take in, but I cannot emphasise enough that your lives are in danger. No matter what you think of my cousin you need to seriously consider my family's offer of protection."

I eyed him suspiciously. "What have your family done exactly that has made this *enemy* so angry that they would want to come after an innocent child?"

"Unfortunately, Tagan killed the son of a very powerful woman where I come from and she wants revenge," he said with a hint of regret.

This was more like the image I had of Tagan. "So he's a murderer?!" I knew he was a waste of space. *Oh Katie, why oh why did you have to get tangled up with someone like that?!*

"You misunderstand," Ahran said in his cousin's defence.

"Well, you either kill someone or you don't." I gave a

humourless laugh. "If he killed someone then he was a murderer."

He looked like I had just slapped him in the face. I'd obviously hit a nerve and it took him a moment to recover.

He shook his head. "You are wrong," he said quietly. "Tagan was a brilliant soldier, he had no choice, it was kill or be killed."

"Tagan was in the army?" I digested this piece of information. I wasn't sure I really want to know any more about him.

Ahran continued. "Yes, he was also the heir to my uncle's extensive estate, which makes Toby the next rightful heir. Capturing Toby would not only be a just revenge in Bazeera's eyes but he would also be a very useful bargaining chip for her to get her hands on my family's land."

I laughed. "This is some kind of joke right?"

"I have never been more serious in my life," he replied without a hint of a smile.

"Okay, so you are telling me that some *woman* wants to kidnap Toby because his father was some kind of lord?" I asked incredulously. The picture Ahran was painting of Tagan as a titled soldier who had fought honourably for his country, jarred with my image of him being a druggy good-for-nothing who slept around.

"Not a lord, a prince."

"A prince!" *Jesus!* I was happier thinking the worst of him, it made it easier to accept that he had deserted my sister.

"Yes, he was a prince from a very wealthy and respected royal family."

"And Toby is the next heir?" I asked, hardly believing what I was hearing.

"Yes," he replied patiently.

It felt like my brain was made of cotton wool. I was having difficulty processing the simplest of his answers. I sat there for some time staring at a mark on the floor. I turned it over in my head. Toby's father was a prince, which means Toby is a prince and heir to some wealthy foreign kingdom. No matter how much I repeated it in my head it didn't sound any less crazy.

"My family would like you and Toby to accompany me back to my family's home where we can offer you full protection," he said, repeating his earlier proposal.

Despite feeling bewildered I started to think about the practicalities. We couldn't just up sticks and leave with this stranger. We had our lives here. "And how long do you think we would need to stay with you?" I asked, playing along.

"As long as it takes for my people to remove the threat," Ahran said with little emotion.

"And how would you do that?" I asked not sure I wanted to hear the answer. I was from a rural community in East Sussex, nothing like this ever happened.

"Until Bazeera is overthrown," he replied matter of factly.

I had a sinking feeling that overthrown was a euphemism for being killed. It all sounded rather too serious and dangerous. What had we found ourselves in the middle of?!

I tried to reason with him. "Surely the police can deal with this. If Toby's life is in as much danger as you say it is then the police or special branch or whoever deals with this kind of thing should be able to do something about this *Bazeera.*"

He frowned and shook his head. "There is no need to involve the police. We are capable of dealing with our own problems."

I still wasn't convinced that they weren't part of the mob. I stood up and started to pace the kitchen. "I can't take Toby out of school, away from all his friends and everything he knows to go off with a stranger for an indeterminate amount of time." I stopped in front of him. "Besides I've got a business to run." I hoped that I might be able to convince him he was being melodramatic.

"I don't think you quite understand what Bazeera is capable of," he warned.

"Maybe not, but we can't just walk away from our lives." I took a deep breath and tried to calm my nerves and temper my frustration. "Look, you've got to try and see this from my point of view. A guy I've never met before turns up on my doorstep and tells me that my nephew is a prince and heir to a fortune and that his life is in danger from some power hungry woman because she wants vengeance and a slice of that fortune."

Ahran shrugged and shook his head as if to say, *'And your point is?'*

"It just all sounds too far-fetched and why should I

believe you anyway, you've not provided me with any hard evidence." I hoped by talking some sense I would be able to convince him that his story was too absurd and that he really shouldn't believe everything he is told either.

I moved towards the door. "Now if you don't mind, I have to go somewhere." I felt more resolute, this sort of thing just doesn't happen in real life. Denial was the best policy until I had proof. "If you can provide me with some irrefutable evidence that what you say is true then perhaps we can talk again." I had no intention of putting Toby at any risk, but this was Hatherley, the most criminal thing that ever happened here was fly-tipping in a field gateway.

Ahran ran his hand over his hair in frustration. He went out into the hallway where I'd hung up his jacket and then came back into the kitchen.

"Look, take this." He handed me a small rectangular tablet.

"What is it?" I eyed it suspiciously.

"It's a cell phone."

"I've got a phone thank you."

"You will need this if you want to contact me."

Somewhere in the back of my mind I wondered why he couldn't just give me his number. "You obviously need some time to think about this. In the meantime, if you feel threatened in any way, do not hesitate to phone one of the two numbers programmed into it. I can get here quickly if necessary. I will give you two days and then I will come back for you both."

I'd had enough of arguing with him. "I'm sorry I am

going to have to go." I tossed the phone on the table as if accepting it would make everything he had just told me true.

I followed him to the front door and offered my hand. "Well Mr Elessar, it's been, er, *interesting*, and if there is anything I'm worried about you can rest assured I will give you a call." I was pleased I had come up with a sensible plan amidst this madness.

Ahran looked at me intently. "I mean it, we haven't got long. If anyone new turns up in your village, or threatens you or Toby in any way, you must call me immediately."

"Yes of course I will," I said in my sweetest and best air hostess voice. "Now if you don't mind." I handed him his jacket and opened the front door as a signal for him to leave.

"Please be vigilant, for yours and Toby's sake." He sounded angry. It wasn't the first time this evening. I'd got the distinct impression that he didn't want to be here and he wanted me to be difficult even less. He had obviously expected us to go with him, but I was damned if that was going to happen without more proof. He hesitated and then turned and walked out into the darkness.

I slowly shut the door behind him. My head ached. As implausible as Ahran's story was, could I afford to ignore it? What would be the point of making up a story like that? Perhaps he was just a very convincing fraud, albeit a very good-looking one. I leaned back against the door and took a deep breath. Were our lives really in that much danger?

THE ALARM WOKE me at 6.30 as usual. I'd eventually got to

sleep about half past three after tossing and turning thinking about Ahran's visit. I slowly put my feet to the floor. My head was pounding as if I had been drinking. I was still struggling to believe what he had told me and the evil voice in my head was doing its usual thing, spouting negativity and insisting that I could be putting our lives in danger if I didn't heed Ahran's warning. "Oh shut up!" I grumbled and went into the bathroom.

I thought about the day ahead. My best friend Bennie had just got back from her latest assignment and she was coming over this evening for a takeaway and a catch up. She had been in Kenya for over a month filming a new litter of lion cubs in one of its nature reserves. I missed her and her sensible counsel even more than usual in the light of last night's unexpected bombshell. She was one of those people who talked sense and at this moment in time I really needed someone to be sensible. After I'd had a shower my headache had lessened and I felt a little better as I headed downstairs. Bennie would know what to do.

Toby was already dressed and sat at the breakfast table eating a bowl of Cheerios with Mungo drooling at his elbow.

"What have I done to deserve the pleasure of your company at this hour of the morning?" I asked cheerily, if a little suspiciously.

"Nothing," Toby said as he slurped down the last couple of spoonfuls of cereal. "I'm going on a school trip today, remember. I've got to be at school by seven thirty."

"Dammit! I'd forgotten all about your trip and I need to

make you a packed lunch," I said, hopping from one foot to the other as I tried to decide what to do first.

"Don't worry, I've made it already," Toby said.

I was always dubious of the nutritional value of a packed lunch made by Toby, but I didn't have time to argue. I hardly even noticed when he put his breakfast bowl on the floor and Mungo began to lap up the leftover milk. It was one of my pet hates. I went over and gave him a hug.

"You are amazing Toby McAllister, do you know that?" I gave him a kiss on the cheek. Ahran's words came back to me and I contemplated life without my little nephew. A lump formed in my throat and tears stung my eyes. I quickly turned away and busied myself with putting some toast in the toaster. I hoped we would never see Ahran Elessar again.

"Yeah, I know," Toby replied.

"And modest too," I laughed, wiping my nose on my sleeve.

"Are you alright Auntie Sophie?"

"I'm fine," I said, dodging his question. "Go and brush your teeth, we'd better get going." We made it to school just in time.

It wasn't as busy at the coffee shop as it had been the day before, so the three of us made the most of the lull and got on with some of the mucky jobs we'd been putting off for a week. I cleaned the coffee machine. Sandie worked on the grills and Audrey tackled the fridge. It was a hive of activity and just what I needed to keep myself occupied. I hadn't told Audrey about Ahran's visit because I didn't want to worry her. I decided I wouldn't say anything until he had proved to me that what he'd said was true. I fully intended to tell Bennie tonight though. I had to share it with someone.

It had been a busy day cleaning and we rewarded ourselves with tea and some unsold cake. We congratulated ourselves with what we had achieved and shut up shop safe in the knowledge that everything was spick and span. I picked Toby up from afterschool club and was regaled with stories of his school trip to the Natural History Museum. He flaked out after his bath not even able to stay awake for a story. I tucked him in and kissed his forehead. We had got through the day without being attacked by evil, vengeful enemies from far off places. I began to think that Ahran's visit had been some kind of stupid prank.

I put some plates in the oven and a bottle of wine in the fridge. It had been too long since I had seen Bennie. I smiled at the thought of my best friend. Her name wasn't actually Bennie it was Cordelia. I remember the day I met her so clearly, it was at the village primary school, the same one that Toby now went to. We were both five. I had been at school for a term and she had just moved into the village with her parents. She had been a real tomboy and figured that nobody at school would be any the wiser if she renamed herself Benjamin. She reasoned that boys had more fun and decided a name change might make her life more exciting. She was an only child. Her parents, Edward and Gwen Blythe-Smith, after twenty three years of trying, had resigned themselves to never being able to have children and then Bennie came along.

Mrs Blythe-Smith became a first time mum at the age of

forty eight. It was a dream come true for her and her husband, but it meant that the first eighteen years of Bennie's life were suffocated by aging parents who were over-protective and unrealistic in their expectations. Bennie had been pretty rebellious in return. She was nearly expelled from the local grammar school on more than one occasion. Her father, a successful lawyer, was over the moon when she got a place on a law degree course at university, it seemed she was finally taking life more seriously. Unfortunately for her parents, her time studying law was short lived when an affair with one of her lecturers brought an end to their dream of Bennie having a successful career in law. Her parents were less than encouraging when she enrolled herself onto a photography course, but two years later she proved them wrong and set herself up as a freelance photographer. Her lucky break came when she met a producer of BBC wildlife films at an industry 'do' and the rest, as they say, is history.

I couldn't wait to see her.

The doorbell rang. I half-ran to the front door. For a split second, I wondered whether it was her and that maybe I should check before I opened it. "Bennie?" I said through the door feeling really silly and not a little bit paranoid. *Damn Ahran Elessar!*

4

After a virtually sleepless night, I woke to the unforgiving demand of my alarm clock and in my attempts to silence it swatted it clean off the bedside table. Yesterday morning I had felt like I was hung over, this morning I *was* hung over. What was I thinking, drinking on a school night? I pulled the duvet over my head and groaned. There was a gentle knock on the door. I ignored it.

"Sophe, it's me, can I come in?" Bennie called softly through the door.

"Only if you've got a cup of tea in your hand," I muttered.

"Check!" she said, entering the room.

"How come you're up and about so bright and early?" I said as I hauled myself up and plumped a pillow behind me, wincing at the pain in my head.

Bennie slid in under the duvet. "I promised my mother I would go Christmas shopping with her today."

"That will be nice," I said supportively.

"Have you met my mother?" She cocked an eyebrow at me.

"She means well, Ben."

I leant forward to take a sip of my tea. "Ah! My head! Why did you make me drink so much last night?" I complained. One glass of wine was my limit or maybe two at a push, but if my memory served me correctly, we had polished off nearly two bottles. "I don't have the stamina I used to have."

"Let's face it Sophe, you've never had the stamina," she laughed. "How do you feel about everything this morning?"

"About the same. At least I'll be seeing Ahran tonight which should shed more light on things."

"You will keep me posted, won't you?"

"Of course I will."

"Well lovey, I'd better get going otherwise my mother will not be amused," she said in her poshest voice.

"Thanks for last night, it felt good to talk."

"Anytime. I'm always here for you." She gave me a quick, minimal Bennie hug. "And don't forget to call me as soon as you've seen Ahran."

"I won't. Promise." She climbed out of the bed and headed towards the door.

"Have fun," I called after her.

"I doubt it," she said with a cross-eyed grimace.

I laughed and automatically clutched my head at the pain. "Ow!"

After I had taken a couple of paracetamol and my headache had eased, I showered, had a second cup of tea and began to feel like I could function for the day. I hoped my head would be clear by the time I had my meeting with the bank manager that afternoon. I wanted a loan to revamp the kitchen at the coffee shop, the cooker was on the blink and during the health inspector's last visit he had recommended I replace the tiles behind the counters with stainless steel splash backs because they weren't strictly in keeping with EU health and hygiene regulations, apparently. Toby went at his usual snail's pace and after much chivvying along we got to the school gate a shade after the bell. I kissed him goodbye and headed to the shop.

The morning brought a steady stream of custom, and before I knew it, it was gone lunchtime. I took advantage of the afternoon lull and sat down with a toasted sandwich and a cup of tea and checked my phone. There were three missed calls from Bennie. I took a bite of my sandwich and called her back. She answered almost immediately.

"I've been trying to get hold of you for the last hour," she said, without so much as a 'hello'.

I swallowed the large mouthful I had just bitten off. "Sorry hun, we've been rushed off our feet. What can I do you for?"

"Well," she said, barely containing her enthusiasm. "After I waved the white flag at my mother in John Lewis' bedlinen department, and agreed to meet her when she had finished hassling the assistant to open virtually every duvet set in the store, I took the opportunity to head to a coffee shop to take advantage of the free wifi and do some digging on Ahran Elessar and Tagan Halsan. I think you'll find the results interesting."

"But we couldn't find much last night."

"I know, it turns out we should have just gone a little further in our search."

Bennie was like a dog with a bone when something piqued her interest, so it came as no surprise that she had continued the line of enquiry that had proved fruitless for us last night.

"Go on."

"Okay," she continued. "There are a number of threads which might shed some light onto who these people might be." She drew a breath. "There is a secretive sect that has some links with the name Halsan."

I laughed "A sect? What like a religious sect?"

"Yes, they call their elders royalty and refer to the chief and his wife as the King and Queen. Maybe the reason we couldn't find anything on a royal family with those names is because they aren't actually royal in the sense that we understand royalty."

"So you think they could be a group of underground religious cranks?"

"Have you ever heard of the Knights Templar?"

"Yes, but I can't say I know much about them."

"Listen to this." She proceeded to tell me what she had found. "*The Poor Fellow-Soldiers of Christ...*blah, blah, blah...*Commonly known as the Knights Templar, were among the wealthiest and most powerful of the Western Christian military orders and were prominent actors in Christian finance...*"

"But wasn't that hundreds of years ago?" I said, interrupting her.

"Yes, but there is evidence of a modern day version of the Knights Templar."

"I'm not sure Ben, it sounds a bit weird."

"But that's the point, this guy turns up and tells you all this stuff about who Toby's father is, that they are rich and that there are people who are after Toby. It *is* weird!"

Before I could make any further comment, she continued. "There's more…*Officially endorsed by the Roman Catholic Church*, so on and so forth." She paused. "Oh wait, listen to this bit, *The Order became a favoured charity throughout Christendom and grew rapidly in membership and power. Templar knights were among the most skilled fighting units of the Crusades. Non-combatant members of the Order managed a large economic infrastructure throughout Christendom, innovating financial techniques and building fortifications across Europe and the Holy Land.*" She paused. "Don't you think this fits in with what Ahran told you about their wealth, the battles they're having with their enemies and so on?"

I thought about this for the moment. "Well, I guess there are some similarities," I said, contemplating what she was saying.

"I think it explains a lot; the secrecy, the money, the feuding. Ahran Elessar and Tagan Halsan are modern day Knights Templars."

She said this so finally and so persuasively, I almost believed her.

"I don't know Ben," I said, sounding more circumspect.

"Okay, what about this idea then?"

I almost laughed. She had sounded so convinced, but the

fact that she was prepared to consider another possibility so easily kind of weakened her Knights Templar theory.

"Elessar could mean Aragorn," she said, once again reading it from some site on the internet *"A character from the fantasy world of J.R.R. Tolkien's Middle Earth."*

"Ben! That's fiction!" I started to wonder whether she was beginning to lose her own grip on reality. "I know this whole thing sounds far-fetched, but that's not even real."

"I know that *der-brain!* But some people who read this kind of stuff really get into it and start to believe it. I once heard of a guy who had surgery on his ears so he would look more like Mr. Spock! You would not believe the ends these people go to in pursuit of their obsession. Did you know that there is even an official religion called the Jedi Church? These sorts of people will do anything to try and become their favourite fictional characters. Maybe Ahran Elessar is some kind of Lord of the Ring enthusiast who has just taken it too far and has begun to believe his own stories."

I had to admit this thought had crossed my mind and then I thought about Ahran for a moment, he had seemed perfectly sane even if what he had said was pretty *out there*.

"No Ben, I don't think that applies here."

"Yeah, you're probably right." She sounded a little deflated. "Okay, I've got one more thing."

I sighed, and looked at the clock. Bless her for trying, but we really weren't getting anywhere. "I need to get back to work lovey."

"Just listen to this," she said undeterred.

I loved her for trying to help me and I was reminded of

what the essence of good friendship was; you could share crazy stuff with each other and you didn't think any less of one another. Although on this occasion she was getting a bit carried away and beginning to test my theory. I smiled at her down the phone. "Fire away," I said patiently.

"There are a number of examples throughout history where the name Elessar or Halsan are linked to famous or high achieving people in their field. Did you know that one of William the Conqueror's middle names was Elessar?"

I dropped my forehead to the table in exasperation.

Bennie took advantage of my silence and continued. "Sir Francis Drake's father was called Edmund Drake-Halsan, but old Frankie boy dropped the Halsan from his name."

I started laughing.

"If you aren't going to listen to me, then I might as well hang up," Bennie said clearly irritated by my derision.

"I'm sorry Ben," I said, trying to sound like I was taking her more seriously.

"I think… *we* could be clutching at straws," I said.

"It's really not as crazy as it sounds, when you start digging there are lots of examples of famous sportsmen, performers, military commanders that are linked to either the name Elessar or Halsan: Roger Bannister; that guy who was the first person to run a mile in under four minutes, Houdini, even Alexander the Great."

"What are you suggesting?" I asked, not quite following.

"I'm not really sure, but there is something remarkable about each of them."

"I don't understand."

Bennie sighed. "Nor do I really," she said, unable to offer any more. "But what I can tell you, is that some searches I made led me to official government pages where any further access was denied."

"What do you mean? Like top secret stuff?"

"Yup, exactly that. I may not have come up with anything concrete, but what is for sure is that there is definitely more to the Elessar/Halsan family than meets the eye."

I groaned. "I don't want to hear that Ben. The last thing I need is to get involved in anything complicated. Why can't life just be simple? *Simple* is highly underrated these days."

"I'm sorry Sophe, but I have a feeling that when Ahran Elessar walked into your life, your chances of a simple life went out the window."

"Thanks for the words of comfort!"

"Look, I'll keep searching and will let you know if I come up with anything else."

"Okay, thanks Ben."

"Make sure you call me when you know more."

"Yeah, I will."

"Love you lots." It was our usual way of saying goodbye.

"Love you too," I said predictably, but with no less meaning. "Bye."

I ended the call.

I spent the next few hours thinking over what Bennie had told me, and by the time three thirty came my head ached, and I was no closer to figuring any of it out.

Once Audrey had assured me she could cope, I left the coffee shop and made my way to the bank.

I didn't like my bank manager, he made my skin crawl and spent most of the time looking at my chest, but after he had given me the Spanish Inquisition, which I suspected was a tactic to make me feel small and insignificant and eternally grateful when he did finally agree to the loan, I shook his hand and thanked him sweetly. After all I had got what I came for. It was a quarter to five by the time I picked Toby up from after-school club and it was cold and dark. I decided to go to the shop and help Audrey close up so she could get home a bit earlier. I parked outside at the front. The street was quiet and the 'Open' sign had been turned to 'Closed', all the lights were off and the shop door was ajar. Something was wrong.

"Stay here Toby, I won't be a minute." I grabbed the heavy Maglite torch I kept in the glove box and locked the car door. I toyed with the idea of ringing Ahran and reached into my pocket for the phone he had given me. It wasn't there and I cursed myself for leaving it sitting on the arm of the sofa in the lounge. *Dammit!* I had a sinking feeling this could very well be one of those times Ahran had warned me about. I walked towards the shop and gingerly pushed the door open whilst my heart beat in my throat.

5

"Audrey?" I called as I hovered in the doorway, straining my eyes in the dark.

No answer. My heartbeat quickened. I flicked the lights on to find the place empty. Strange, very strange. Why had the front door been left open? My eyes scanned the coffee shop. Nothing appeared to be out of place.

I went out the back to check the back door had been bolted and almost fell over a heap on the floor in the darkened kitchen. I turned the light on and to my absolute horror realised it was Audrey; she was lying on her back with her head at an awkward angle against the wall and her face was covered in blood.

"Oh my God," I whispered, sinking to my knees next to her. A strangled cry came from somewhere deep in my throat. I thought she was dead at first, the way she was lying looked so unnatural as if her neck was broken, but I could just about make out the almost imperceptible yet reassuring rise and fall of her chest. A debilitating wave of nausea washed over me and for a few moments, paralysed by shock, I stared at my dear friend.

I fumbled for my phone in my pocket. "I need an ambulance now," I cried as soon as the line clicked for the emergency services. A calm and business like voice answered and started asking me questions, most of which I barely heard. "Just get an ambulance here *please*." The unflappable voice on the other end of the line asked me for the address and once I had given it she reassured me that an ambulance was on its way. I breathed a sigh of relief and hung up.

"Audrey, can you hear me?" I picked up her limp hand feeling the need to cradle her head in my lap to make her more comfortable, but I vaguely remember something about not moving her in case her neck was injured. I sat staring at her lifeless body, tears streaming down my face feeling utterly helpless.

Oh God, Toby! He was still in the car. I couldn't leave him out there on his own. I wiped the tears from my face, took my coat off and gently laid it over Audrey's still form. I hesitated before dashing back through the shop thinking through my options. I would ask Sandie to collect him, I didn't want him seeing Audrey like this.

I breathed a sigh of relief when I got to the door of the shop, he was still sitting in the car, his head bent over the glow of his iPad. I stood at the door and kept my eye on my nephew as I called Sandie. She was more than happy to come and get him. I simply told her that Audrey had been taken ill and that an ambulance was on its way.

I was just about to put the phone down. "Oh and Sandie, is Dan with you?" This recent turn of events had made me feel jittery and I didn't think it was a bad idea if Dan, her rugby playing boyfriend, came with her.

"Yeah, Why?"

"Oh it's just um, that er, Toby wanted to talk to him about who was playing for England in the Six Nations this year. Could he come with you so Toby could have a chat with him?" That sounded as good a reason as any. I was reluctant to tell her that I would feel much happier if she had some muscle with her just in case.

"Yeah, no worries," she replied.

"Great, thanks very much."

Toby looked up as I opened the driver's door. "What's the matter?" he asked.

"Audrey isn't very well and I need you to go with Sandie, she's coming to get you and will take you home. I'm going to the hospital in the ambulance."

"Can I come? I've never been in an ambulance," he said hopefully.

"No, you go home with Sandie, she'll get you some tea and put you to bed."

"Oh!" he complained. "How long are you going to be?"

"I don't know yet, but I'll come in and kiss you good-night when I get back."

I was torn. I didn't want to leave Audrey, but neither did I want to leave Toby in the car on his own. I contemplated whether I should phone Ahran. I hesitated before dialling Sandie's number again.

"Sandie, it's me again, could you do me another favour? Could you stop by my house and pick up the phone that's on the arm of the sofa in the lounge? There's a key under the pot by the back door."

"Yeah sure, see you in a bit."

I pressed the hang up button. "I'm just going to wait by the door Tobes."

"'Kay," he replied, not looking up as he resumed his game. I stood in the doorway of the shop and kept watch over Toby and Audrey at the same time. I hoped I might see some movement from her but she remained sickeningly still.

When Sandie and Dan arrived I gave Toby a hug. "Go on, be a good boy."

He went with Sandie reluctantly and Dan drove my car back home.

I ran back into the shop and knelt down next to Audrey picking up her hand in both of mine. She felt cold. I tucked my coat around her as best I could.

"Oh Audrey, I'm so sorry this has happened to you," I whispered.

There was a huge gash on her left temple and the blood from it had smeared and dried on her face. "Where are you ambulance?" I demanded impatiently, and as if in response, the ambulance's siren came blasting down the street. It stopped outside, its blue lights bouncing around the walls of the shop. Two paramedics came in and set to work with their preliminary checks and fired questions at me before carefully lifting Audrey onto a stretcher and carrying her out into the ambulance. All I could do was stand and watch. The sight of my dear friend, lying motionless on a stretcher with her head in a brace looking ashen and bloody, was something I never wanted to see again. I locked the door and jumped into the back of the ambulance.

It seemed to take forever to get to the hospital. "Is she going to be alright?" I asked shakily.

"I can't really give you an accurate answer," replied one of the paramedics. "The doctors need to take a proper look at her. But I'll be honest with you, she's not in great shape."

Tears began to stream down my cheeks. What psycho would beat up a poor defenceless woman? *Bastards, bastards, bastards!* I felt angry and guilty that Audrey was in this condition. Ahran's warnings came back to haunt me, but I quickly shoved them to the back of my mind. If I hadn't left her on her own this might never have happened. "Nearly there," the paramedic said kindly.

We pulled into the ambulance bay at the hospital and as soon as the back doors were open there were half a dozen people tending to Audrey. All I could do was answer their questions and follow on helplessly.

"I'm sorry, you can't come in here," one of the nurses said, as she put her arms around my shoulders and steered me away from the double doors Audrey and the team of medical staff had just disappeared through. "There's a coffee machine over there," she said, pointing to a drinks machine near the door. "Why don't you get yourself a hot drink and sit down? As soon as I know anything I will come and update you."

I nodded and did as she said. I took a sip of sweet hot coffee and sat down. The tears had stopped and I stared numbly at nothing in particular. I don't know how long I had been sitting there when an unfamiliar ringtone rang in my pocket, making me nearly jump out of my skin.

Damn! I had meant to call Ahran, but during the drama of the ambulance ride I had forgotten all about it. He must have gone to the house like we had arranged.

"Hello?" I answered tentatively.

"Why didn't you call me?" he asked angrily. His accent sounded stronger than I remembered. I didn't like his tone at all. "For your information, my dearest friend is lying on a hospital bed fighting for her life, so forgive me for not informing you of my every move." Why should I care his journey had been wasted? "We will just have to rearrange our meeting," I said icily.

"What happened to her?" he asked in a more controlled voice.

"She was attacked in the shop," I snapped back.

There was the briefest of pauses.

"You do realise that what happened to your friend was meant for you?"

I went cold. "What do you mean?" I closed my eyes knowing what his response would be and fearing it all the same.

"I'm pretty sure their intention was to kill you, but your friend was in the wrong place at the wrong time. You are lucky she isn't dead or that it's not you."

"Was it Bazeera?" I asked in a shaky voice, knowing that his warnings were begin to stack up.

"I'm almost certain she was behind it. After I'd been to your house, I went to your shop to see if I could find anything that might give me a clue as to what had happened.

There was no sign of anything missing, there was money in the till and nobody had touched your safe. The person who attacked your friend was only after one thing and that was *you*."

I hated the thought of what Audrey had suffered, but I daren't think about what might have happened if I hadn't had my appointment at the bank. Where would *that* have left Toby?

I felt like I might throw up. Whatever evidence Ahran had come to show me this evening now paled into insignificance. Mine and Toby's lives were seriously in danger and as much as I didn't like to admit it, we were going to need all the help Ahran was offering.

"Sophie, are you still there?" he asked, breaking my train of thought.

"Yes, I'm still here," I said quietly.

"Will your friend live?"

I balked at his directness. "I don't know," I looked at the clock; it had been nearly three hours. "Nobody has told me anything yet."

"I'm on my way to the hospital," he announced.

"No, stay there with Toby. Keep him safe," I argued.

"It's okay, my sister Elaya will be at your house shortly."

I thought about Ahran's size and strength, surely he would make a far better bodyguard than a girl. "I'd rather you stayed with him."

"Don't worry, Elaya can protect your nephew as well as I can." I pictured one of those American female wrestlers I'd seen on WWE wrestling Toby liked to watch on a

Saturday morning and felt more comforted. "Besides how are you going to get home, your car is parked on your drive."

He had a point.

"Well I am not leaving until I know Audrey is alright," I said stubbornly. I felt out of control. The plan I'd had where I called the shots had now been completely blown out of the water.

"Of course. I'll be there as soon as I can." He hung up.

Despite the sickening worry I felt for Audrey I felt traitorous butterflies in my stomach at the thought of seeing Ahran again.

I put the phone back in my pocket. A couple of minutes later my phone rang in my other pocket. I looked at the caller display. It was Marcus. My heart sank. I didn't want to have to explain anything to him for the time being.

"Hi Marcus."

"Sophie, are you alright? How's Audrey?"

I was supposed to have called him to tell him what I wanted to see at the cinema at the weekend, but so much had happened I had hardly given him a second thought.

"Not good I'm afraid. I'm still waiting for the registrar to come out and tell me how she is." I fought back tears.

"I hadn't heard from you and when I called the house, Sandie told me where you were. What happened?"

"It looks like Audrey was attacked as she was shutting up the shop."

"Why on earth would someone want to attack her?" he asked incredulously.

"I don't know, maybe they were after the takings?" I

cringed as I lied. "Perhaps the police will be able to tell us more tomorrow." I knew the hospital was obliged to inform the police and it wouldn't be long before they came to ask questions.

"Look, do you want me to come to the hospital? I'm sure there's somebody there I know, I could try and speed things along a bit."

It was very sweet of him to offer, but the last thing I wanted was for Marcus to meet Ahran and start asking questions about who he was and why he was here.

"Oh! It looks like the registrar is on his way over now," I lied for the second time. "I've got to go, I'll give you a call when I know more." He barely had time to say goodbye before I hung up. I felt guilty, but really didn't need the added complication.

A few moments later a text came through. *'Let me know if you want me to come and pick you up. Mx.'*

My guilt stepped up a gear.

What was I going to tell him? I stared at my phone for a long time, my thumb hovering over the screen whilst I thought about how to reply. Eventually I gave up and stuffed it back in my pocket. I couldn't come up with anything that didn't give too much away, I decided to give it some thought and text him later.

I sat and watched another medical team rush in from the ambulance bay. I caught a glimpse of a child lying on a trolley, one of the nurses was holding up a drip attached to his or her little arm. A couple clung to each other sobbing as they followed their child. I turned away, tears stinging my eyes. The thought of Toby lying on one of those trolleys made me feel sick to the stomach. I closed my eyes and drew in an unsteady breath. I hated hospitals. Other than when I had been Katie's birthing partner, every other trip I'd made to a hospital had brought pain and loss. I found the smell and atmosphere cloying and every minute I spent in one made me feel more and more claustrophobic. I fidgeted in my chair. How many more torturous minutes would I have to wait before anyone gave me an update on Audrey's condition? I couldn't fight it any longer, I needed to go outside. I concentrated on walking at a normal pace and tried not to break into a run as I made my way to the front entrance.

I finally made it outside and sucked in the night air leaning my back against the wall to steady myself. I closed my eyes. The air was cold and it made my lungs ache.

I took another deep breath and opened my eyes to see Ahran striding towards me. He was dressed all in black; black boots, black jeans and a black, leather motorcycle jacket. His short blonde hair stood out in contrast. He cut quite a picture as his long legs ate up the distance between us. My pulse jumped at the sight of him. His broad shoulders blocked my view as he stopped in front of me. *Flippin' heck, those eyes!*

"Have you heard anything?" he said, without even saying hello. There it was again, that look as if I irritated him. What *was* his problem? It bugged me no end that I found him so bloody attractive.

"*Hello* Ahran," I said, unable to hide my sarcasm. "No, I haven't heard anything. You obviously aren't familiar with

English hospitals; it's customary not to tell anyone anything for hours on end."

"Come on," he said, taking my elbow and frogmarched me through the hospital. Pulling my arm away from him, I stole a sideways glance at his profile and noticed the muscle at his jaw flexing. He seemed really pissed off. I started to seethe. *Who the hell did he think he was?* I was just beginning to get my life sorted out and then he turned up and it had all started to unravel again. Self-pity began to mingle with anger. I hadn't asked for any of this, all I'd done was try to establish a more settled life and do what was right for Toby. I did my best to demonstrate my annoyance whilst we walked, although frankly this was difficult as I struggled to keep up with his pace.

I tried not to notice the female attention Ahran's presence attracted in the A&E waiting room. As we approached the reception desk, the receptionist looked at me, then at Ahran, and then back to me. I got the distinct impression she was wondering what the likes of me was doing with the likes of him. His leather jacket creaked as he leant forward and I got a waft of aftershave, leather and that smell of the sun again. It was a distracting combination of scents and I took a step away. He started to ask about Audrey, instantaneously switching from Mr Angry to Mr Charming. On the two occasions we had met he had been positively hostile. My annoyance increased. A nurse joined the receptionist and together they fawned over him. I used the excuse of getting another cup of coffee to distance myself. Some women were *so* transparent.

I got my coffee and sat down. Another nurse had joined

the merry twosome at the reception desk, drawn to Ahran like bees to a honey pot. Fawning nurse #1 gave Ahran a dazzling smile and went through the double doors they had taken Audrey through several hours earlier, whilst fawning nurse #2 continued to fawn with the fawning receptionist. I turned away in disgust.

It couldn't have been more than three minutes when the nurse came back through with the registrar. *How did he manage that!?*

Ahran gesticulated towards me and he and the registrar came to where I was sitting, leaving the three fawners to admire Ahran's tidy behind. I couldn't believe I had been there nearly three hours and had heard nothing, and yet Ahran had managed to get the head honcho to come out in under three minutes. The registrar was laughing at something Ahran had said as they approached me.

The doctor's face turned serious. "Miss McAllister, sorry you have had to wait so long, my team have been working hard to stabilise Ms Goodfellow. She has several cracked ribs, a broken wrist, severe concussion and we think she's suffered a stroke, probably brought on by the trauma of the attack."

"Oh my God," I said quietly, my hand covering my mouth in shock.

"We can't be certain about the extent to which the stroke will have affected her, but she should make a complete recovery from her other injuries," he continued.

"Can I see her?" I croaked, my mouth suddenly feeling parched.

"Not tonight I'm afraid. Ms Goodfellow has been

moved into intensive care so that she can be closely moni-
tored, she is heavily sedated."

I wasn't sure what I had expected to hear, but Audrey's
condition sounded bleaker than I had feared. I stifled a sob.
Ahran stepped forward and put his arm around me, I was
grateful for the support.

"Why don't you go home and get some rest and give us
a call in the morning?" the registrar suggested.

I nodded barely able to see the doctor through my tears.
He gave me a sympathetic smile.

"Thank you," I said. He gave a curt nod in response and
headed back towards the emergency room.

I turned and sobbed into Ahran's chest. I felt him tense
and then he put his arms around me. His embrace was reassuring and I forgave his previous abruptness just a fraction
as I welcomed his sympathy.

"Come on, let's get you home," he said gently. It was
the nicest he had been to me so far.

I allowed him to steer me out of the hospital. It was
bitingly cold outside and in stark contrast to the hot dry air
of the hospital. I took a couple of deep breaths welcoming
the cold burn of it again. We silently made our way to
Ahran's car. I sat in the passenger's seat and let my head fall
back onto the headrest, the leather seat felt cold. Ahran
made his way around to the driver's door. I took in a deep
breath, the car smelt of him. I closed my eyes and allowed
the events of the evening to sink in.

Ahran started the engine and the warmth of the heated
seat began to seep through my jeans.

"Are you alright?" he asked, the glow of the orange street lamp overhead casting a funny light into the car.

"I feel a bit better now I've come outside," I replied, turning to look at him.

"You'll feel better once you've had some sleep." He had an odd look on his face.

I glanced at the clock on the dashboard, it was gone ten. It seemed very quiet and intimate in the car compared to the noise and bustle of the hospital. "Ahran, I want to thank you. You didn't have to come to the hospital and I don't know what you said to those nurses, but it had the desired effect."

Ahran gave me a lop-sided grin, it was the first time I had seen him smile and it did funny things to my insides. I struggled to tear my eyes away from his. I really didn't want to dwell on my reaction to him. I was tired, I'd had a traumatic evening and my guard was down, that was all.

"It was the least I could do, if I had been more vigilant I could have prevented your friend from being attacked. At least now we know that Bazeera means business and we cannot take any chances. I want you to seriously consider coming to stay with my family, it is the only way we can assure the safety of you both."

I knew this evening had left me with little choice and I felt despair wash over me. Toby and I would be safe from Bazeera if we stayed with Ahran's family, but I was also painfully aware that Toby was heir to a large and wealthy kingdom, once he was there they would not let go of him easily.

"Can we talk about this in the morning?" I asked wearily.

Ahran hesitated as if he wanted to say more, but he just nodded and reversed the car before pulling out of the car park. He drove fast and I willed myself not to look at the speed dial preferring not to know what breakneck speed we were travelling at. A couple of times I looked over at his profile, he was deep in thought. All I hoped was that he was concentrating on the road. Nevertheless, I was thankful for his silence. It surprised me how comfortable I felt with him. I usually felt the need to say whatever inane thought came into my head with people I'd only just met, I didn't like uncomfortable silences, but for some reason I didn't feel like this with him. Maybe it was because he hadn't gone out of his way to be too friendly with me. I wasn't sure, but I was happy to be left alone with my thoughts.

We got back to the house in record time. Ahran parked behind my Land Rover in front of the garage. I couldn't have been more pleased to see the welcoming glow of my porch light. All I could think about now was my bed.

"Thanks for driving me back," I said, daring to look into his eyes. Why did I find them so hypnotising?

"It was the least I could do," he replied.

I went to get out of the car.

"If I could change any of this I would."

I turned back to look at him. He hadn't made any attempt to move and I wasn't sure what he was referring to exactly.

He held my gaze, but didn't elaborate any further.

Suddenly the atmosphere between us changed. It no longer felt so easy going and comfortable.

"Let's go inside," I said, clearing my throat and got out of the car.

Ahran joined me on the garden path and we walked to the front door. A woman was standing under the porch waiting for us. Where had she come from? She was absolutely stunning. She had short blonde, spikey hair, delicate features and must have been at least six feet tall.

6

Ahran spoke to the woman in a language I wasn't familiar with.

"This is my sister, Elaya," he said, making the introductions. She didn't look anything like the American female wrestler I had imagined. The Elessar family obviously had good genes. "Elaya, Sophie McAllister."

She offered me her hand. "Hello Sophie." Her voice was slightly husky and more heavily accented than Ahran's. Her handshake was extremely firm and she eyed me curiously.

"How is your friend?" she asked.

"Not great. She's in intensive care."

"I'm sorry."

"Thanks. Shall we go in, it's cold." They were both making me nervous and I scrabbled around in my bag for my keys. "Aha! Here they are," I said awkwardly.

The house felt warm and I closed the door against the biting cold. "Can I take your coats?" I offered. They both handed me their jackets and I hung them up with mine.

Sandie came and stood in the kitchen doorway. "Hi," she said, looking from Ahran to Elaya with a confused expression on her face. She clearly recognised Ahran. She had been right, he wasn't easy to forget.

"Hi Sandie, this is Ahran and Elaya Elessar. They are, er, friends of mine."

"Hello, nice to meet you," she said, looking even more confused, but was too polite to say anything.

They shook her hand, but didn't respond. Sandie looked decidedly uncomfortable and blushed. Being in the presence of such beautiful people was most definitely disquieting.

"How's Toby?" I asked.

"He's fine; he went out like a light as usual. How's Audrey?" she asked.

"Not great, we should know more in the morning."

"Poor Audes," Sandie said sympathetically. "Will you let me know how she is?"

"Yes of course. Thank you for helping me out at such short notice." I took a twenty pound note out of my purse and held it out to her. "I really appreciate it."

"No problem, any time," she said, shaking her head at the money. "Don't worry about it, I'm just happy I was able to help out."

Dan came and joined her.

"This is Dan, Sandie's boyfriend," I said, introducing him to Ahran and Elaya. They both nodded.

"Ok, well, we'll be off then," Sandie said. The small hallway suddenly felt very crowded.

"Go through," I said to my guests. I turned back to

Sandie and Dan. "Thanks again." I saw them out and took a deep breath before returning to the kitchen where Ahran and Elaya were waiting. They were having a hushed conversation which came to an abrupt end when I entered the kitchen.

"Would you like a tea or coffee?" I asked.

"No, thank you," Elaya replied.

"Not for me," Ahran said.

I felt a sudden wave of exhaustion. I doubted whether they would leave Toby and me on our own now, and to be frank I didn't want to be left alone after Audrey's violent attack.

"You are both very welcome to stay the night," I offered, trying to make them feel more at ease.

They exchanged a few words, but just Ahran answered. "Thank you. Elaya will go home, I will stay. From now on, one of us will be with you at all times until you and Toby can come and stay with our family."

I couldn't help but feel irritated that the decision had been taken out of my hands.

"Goodbye Sophie," Elaya said, shaking my hand again. "I hope you and your nephew are able to return with us soon, it is not safe for you here."

"Yes, so it would seem," I replied.

Elaya's expression softened a little.

"It was nice meeting you. Oh and thank you for your help," I said.

She acknowledged my gratitude with a nod and a smile. She really was beautiful, I felt decidedly plain stood next to them both.

Elaya and Ahran exchanged a few more words and Elaya left.

"Well, I need to go to bed," I announced.

Ahran looked as if he was contemplating what to say next. He took a deep breath. "There is more I need to tell you."

"Can't it wait until the morning?" I said, stifling a yawn, but the expression on his face began to ring alarm bells and my curiosity got the better of me. "What is it?"

"You have to promise that what I am about to tell you, you will keep to yourself, because if you don't, we will have far worse problems on our hands than the ones we already have. Please don't even tell Toby, he will know soon enough."

I sat down at the kitchen table. What could it possibly be? I wasn't sure I could take much more.

He seemed to be taking his time to choose his words carefully as he pulled out a chair for himself. "I am from a place called Ramia."

I had never been any good at Geography so I wasn't particularly surprised when I didn't recognise the name.

"I've never heard of it, where is it?"

"You wouldn't have heard of it because it isn't *exactly* in this world," he said carefully, watching for my reaction.

I shook my head slightly feeling confused. "What do you mean it isn't *exactly* in this world?"

"The place I am from is...not on this planet."

I struggled to suppress a laugh and made a funny snorting noise in the back of my throat.

He ignored me and continued straight faced. "My world is in a parallel universe," he said slowly.

"Riiight, so you are some kind of Dr Who Time Lord?" I said, nodding slowly. I knew I was tired, but the man had clearly gone mad.

Ahran looked offended. "No, not at all, Dr Who is a character in science fiction and as far as I'm aware you can't travel through time, but you can travel between universes," he confirmed.

There wasn't a hint of a smile on his face. He really was serious. Oh. My. God. I was dealing with a nutcase. Why did I let him and Bennie convince me that what he had told me was the truth? Audrey wasn't beaten up by someone who was after me, it had been a coincidence. *Oh hell!* What if it wasn't a coincidence? What if *he* had beaten Audrey up in order to gain my confidence? I'd been a complete idiot. I had started to believe this elaborate ruse and now I had let this psychopath into my home.

I stood up feeling sick and shaky.

"Well Ahran, that's fascinating, but it really is getting late, thanks for picking me up from the hospital, there really is no need for you to stay I'm sure we will be fine. How about I call you in the morning?" I said with forced cheeriness. "Let me show you out." I started to walk towards the front door in the hope he would follow me, frantically looking for something I could defend myself with. When I realised he hadn't moved I dived into the lounge searching for anything that would serve as a weapon, my breathing came hard and fast as the panic set in. I caught sight of the cast iron companion set stood next to the log burner. I lunged forward and grabbed the fire poker.

"Sophie?"

Ahran's voice came from behind me.

I spun around wielding the poker. "Don't you dare come near me or I swear I'll stab you with this." I was aware he had a distinct height and strength advantage and I probably didn't stand a chance, but I was prepared to die trying anyway.

"Sophie, don't be ridiculous, I'm not going to hurt you." He raised his hands as if he was placating someone who was about to do something very stupid.

I moved forward waving the poker from left to right as if it was some lethal light sabre. "Get out of my house," I said as menacingly as I could.

"Sophie, calm down. I know what I have just said is difficult to believe, but I swear it's the truth." He took a step towards me.

It was now or never and I charged at him growling like a woman possessed. I didn't care, I wasn't going down without a fight. But before I knew what had happened, Ahran had grabbed the poker, bent it in half, clamped my hands behind my back, spun me around and pulled me off balance, which caused me to slam back against his chest and the air to leave my lungs in a rush.

"You *bastard!*" I said through gritted teeth. "If you touch one hair on Toby's head I *will* kill you," I threatened. I struggled to break free, but he held me firmly. I aimed a backwards kick at his shin and made perfect contact.

"Ah!" His grip loosened slightly. "You are stronger than you look," he said with a hint of admiration in his voice.

I struggled, but it made no difference. Negotiation was the only thing I had left in my rather pathetic armoury.

"Look," I said. "If it's money you're after, I can get money, just please don't hurt the boy." I was starting to feel desperate; I didn't care if I was harmed. "Please don't hurt Toby." My voice broke.

Ahran released my hands and turned me around. I found myself sobbing into his chest, for the second time that night.

"Please believe me Sophie, I have no intention of hurting you or Toby, I've been sent here to protect you."

I pulled back and looked up into his face, his expression was wary. I stared at him for a moment or two wondering whether to believe him.

Ahran hesitated, clearly unsure whether I was about to lash out at him again. When he seemed satisfied that I had calmed down enough not to go in for a second strike, he relaxed.

"Sit down," he said.

Suddenly, I felt too exhausted to argue and did as he said. He came and sat in the chair opposite me.

"Are you some kind of alien?" I said, not quite believing I was asking him this question.

"Not in the 'little green man' sense," he said with amusement in his eyes, "But, I am different to you."

What did he mean different? He looked like any normal human being to me, okay, not *normal*, his looks were extraordinary, but he had the usual outward attributes of a human being.

"So you're not human?" I asked.

Ahran frowned. "No, I am human, but I have certain...advantages."

I looked at the bent poker lying on the floor. "Well, you're strong, I'll give you that," I said, eying the mangled piece of metal.

"Strength is one of them," he confirmed.

I thought back over the last few minutes. "And fast," I added.

"Much faster than any athlete. I also have heightened senses: sight; smell; hearing and taste."

"So you are some kind of superhuman?" Now that my fear had subsided, my interest increased.

"Yes," he replied, looking relieved I was now listening to him.

"And you really come from another world?" I asked.

"Yes."

I sat there unembarrassed, staring at his beautiful face for a while, trying to take in what he was telling me.

"How is this at all possible? Why have I never met anyone like you before? It's like...like something out of a film, like Superman or Star Wars and that stuff is just made up," I babbled.

"Well, unfortunately I can't fly," he said with a hint of a smile.

"How did you get like this?" I said, gesturing towards him.

He chuckled. "I was born like it. The origins of my race are human, but we are more evolved than yours." He didn't say this as if he was gloating, just a statement of fact.

My mind buzzed with questions. "So Toby's father was like you?"

"Yes, Toby is half Ramian," he answered, following my line of enquiry. Things were starting to click into place. It explained so much. Why Toby was so good at sport, why he could identify a bird in the sky a hundred metres away and why he could hear a car approaching way before I could. I'd never really questioned it before, he was just Toby and like any doting aunt, I adored him. "He's hardly had a day's sick in his life," I mused out loud.

"It is rare that we are sick. We are resistant to most bacteria and viruses and if we are injured we heal quickly."

"Are you immortal?" My mind starting to go into overdrive.

Ahran laughed. "No, although our life span is longer than yours, typically we live to about two hundred although some have lived to nearly two twenty, but only if they have lived entirely in Ramia. We age much quicker on Earth, it's to do with atmospherics. Our atmosphere has a higher concentration of oxygen and is much cleaner. Your atmosphere is full of toxins," he said, sounding slightly judgemental.

"How many are there of you here?"

"It varies, not all Ramians are allowed to travel here, you need to gain special permission, but there could be up to several thousand Ramians on Earth at any one time."

My eyebrows shot up. "Several thousand?! How come no one knows about you all?"

"It's our best kept secret. There is much in our world that would be very precious and beneficial to your kind and we would be in danger if Sapiens discovered us and our planet."

"So does everyone look like you?" I gazed at his perfect features. What I really wanted to ask was, '*Are all Ramians as attractive as you are?*'

"We are generally taller than your kind, but other than that we don't look any different."

"Oh right," I nodded somewhat relieved, although not convinced that his looks were on a par with any man I had seen on Earth.

"How old are you?"

"Sixty five."

I snorted and laughed. "Well, I have to say, you look good on it," I said, my eyes scanning up his body.

"I am still a relatively young adult where I come from."

"So if I lived in your world I would live longer?" This presented possibilities.

"Yes, although not as long as a Ramian." He hesitated. "You must keep what I've just told you to yourself for Toby's sake, if anyone ever found out that he is half Sapien, half Ramian, he would be of great interest to your scientists and government. Could you imagine how powerful it would make this country if they found the DNA answer to a superior human being?"

I looked at him blankly. Dr Who or no Dr Who this was most definitely the stuff of science fiction.

"You must have heard of cloning?" he asked.

"Oh yes, right," I said nodding. It was so much to take in I felt punch drunk. I yawned feeling brain and bone weary.

"You are tired. This is difficult for you to take in on top of an already traumatic day, why don't you go to bed. We can talk more in the morning."

I sat there letting what he had told me percolate through my mind. *His eyes really were a lovely shade of blue and his face was beautiful yet masculine.* And then a thought struck me, "You can't read minds can you?"

"No. I wish. You just look exhausted." His face softened a fraction.

Thank God for that!

"Now that you mention it I feel wrung out." My mind drifted to poor Audrey lying in a hospital bed battered and bruised; it seemed an age ago that I was sat in the waiting room unaware of any of this. "Well, this certainly has been an interesting evening," I said, shaking my head in disbelief.

"You must understand that Bazeera and her soldiers are dangerous people and you would not stand a chance against them." His tone had become more business like once again.

"I can see that now," I said wearily and yawned again. "I'm sorry I really need to go to bed." Although, there was a part of me that questioned how I was ever going to be able to sleep after finding out about other worlds and superhumans.

"Yes of course," he said, standing up.

I got to my feet. "The spare room bed is made up. It's up the stairs, the second door on the right. There are towels in the airing cupboard in the bathroom. Please make yourself at home."

I felt shaky and wobbly.

Ahran grabbed my arm and held me steady. A funny

expression flickered across his face. He was not an easy person to read. One minute he was cool, brusque, almost hostile, the next minute he was gentle and compassionate. I struggled to keep up.

"I'm fine...stood up too quickly...head rush," I explained, although his closeness wasn't helping matters. "Night then," I said, stepping away from him.

"Goodnight Sophie," he said quietly and made his way upstairs.

I walked into the kitchen in a state of disbelief, let Mungo out and leant against the counter waiting for him to do his business outside. I rubbed my eyes. Well, it had been quite an evening. I can honestly say I would never have guessed any of it in a million years. *Toby is half superhuman!* It just sounded so ridiculous. I shook my head again. Not only did I need to digest everything Ahran had told me, but I had to contend with him sleeping in the room next to me. The odds of getting a decent night's sleep tonight were definitely stacked against me.

Mungo started howling like he was some very important link in the local dog telegraph and I opened the back door. "Mungo! No one is interested in what you've got to say," I said sharply and he trotted in. He had the decency to look sheepish. I gave him a biscuit and he curled up in his bed.

I switched off the lights downstairs except for the lamp in the hallway and headed upstairs myself. I caught sight of myself in the bathroom mirror. I was pale, my eyes looked puffy and my lips were slightly swollen. That always happened when I cried. I pictured Elaya. I must seem pretty mediocre if she was the type of woman Ahran was used to.

What the hell was I thinking? Good looking or not, he ran hot and cold and wasn't even from this planet! I really needed my head seeing to if, in addition to everything I had learnt about Toby this evening, I thought I had any chance with Ahran.

I took my phone out of my back pocket. There were three missed calls from Marcus.

Bugger! It was a timely reminder that I was in fact seeing someone. I cowardly chose to send him a text.

Sorry I missed your calls, my phone was on silent. I met a neighbour at the hospital and she gave me a lift home, thanks for the offer anyway. Sx.

I cringed as I sent it, he deserved better than that, but then it wasn't every day you find out your nephew is half superhuman. Somehow I would make it up to him.

I went in and checked on Toby. He was lying on top of his duvet and I carefully tucked him back in. I stood and watched him sleeping for a minute or two. He had no idea who he was and the legacy his father had left him. What did the future hold for him? I wished I could feel some of the optimism I had felt a couple of days ago, but what I had found out this evening had changed everything. Our lives were never going to be the same again. So much for trying to lead a normal life.

7

I prayed that the morning had brought an improvement in Audrey's condition. I got up and opened the curtains and heard movement in the spare room next door. I glanced at myself in the dressing table mirror. After only a few hours' sleep my eyes still looked puffy. Maybe a shower would help.

I opened my bedroom door and came face to face with my half-naked house guest. He'd obviously had the same idea if the towel under his arm was anything to go by. "Oh, um morning." I was caught off-guard, distracted by his spectacular bare chest. My gaze travelled down the most magnificent body I had ever had the good fortune to come across in the flesh. His chest was broad, like an Olympic swimmer's and every muscle in both his chest and abdomen were clearly defined. His skin was a natural bronze and there was a smattering of fuzzy dark blonde hair that dipped down into his boxer shorts. Before my eyes could betray me any further, I forced myself to look up into his face. I knew I was blushing, I could feel the heat spreading up my neck and across my cheeks which only made me blush more.

"Morning," he replied. There was that look again, as if I was a source of irritation.

I cleared my throat. "Did you sleep well?"

"Yes," he said in a clipped tone, his expression closed. *Great!* We were back to frosty again.

"Good, good. Hope you don't mind, I'm just going to jump in the shower," I said breezily.

Before he could answer I dashed into the bathroom. I should have offered him the bathroom first, but his state of undress was too distracting and I wasn't quite sure how to handle his unnerving mood swings. It seemed a good idea to remove myself as quickly as possible before I said anything stupid.

I was thankful for the sanctuary of the bathroom, but felt a surge of anger as I leant up against the closed door. I was angry at myself for acting like a naive virgin who had never seen a semi-naked male body before, but I was angrier at him. He had come here and delivered several bombshells of atomic proportions, the least he could do was be a bit nicer. The compassion he had shown last night had obviously been an act because in the cold light of day he was back to being cold and aloof. Frankly, I felt I deserved more. He had no idea what it was like to be told that there were other universes and extra-terrestrials who travelled undetected to and fro between your world and theirs. And then, to top it all, that your dear, precious little nephew, who was your reason for existing, was one of them.

I took a few deep breaths to compose myself. I was

going to have to develop a thicker skin and get used to him being around, because for the time being, Toby and I needed him. I switched the shower on and got in, welcoming the almost scalding heat.

When I had finished and my skin was hot and red, I wrapped myself in a towel and cracked the bathroom door open to see if the coast was clear. Fortunately, his door was shut and I dashed back to my room. I was going to call out to him and tell him that the bathroom was free, but then with his superhuman hearing, he would probably know that already.

I sat in front of the mirror and dried my hair. I would have to offer Toby some kind of explanation as to who Ahran was; it wasn't as if I was in the habit of having men stay over. I decided I would just say he was a friend from London who had dropped in unexpectedly.

For once my hair actually behaved itself and it hung in soft waves below my shoulders. I wriggled into a pair of Levi's, a fitted white t-shirt and a cerise pink, V-neck, lamb's wool sweater that clung in all the right places. I always felt good in it, the colour suited me. I quickly applied some mascara and some tinted lip gloss and gave myself the once over in the full-length mirror. I didn't usually put this much effort into my appearance for the school run, but for some reason this morning I felt the need to try a bit harder. I forced a smile at myself before going into Toby's room to open his curtains. "Time to get up sweetheart." I stared at his little, sleeping, half-superhuman form. He was fast asleep and completely oblivious to how his life was about to change.

I left him to come round and went downstairs. Even though I still hadn't come to terms with going to Ramia with Toby, I began to think about all the things I would have to do if we did. Audrey usually had Mungo if we went away, but she wasn't going to be able to help in her current condition, and what would I do about the shop?

And then it hit me. This wasn't just some trip abroad for a bit of sun, sea and sand, we were going to another bloody universe! Well, I assumed we were, unless Ahran's family had some kind of set up here on Earth. This was a fundamental piece of information that Ahran had, as yet, neglected to tell me, although admittedly, I hadn't asked. Bennie would have gone mad if she'd known. I switched the kettle on and tried to think about how one might travel to another universe. Unfortunately, my lukewarm liking of futuristic films had left me severely lacking, all I could come up with was a round spaceship with blue flashing lights. *Great!* I had found myself in the starring role of the sequel to Close Encounters of the Third Kind. I didn't like flying at the best of times, but the thought of travelling in some kind of flying saucer took my anxiety to a whole new level. Wasn't there a decent risk of burning up as you left the Earth's atmosphere? *Please* let Ahran's family have some kind of second home somewhere on Earth. Now, if it was a palatial villa in the Seychelles, I could be more easily persuaded.

The hot water system fired up and interrupted my flow of thoughts. I quickly blocked the image of rivulets of water running down Ahran's naked body and put the breakfast things out on the table. I really needed to have sex with

Marcus. Having had such a long period without it was making my imagination run wild. Funny that I hadn't felt like this until Mr Elessar had turned up.

I didn't feel particularly hungry, but put some bread in the toaster anyway. Mungo hadn't moved from his bed and I absentmindedly wondered how long he would go without having a pee if I didn't force him out of the back door. "You need to go out," I said. He just about managed to open his eyes and looked at me as if to say *'It's freezing out there! Are you out of your mind?'*

"Mungo!"

He got up slowly, had his usual stretch and trotted out the back door ignoring me as I stood there holding it open for him. "I thought Weimaraners were supposed to be lively," I muttered to myself.

Now, what do superhumans eat for breakfast? I scanned the cereal cupboard. The phone rang and I glanced at the clock. Surely it was too early to be the hospital, unless something dreadful had happened over night. My heart skipped a beat. I snatched up the cordless phone from the windowsill.

"Hello?" I answered anxiously.

"You were supposed to phone me last night," said a groggy, slightly disgruntled voice on the other end.

I took a deep breath and relaxed. "I'm sorry Ben, a lot happened yesterday." I cradled the phone between my ear and shoulder and buttered my toast. "Audrey was attacked in the coffee shop and I spent most of the evening in the hospital."

"*Jesus!* Is she alright?"

"We don't know yet, in fact I thought you might be the hospital phoning to give me an update. When I left last night they had just moved her into intensive care. She's had a stroke and is unconscious. Hopefully, they should know more this morning."

"Oh God Sophe, I'm so sorry, is there anything I can do?" she offered.

"Thanks, but there's nothing anyone can do at the moment, we'll just have to wait and see how she is when she comes round."

"Bloody hell. I can't believe it. Give her a big hug from me. I'll send some flowers or something."

"I'm sure she'd appreciate that, thanks Ben."

She paused. "So you didn't see the mysterious Ahran Elessar last night then?" she asked.

I contemplated lying, but knew she would suss me out. "He met me at the hospital and brought me home."

Just at that moment Ahran walked into the kitchen looking fresh faced and gorgeous, in a dark navy shirt and dark jeans. *Oh dear Lord!*

I smiled at him and pointed to the phone as if it wasn't obvious what I was doing.

He stood in the doorway looking at me, his head cocked to one side, an unreadable expression on his face.

I put my hand over the phone. "Help yourself to breakfast."

"He's still there?!" Bennie's high pitched voice screeched from the other end of the line.

"Yes," I said, irritated by the conclusions that I knew she

was drawing and feeling embarrassed knowing that Ahran could probably hear her.

Was that a smile I saw on his face?

It was too awkward putting Bennie straight in front of him and so I opted to say nothing. I would have to tell her an edited version of what happened last night, later. Even though she was my best friend, I knew I couldn't tell her about Toby's origins.

I picked up my breakfast and moved into the lounge for some privacy. I lowered my voice and wondered just how good his hearing was. "Unfortunately, everything he told me about Toby being in danger is true. He seems to think the person who attacked Audrey was after me." I bit off a mouthful of toast.

"Oh my God Sophie! What did the police say?"

"I haven't spoken to the police yet, although I expect I'll see them this morning."

"So, what are you going to do?"

"I don't know yet. Look, I'm going to have to go, I need to get Toby up and off to school, can I call you later?"

"Okay, but make sure you do," she insisted.

"Yeah of course. Bye hun." We both hung up.

I went back into the kitchen and tipped the remainder of my breakfast in the bin. Ahran was buttering six pieces of toast. I suppose it didn't come as much of a surprise that he had a big appetite. "Did you find everything you need?" I asked.

"Yes, thanks," he replied and carried his plate and a glass of milk over to the table.

"Good, um, I'm just going upstairs to get Toby up," I

said when I realised I was staring at him. "He and I need to have a little chat before he comes down." I refrained from saying that Toby wasn't used to seeing men here. "You know, try and give him an explanation as to why you're here."

He nodded and took a sip of his milk.

I climbed the stairs and went into Toby's room. He had managed to drag himself out of bed and was getting dressed. I sat on the chair by his desk. "Toby, there is a man downstairs, his name is Ahran and he is going to be staying with us for a little while."

"What happened to Dr Marcus?" he asked

"Oh Ahran isn't my boyfriend." I couldn't help wondering whether Marcus was anymore. "He's just a friend from London and needs a place to stay for a little while." I hadn't been able to think of anything else that wouldn't have him asking lots of questions.

"Did he used to be your boyfriend?"

"No." I stood up and pulled the collar of his polo shirt out of his sweater. "Come downstairs and have some breakfast and you can meet him."

I left him to finish getting dressed. Ahran was still sat at the kitchen table looking relaxed and at home in my kitchen.

"You need to make arrangements to leave," he said. "The quicker we can get you to King Halsan's the better."

"Is King Halsan Toby's grandfather?" I asked.

"Yes. He is an important and powerful man. His home is extremely well-protected, you will be safe there."

After the superhuman, alien shocker, I had forgotten that Toby was royalty as well.

At that moment, Toby came running down the stairs. "Hello," he said, greeting Ahran as he came into the kitchen.

"Hello Toby," Ahran replied, studying him as if he was a new and fascinating exhibit at some museum.

I busied myself pouring out Toby's cereal and milk and he sat down at the table. "So, do you like sport?" Ahran asked. I couldn't help but smile to myself, super-evolved being from another planet or not, it was such a *guy* question.

"Love it, my favourite is rugby."

I put Toby's bowl of cereal in front of him.

"I liked rugby, we played a game similar to it at school. What position do you play?"

"Flanker," Toby said through a mouthful of cereal.

"Finish what's in your mouth before you speak," I corrected. If there was a chance he might be a king one day, I was going to have to be stricter about his table manners.

"Is it just rugby you play?" Ahran continued.

"No, I play football and cricket in the summer," Toby answered.

"Your dad was a good cricketer."

My head snapped round and I glared at Ahran. *What the hell was he playing at?*

By the look on his face I could see he'd realised his error too.

Toby stopped eating and looked at Ahran. "You know my dad?"

Ahran looked uncomfortable.

What should I say? I didn't want to lie to Toby, but nor was this the time to go into a lengthy explanation about who his father was, his untimely end and the legacy he had left Toby. He deserved to know the whole story, but just not yet.

I pulled up a chair in front of Toby and took hold of his hands. "Sweetheart, Ahran is your father's cousin and he wants to tell you about your dad, but you've got school today and we need to get going." Toby was about to protest. "We haven't got time to talk about it now, but it is very important that you hear what Ahran has to say. So when you get home from school tonight, when we've got more time, we can talk about it properly then, I promise."

Toby wasn't prepared to let it go that easily.

"But I want to know about my dad now," he demanded.

"Let us talk about it when you get home from school. Auntie Audrey is very sick and I need to go to the hospital this morning to see her and I don't want to be late." Toby loved Audrey like a grandmother and I knew he would understand.

"Okay, but can you pick me up straight after school?"

"Yes, of course I will."

He seemed satisfied with that.

"Now go upstairs and clean your teeth." He did as he was told and ran upstairs.

"I'm really sorry about that, I wasn't thinking," Ahran said.

I sighed. "Don't worry. He will have to know sooner or later, I just would rather have broken it to him slightly differently."

"You dealt with it well," he said, complimenting me.

I was cross with myself for liking his praise. "Toby is a smart and sensible boy," I said, brushing it off.

I collected the dishes and started to wash them up. I noticed Ahran didn't offer to help. He was probably used to having servants do everything for him, I thought sulkily. Well, he wasn't royalty here. I handed him the tea towel. He looked at it blankly.

"Would you mind drying up?" Surely he knew what a tea towel was?

"Oh yes, yes of course." He stood up and took the towel out of my hands.

We worked silently for a minute or two.

"Will he be safe at school?" It was something that had been bugging me.

"It's highly unlikely that Bazeera's people will try anything in such a public place, they will not want to draw attention to themselves. Elaya will watch the school. But you and Toby really need to come back to Ramia as soon as possible," he urged.

"I know I...." I stopped as Toby came into the kitchen.

"There you are. Ready?" I put the last of the dishes on the drainer. I threw Ahran a warning look not wanting to continue our conversation in front of Toby.

Ahran offered to take us to school in his car, but I knew it would set tongues wagging. He followed us closely behind instead. I looked in my rear-view mirror a number of times. After what had happened in the shop, it was reas-suring to know he was there. When we arrived at the school gates I kissed Toby on the cheek and he walked in with Adam.

On my way home, I stopped off at the shop and left a note on the door to say that we would be closed temporarily due to unforeseeable circumstances. Wasn't that just the understatement of the year! Who could have foreseen any of this?! I drove the short distance from the shop, to home, thinking about all I needed to do. I would no doubt have to speak to the police at some point. I wondered if they would want to see the crime scene. Would they do forensics? It was a horrible thought thinking that my coffee shop was now a 'crime scene'.

I rounded the corner of my road and checked that Ahran was still behind me, when my eyes returned to the road I saw the police car parked outside my house.

I parked on the drive and Ahran pulled up behind me. I took a deep breath and got out of the car. "Morning officers," I said as I walked up my front path. Two male police officers had gotten out of the panda car and were stood waiting under the porch.

"Miss McAllister?"

"Yes."

"I'm Constable Mark Wagner," said the taller of the two, "And this is my colleague Constable David Harmsworth. We understand that one of your employees was attacked at your coffee shop late yesterday afternoon."

"Yes, she was," I confirmed. Ahran was now standing next to me.

"May we come in and ask you a few questions about what happened yesterday evening?"

"Yes of course." I knew I had nothing to feel guilty about, but my pulse quickened anyway. Policemen always made me nervous, especially now that I had a whopper of a secret to keep. I glanced up at Ahran, but his face was expressionless.

I unlocked the front door. "Please come in." I led the two constables into the kitchen and Ahran followed. "Take a seat," I offered. They both obliged. Ahran continued to stand and leaned against the work surface. Constable Wagner looked at Ahran and then back to me, his unspoken question hanging in the air. Ahran was a big presence in my kitchen and it was hard to ignore him.

"Oh this is my, er, friend, Ahran Elessar."

Constable Harmsworth wrote something in his notebook. I felt the need to explain. "Ahran knows about the attack, he was with me at the hospital."

They both nodded.

"We're not a couple or anything," I said, sounding flustered, not sure why I felt the need to tell them this. A change of subject was needed before I made myself look even more stupid. "Can I get anyone a tea or coffee?"

All three men declined. I made myself one anyway. I needed tea at a time like this. The policemen waited until I had finished and joined them at the table before they resumed their questioning. Wagner asked the questions and Harmsworth continued to write in his book which I found distinctly unnerving. I was dying to know what he was writing.

"You found Ms Goodfellow after the attack?" It was both a question and a statement.

"Yes, that's right," I replied. "I left Audrey in charge whilst I went to meet with my bank manager. When I'd finished I went back to see if she needed any help closing up and found her lying on the floor at the back of the shop. I called the ambulance straight away."

"I see," he said, which just made me feel more guilty.

"Can you think of any reason why someone would want to attack Ms Goodfellow?"

"No, absolutely none, she is the nicest lady you could ever wish to meet," I said, shaking my head.

The policeman paused. "Do *you* have any enemies Miss McAllister?" I fought the urge to look at Ahran.

"No, not that I'm aware of," I said, lying through my teeth. What else could I have said? Yes, there is some mad woman from a parallel universe who wants to kidnap my nephew to use as a pawn in a bid for power and land. Ordinarily, I would never have lied to a policeman, but Ahran was watching me like a hawk. I came to the uncomfortable realisation that Toby and I were totally reliant on him and his family, there was nobody else we could turn to, not even the police.

"Was anything taken after the attack Miss McAllister?"

"Not that I'm aware of," I answered.

Ahran interrupted. "I'm afraid there was. After I found out what had happened I went to the coffee shop to see if anything had been stolen and the till draw was open and empty."

I choked on my tea. They all looked at me. "Sorry, went down the wrong way," I spluttered.

Ahran continued. "I didn't want to tell Sophie last night because she was too upset. It looks like Ms Goodfellow was the unfortunate victim of a robbery," Ahran said, sounding regretful and sincere.

Both constables nodded, seemingly in agreement. What was it about Ahran that had everyone eating out of his hand?

"Do you know how much was in the till Miss McAllister?"

"About fifty pounds, we don't keep a lot of cash, most people pay by card these days," I explained.

Wagner seemed satisfied with our answers. "Our forensics will need to go in and do a sweep of your shop; they should be there this afternoon. Will you be able to let them in?"

"Yes of course."

"Can they call you on your mobile?" Wagner asked, reading out my number from his notebook. They must have got it from the hospital.

I nodded.

"Okay, that will be all for the moment Miss McAllister, Mr Elessar, thank you for your help."

Harmsworth finished off whatever he was writing in his notepad, looked up and smiled. They both stood up. "I hope your friend makes a speedy recovery," Wagner said as I walked them to the front door.

"Yes, thank you, so do I."

I shut the door behind them and breathed a sigh of relief. I re-joined Ahran in the kitchen. "You told me nothing had been stolen," I said, rounding on him.

"And as I said last night, nothing had been taken. I took the money out of the till to make it look like a robbery. We want the police to think this was a straight-forward burglary and that Audrey got in the way. My people can take care of Bazeera," he said, sounding just like the mafia hood I had accused him of being when we first met.

"Where's the money?" I hadn't meant it to sound like an accusation.

"In a bag under the stairs." Anger flashed briefly across his face, he was clearly offended.

"I'm sorry. I didn't think you had kept it," I said, backpedalling.

He didn't respond, but his expression remained cool and it made me feel uncomfortable. I changed the subject. "Don't you think it is going to look kind of suspicious if Toby and I just take off now?" I hoped he would agree that this was a good reason for me and Toby to stay.

I was disappointed.

"Not at all, you can tell people that you are going on vacation for a while to get over an upsetting turn of events. There is nothing odd about that."

I didn't like to admit it, but he had a point, a robbery in Hatherley would shock its inhabitants and keep them gossiping for weeks, they would expect the shop to close for a while, especially whilst Audrey was in hospital.

The phone rang interrupting our discussion.

I glanced at the clock. It was nearly ten.

I picked it up. "Miss McAllister?"

"Speaking."

"It's Dr. Bhandari here." It was the registrar from the hospital last night. My heart sank, it was virtually unheard of for a doctor to call, unless it was bad news. *Please no, Please no!*

"Is Audrey alright?" I braced myself for his response, my heart now in my throat.

"There's been no great change in her condition I'm afraid. Ms Goodfellow still hasn't regained consciousness, but she remains stable."

I felt a lump forming in my throat.

"She's in a coma?"

"Yes she is."

I clamped my hand over my mouth.

The doctor filled the silence. "This is not necessarily a bad thing Miss McAllister, a patient who has had a head injury will often fall into a light coma. It's the body's way of protecting higher brain function. We suspect that she has sustained damage to the part of the brain called the reticular formation, but we are optimistic that she will gain full consciousness within the next few days."

His optimism made me feel a sliver of hope. They didn't usually say that kind of thing if they weren't sure, although I hated the idea of my dear friend lying in a vegetative state in intensive care even for a day.

"Do you know yet whether there will be any lasting damage?"

"I'm afraid it is too early for us to tell, as you know she suffered a stroke and until she's awake it's almost impossible for us to properly assess any damage that has been caused."

"Can I come in and see her?" I asked.

"Yes that's fine. It's beneficial for a coma patient to have contact with loved ones."

I felt relieved that I would at least be able to visit.

"In that case, I will be in later on. Thank you for phoning doctor."

"Goodbye Miss McAllister." And with that he put the phone down.

I was so thankful that it was not as bleak as I had feared. "I can't believe Audrey's doctor phoned just to give me an update, what did you say to him last night?" Still marvelling that I had been phoned by the doctor in charge of Audrey's care.

"I just said that I would be grateful if he could report on her condition in the morning," Ahran replied.

I shook my head disbelievingly. "Thank you." As much as I didn't want to admit it I don't know what I would have done without him over the last twelve hours.

Ahran looked slightly uncomfortable. "So she's still in a coma," he said, diverting the attention away from himself.

I nodded and my bottom lip began to quiver.

His expression softened. "As the doctor said, this is normal for someone who has suffered the injuries Audrey has." He was trying to reassure me, but his sympathy only made me want to cry.

I buried my face in my hands and sobbed.

"She's going to be fine, it will just take a little while," he said gently, and I felt his arms around my shoulders. His warmth seeped through my sweater.

"I hope you're right," I said through my tears. He pulled me further into his arms. This man was little more than a stranger to me, but I took the sympathy he offered and cried into his chest.

"I'm sorry. I keep doing that to you," I said, pulling

away. "I've made your shirt all wet." I went to get some kitchen roll to pat it dry.

He caught my wrist and turned me back towards him. "Please. It doesn't matter."

We stood there for a few moments looking at one another. Just as he turned away, I saw the flicker of conflict across his face. I stared at his back feeling confused. He gripped the edge of the sink and looked out the window. Showing his humanity seemed to unsettle him. I didn't know what to make of it. All I knew was that when Ahran was being supportive and compassionate, I could feel myself being drawn to him like a moth to a flame, but when he was cool and abrupt, it only served to put my back up. I grabbed a tissue and blew my nose.

"We should go to Ramia tonight," Ahran said, turning around.

"Tonight?! That's impossible."

"Sophie, you've seen the condition Audrey is in. This really is a matter of life and death."

I contemplated Toby coming to any harm and it brought me up short. I knew I had to do what Ahran asked and soon. "Okay, okay, I get it. But I really would like to know what we are getting ourselves into. Is there any way I can meet King Halsan before we go and stay?"

"Halsan won't come to Earth."

I tried not to feel offended.

"But I suppose I could take you to him," he said, considering my request.

"What about Toby?"

"Elaya is at the school, she will protect him."

I looked at the clock it was nearly ten thirty. I had no idea how long it would take to get to Ramia and back and I wanted to visit Audrey before I picked Toby up from school. "We can't go today," I said adamantly. "How long does it take to get there anyway? Isn't it in a completely different universe?" I couldn't fathom how far away that was.

"There are other modes of travel than the ones you are thinking of Sophie."

I felt even more confused. What ways other than a rocket or a spaceship were there?

"We travel to and from my world through a portal," he explained.

"What do you mean, like some kind of gateway?" I'm sure this had been on Deep Space Nine the only time I had sat and watched it with Toby. I wish I had paid more attention.

"Yes, exactly that, we have created one in the woods just behind your house."

"In *my* wood?" I was shocked.

"Yes, a wood is a good place for a portal. We are more able to travel through it undetected."

I nodded as if we were having the most normal conversation in the world. "Oh, right." I said, my eyes wide. This explained why Ahran and Elaya were able to get here so quickly.

"It would be very strange if someone just materialised in the middle of a busy shopping mall," he continued.

It was just as odd materialising in a wood, I thought to myself.

"So what do we do? Just walk through it and bingo we are there?"

"Yes, pretty much," he said without any further explanation.

It seemed so easy. I had expected spaceships and flashing lights maybe it wouldn't be so bad after all.

"What's Ramia like?"

"Dinara, which is the kingdom I am from, is very beautiful, you can see for yourself if we go now."

"Now?" I said in a high-pitched voice.

"The sooner we go, the quicker we can get back."

"We can't go today," I argued. "I want to see Audrey and I need to speak to Sandie and I need to pick Toby up from school at 3.15." I knew I was stalling. Suddenly, I didn't feel comfortable travelling to another universe through a portal. What if I disintegrated or something? It was alright for Ahran he was a superhuman and used to it, I was a mere, what did he call me? Sapien?

"We could be there and back in a couple of hours," he reasoned.

I stared at him feeling a little dazed, I'd run out of excuses. "Okay, if you are sure we won't be long," I said hesitantly.

Oh hell! What had I just agreed to?

"Just give me a minute." A hefty dose of fear was beginning to settle in. I went upstairs to the bathroom and looked at myself in the mirror. Wild panic was now galloping through my veins. "I can do this," I said to my reflection, trying to ignore the terror in my eyes. *Please don't let me burn up!* I prayed and splashed some water on my face.

After I had patted it dry I grabbed my bag from the bedroom checking I had everything I needed. What did I need for a trip to another universe? I hadn't a clue, but before stalling much longer and changing my mind, I rejoined Ahran downstairs.

"Shall we go then?" I said nervously. Ahran nodded and followed me out of the back door. I locked it and put the key under a nearby plant pot.

The thirty acres of woodland behind the house belonged to me and I often walked through it with Mungo. Little did I know that anything like a space travelling portal existed in it. We walked through the back gate. Ahran took the lead and we started down a worn footpath.

"Are you okay?" he asked.

"No," I said shakily. I scrutinised my familiar surroundings suspiciously and couldn't see anything that resembled a portal, not that I had any idea what one looked like anyway.

"You will be fine," he said with a hint of a smile. I narrowed my eyes at his back as we continued to walk down the path. *That's easy for you to say!*

We veered off the path and I carefully picked my way through the dense undergrowth, trying to avoid the tree roots and the tangle of brambles that clawed at my ankles. I tripped a couple of times, crying out as the brambles hooked my flesh. Ahran slowed and offered me his hand. I hesitated before taking it. It galled me that he didn't seem to be having any trouble walking through the vegetation.

"Not far now," he confirmed. "I should perhaps mention that people are affected differently when they travel through portals. It is a bit like travel sickness, some people get really sick and some people are not affected at all. Do you get travel sick?" he asked.

"Not generally," I said, wincing for the umpteenth time as a sharp stick jabbed into my leg. "I'm not great on boats though," I said, not feeling heartened by this most recent piece of information.

"You won't know how you are affected until you travel through one," he explained.

My stomach started to churn at the thought and I had a horrible feeling I might be one of those people who got sick.

"It's over there," he said, pointing to a big oak.

"What, that tree?"

"No," he said chuckling.

"I'm glad I amuse you," I said, narrowly avoiding a tree stump.

"It's just in front of the tree."

I squinted to see if I could see anything that resembled a space travelling portal, but my not so superhuman eyes let me down. "Oh of course, silly me, so it is," I said, defaulting to sarcasm to hide my nerves.

We approached the oak he had pointed to and he held out his hand. I took it and gripped his arm with my other hand as if my life depended on it. Which, I thought to myself, it actually did.

"You won't let go will you?"

"No, of course I won't."

He stopped and looked down at me.

"Okay, take a few deep breaths. Are you ready?"

"No, but yes," I said, my stomach feeling like a boa

constrictor had wrapped itself around it. I eyed the indistinct spot in front of the tree nervously.

"Let's go then," he said.

I felt like a World War One infantryman who had just been ordered to go over the top and I clung to Ahran as we walked towards the gateway. As we neared it, I spontaneously put my hand out thinking we were going to walk right into the tree trunk, but instead we kept on walking, hitting nothing. Suddenly, the only thing I was aware of was darkness and the feeling I was in a lift that was hurtling towards the ground.

It was a *really* unpleasant sensation.

I gripped Ahran's hand as tightly as I could and screwed my eyes shut. My stomach began to heave as I lost all sense of gravity. We took another step and I jolted forward as if I had misjudged the distance stepping off an escalator.

After the darkness of the portal I was not prepared for the intense brightness and clamped my hand over my eyes trying to shield them. "Ah, that's bright," I exclaimed. I don't know what was worse, the nausea or the near blindness I felt. I did a quick mental check. Thankfully I hadn't burnt up on entry. In fact, not one hair was singed. I took a deep breath and inhaled the smell of warm undergrowth.

"Here, put my sunglasses on," Ahran said, placing them in my other hand. "You will need them until your eyes have adjusted. Our sun burns much more brightly than yours."

I put them on, but didn't open my eyes immediately.

"How are you feeling?" he asked.

"Not great," I said as my stomach began to heave. I reached out to steady myself, grateful when my hand made contact with his arm. A second wave quickly followed the first and I bent forward and threw up. When I had finished I spat out some biley dribble. "Ugh! Sorry."

"Sit down and have some water," he said, placing a small bottle in my hands. I didn't argue and gingerly sat down resting my forehead on my knees and took a few deep breaths.

"That was horrible," I croaked. "I thought I might react like that." I felt disgruntled at my bad luck and laid my head back on my knees.

After a few moments the nausea subsided enough for me to sit up straight and sip from the bottle Ahran had given me.

"Take your time, you should find it gets easier the more you do it," he reassured.

For the time being, I didn't want to contemplate going back through the portal. Gradually, the nausea began to pass. I slowly opened my eyes, unprepared for what I was about to see.

"Wow!"

We were sat on high ground looking down into the most beautiful valley I had ever seen. It was flanked by two ranges of enormous snow-capped mountains. Lower down they were beautifully lush and green. Wispy clouds ambled from mountain to mountain whilst the river below mirrored the startling blue of the sky above as it snaked into the distance. Nestled along its banks was what looked like a small town in a uniform, grid-like pattern. The air was crystal clear and it felt like someone had just removed a fuzzy filter from my eyes. The colour of the lake, grass and trees was so vibrant and the sky was the most brilliant of blues. I greedily drank it all in. "It's so beautiful," I said breathlessly. "Where are we?"

Ahran had been watching my reaction. "This is Dinara, and we are in the grounds of the King's private estate."

I breathed in a lungful of air and it felt like it was doing me good from the inside out.

"Dinara is particularly known for the purity and clarity of its atmosphere. We have very strict rules about pollution." We sat there for an immeasurable amount of time as Ahran waited for me to have my fill of this new world.

"How do you feel now?" he asked.

"A lot better than I did thanks. It's so warm." I felt overdressed in my pink sweater and I peeled it off, my t-shirt riding up underneath as I pulled it over my head. Ahran's eyes lowered to my midriff before I could pull the hem back down to meet the top of my jeans. I felt a certain sense of satisfaction that he wasn't quite as immune to me as I had thought he was.

"Now I know why you always smell of the sun," I said, tying my sweater around my waist, although immediately regretted saying it because it sounded like I paid far too much attention to him.

He smiled and stood up, offering his hand to help me up. "Shall we continue?"

He pulled me to my feet effortlessly. He had removed his jacket and had casually slung it over his shoulder like he was about to do a photo shoot. I dragged my eyes away from the way his t-shirt stretched across his broad chest.

Dear Lord! How was a girl supposed to keep her eyes to herself?

"Whoa," I said, feeling woozy and losing my balance. Ahran put his hands out to steady me.

"Our atmosphere has a slightly higher concentration of oxygen and it can make you feel a little light-headed to begin with, so just take it easy, you will adapt."

Most of the physical contact I'd had with Ahran so far had been as a result of me collapsing or tripping or crying on him. I made a mental note to try and be more robust, besides all this close contact was not doing my nerves any good. Fighting the urge to lean into him, I pulled away. "I'm okay. I'm not usually this feeble, it's just that a lot has happened over the last couple of days," I said, making my excuses.

He smiled and took my hand. "Come on, that's the palace down there," he said, pointing to an extensive building that was nestled into the hillside.

"Why isn't the portal inside the palace?" I asked as we began to make our way down a path.

"The frequency of a portal causes too much interference; it needs to be a certain distance away from buildings."

"Oh, I see." Well, at least I tried to. "Does King Halsan know we're coming?"

"Yes, I contacted him before we left; he is looking forward to meeting you."

I liked the idea of royalty looking forward to meeting me. In spite of my initial apprehension, I was starting to enjoy myself. The sun was warm, the scenery was a sight to behold and I liked the feel of my hand in Ahran's more than

I cared to admit. We descended the hillside and I noticed the light glinting off reflective surfaces at various points on the opposite hill.

"Are those houses built into the side of the mountain?" I asked squinting.

"Yes, a lot of houses are underground or partially under-ground here in Dinara. They are more energy efficient and have less of an impact on the landscape. Everything we build has to have minimal impact on the environment," he explained.

I compared this stunning place to Earth and felt embar-rassed that we were only just beginning to realise the impor-tance of looking after our planet.

Before long, we were walking along a gravel track. At the end of it, there was a pair of large wooden gates flanked by high stone walls that traced around the hillside. It was a non-descript entrance like that of a multi-million dollar Hollywood pad. There were cameras dotted around the entrance and along the wall and as we approached, the gates slowly opened. I was beginning to feel more than a little nervous. We walked through the gateway into a large grav-elled area. To our left the grounds were terraced and led up to an extensive, modern, wooden and glass, largely single storey building that adhered itself to the contours of the hill. It had a wonderful vantage point of the lake and town below. There was a beautiful fragrance coming from the unrecognisable blooms in the flowerbeds and I could hear running water, but I couldn't see where the sound was coming from.

A middle-aged man in a dark suit came out of the

building and trotted down the wide steps to meet us. This must be King Halsan, I thought and wondered whether I should curtsey.

"Ah Ahran, good to see you, we haven't seen you here for a while," the man said as he approached, his spoken English was clearly a gesture for my benefit and demonstrated his excellent manners. He wasn't as tall as Ahran, but he was in good shape for a man of more senior years. His fair hair was peppered with grey and he had a kind face. The man bowed his head towards Ahran, and Ahran responded with a slight dip of his head which didn't seem quite as reverential as I thought it should have been.

"Sulaan, I'd like you to meet Sophie McAllister."

Okay so this *wasn't* the king.

"Miss McAllister, we have been anticipating your arrival." He bowed his head for a second time. Sulaan must have been the King's butler or footman or whatever you called someone like him in an alien royal household.

"Sophie, this is Sulaan, the King's premier aide."

I noticed he didn't extend his hand so I just nodded awkwardly.

"Er, hello, pleased to meet you." I had no idea what the standard etiquette for meeting the King's *premier aide* was, come to think of it I was pretty clueless as to how to greet a King. I hadn't thought to ask Ahran to brief me on the finer details of meeting and greeting his head of state.

"If you would like to follow me the King is waiting for you," he said turning. We followed on.

I gave Ahran an uncertain look and he winked at me. *Playful Ahran*. Now that was new. I was trying so hard to fight my attraction for him. It was so much easier when he was being abrupt.

We walked into the palace together and it was like we had just stepped into the pages of 'Hello!' magazine. I pushed the sunglasses I was wearing up onto my head. The entrance was opulent in an understated way. There were several cream chaise longue chairs lining the walls on either side which were interspersed with ferns and other greenery. Hanging on the walls were large pictures of subtle abstract art and there was a large modern chandelier which hung from the double height ceiling. Sulaan's shoes clicked on the polished marble floor as we walked through the entrance. We turned down a long corridor. On the right-hand side were doors leading to modern, spacious rooms with views out onto the valley. To our left there didn't appear to be a wall as the corridor circumnavigated an enormous open air rectangular courtyard. In the middle of the courtyard was a large shallow rectangular pool with a water fountain. This must have been the source of the running water I had heard out on the terrace. It was deliciously cool and tranquil inside.

I found it difficult keeping up with Ahran and Sulaan, their strides were so much longer than mine. We walked through a number of other glass corridors fringed by rooms. The ones I had a chance to peek into were large, understated and tastefully furnished. I marvelled at how the place managed to stay so cool in spite of all the glass. I managed to get a good look at one of the dining rooms. It had a huge glass dining table with a number of large leather chairs around it. In contrast to the simple lines of the table, was an intricate glass chandelier hovering over its centre. I thought about my cosy little cottage back home, this place could not have been more different. It wasn't particularly to my taste, but it was beautiful and expensive.

"Nearly there," Sulaan announced. We had been walking for a good few minutes.

I suddenly wished I'd put on something a bit smarter rather than jeans and a white t-shirt.

"Okay?" Ahran asked.

I had butterflies at the prospect of meeting Toby's grandfather. I nodded.

We walked down to the end of the corridor to another nondescript door and Sulaan knocked and waited.

This is it!

Ahran must have sensed my nerves because he smiled at me flashing his lovely white teeth. A voice from inside invited us in and Sulaan opened the door. Ahran gently took my elbow and steered me into the room. Sulaan didn't follow and quietly shut the door behind us .

9

The room was bigger than the whole of the downstairs of my house. We were facing a glass wall with that spectacular view out onto the valley. In front of the window was a large desk, and sat behind it was a man, who bore a remarkable resemblance to a fifty-something Sean Connery, although he was perhaps a little broader. He stood up and came out from behind it. He was tall with short greying hair that must have been dark brown once, and he had a closely cropped greying beard. He wore a pair of light casual trousers and a loose white, short-sleeved linen shirt. He carried himself with the confident air of someone with authority. *This was King Halsan.*

He wasn't what I had expected at all. What had I been expecting? A wizened old man, wearing an ermine cloak and crown and holding a sceptre? I wasn't sure. I hadn't had time to give it much thought. He walked towards me with his hand extended, showing surprisingly strong looking forearms. *So they did shake hands here.* I felt relieved this was the standard formal greeting, I wasn't sure I'd have been able to pull off a curtsey.

"Miss McAllister, I am extremely pleased to meet you." His voice was deep and reverberated around the room, but instead of the Scottish lilt I had been half expecting he spoke with the same accent as Ahran. His eyebrows were darker than his hair and beard and he had beautiful brown eyes. They struck me as familiar and then I realised why, Toby had a replica pair. He was an inch or two shorter than Ahran, but he was a handsome man and all in all, rather impressive. I was more than a little star-struck.

I cleared my throat. "Sophie, please call me Sophie." I shook the hand he offered, his handshake was firm and confidence inspiring.

King Halsan turned his attention to Ahran. He shook Ahran's hand and clapped him on the arm at the same time. He was obviously fond of his nephew.

"Ahran, it has been too long, good to see you." Like Sulaan, he spoke in English in my presence and I was thankful, it made me feel a little less like a fish out of water.

"Thank you for bringing Sophie here safely," the King said, expressing his gratitude.

"Good to see you too my Lord, it was the least I could do," Ahran replied.

"Now I expect you young people are hungry," the King said, playing the role of perfect host.

I hadn't thought about food, but now he mentioned it, I was starving.

"Yes, food would be good, my Lord," Ahran replied. I

suspected that the six pieces of toast he'd had for breakfast were no longer sustaining him.

"Come then, let us eat. Sulaan has arranged some lunch for us in the dining room."

"How was your journey?" the King asked as we walked towards the door.

I figured it probably wasn't polite to report that I had puked my guts up. "It was a little shaky, but I made it through in one piece," I replied.

"I have never travelled through a portal myself, I leave that kind of travel to the younger generations, but I've heard it can be quite unpleasant."

"It wasn't the most enjoyable experience I've ever had," I confessed.

"No, indeed. Still, you are in safe hands with Ahran here."

I glanced at Ahran who gave me a crooked smile which made my heart do a double beat. The King exuded strength and power and yet he was welcoming and gracious. I started to feel more relaxed. He pulled the door open and gestured for us to go ahead of him.

"Leylana will be joining us for lunch, she is on her way back from the town," the King said. "Leylana is my wife," he explained in response to what must have been a blank look on my face.

I nodded. There had been no mention of a Queen. So Toby had a grandmother too. It made me feel a little easier at the thought of having another woman around. We started to make our way back down the corridor.

"We will be celebrating our 100th wedding anniversary

soon," he said with a hint of pride in his voice. "She has spent the morning in town making arrangements for the celebrations."

"Wow! A hundred years, congratulations!" Was I being too informal? I groaned inwardly, I felt completely unprepared for meeting Toby's royal grandparents.

The three of us walked back the route we had come with Sulaan.

"So how is my *grandson*?" The King said the word tentatively, clearly unaccustomed to saying it.

For a moment, it didn't register who he was referring to. The palatial surroundings and being in the presence of a King was so far removed from my life back home I failed to make the connection straight away. "Oh Toby," I said after an embarrassing pause. "Yes, he's good. He's at school at the moment."

"I hope we will meet him very soon. We cannot guarantee your safety whilst you remain on Earth."

Now that I had at least seen the place, the idea of coming to stay here didn't seem quite so bad.

"Here we are," announced the King.

We had arrived at the dining room we had passed earlier. It was as if a banquet had appeared by magic. I had never seen so much food for four people. There were plates of cold meat, bowls of colourful and sumptuous looking salads, about eight different types of bread rolls and an array of fruit, some of which I didn't recognise. I felt my stomach rumble and wondered, with their Ramian sense of hearing, whether the King and Ahran had heard it.

A servant pulled out a chair for me. "Thank you," I said

and sat down. Ahran sat opposite but one, leaving a space for the Queen. The King took a seat at the head of the table and unfolded his napkin, laying it across his lap. A solemn looking man dressed in a smart grey uniform appeared as if from nowhere and offered him a selection of rolls. Suddenly someone appeared at my elbow offering me an array of cold meats.

"Yes please." The girl, in a matching grey uniform, served a couple of slices onto my plate with a polite smile.

Neither the King nor Ahran spoke as they concentrated on selecting their food; it was obviously a serious business. I followed suit and just as I was about to butter a roll, a tall elegant lady swept into the room.

"Ah, there you are, my dear," the King said, standing up as the woman approached. She put a hand on his shoulder and kissed the King on the cheek.

"I'm sorry my darling, I got held up, it took longer than I thought," she said in English, taking her cue from her husband. Everyone so far had spoken my language flawlessly.

The woman looked younger than the King. She was tall and slim with rich, brown, beautifully coiffured hair that fell in thick, soft waves around her shoulders. She wore a cream trouser suit and was the epitome of elegance. I could have kicked myself for not giving more thought to who I would be meeting and dressing more appropriately.

"Leylana, I want you to meet Miss McAllister," the King said.

"Sophie, please," I corrected.

Leylana came around to my side of the table and I stood

up. The skin around her eyes was gently lined, but the rest of her face was smooth. She had large brown, almond shaped eyes and she was gorgeous. Everyone here was so beautiful and it made me feel like one of the ugly sisters.

"Sophie, I am absolutely delighted to meet you," Leylana said warmly, extending her hand.

I shook it gently. "It's good to meet you too." By a strange twist of fate, these people were Toby's family and so far they had been nothing but warm and welcoming. Maybe I could actually get to like them.

Leylana turned her attention to Ahran and he stood up to receive her hug.

"Ahran, it is so lovely to see you, why haven't you been to see us sooner?" she said, scolding him.

"I am sorry Aunt Ley."

It was touching to hear him use a shortened version of her name; it was so much less formal than *My Lady*. Ahran had been polite and respectful towards the King, but there was obvious warmth between him and his aunt. "I've been concentrating on the purchase of the farm, there have been various issues." He frowned.

I listened with interest. It was the first time I'd heard Ahran talk about his life. He was buying a farm. That surprised me. He didn't strike me as a farmer.

"Has the purchase gone through now?" Halsan asked as Leylana took her seat next to Ahran.

"Yes, I received notification a few days ago."

"I am pleased to hear that, it is about time you settled down," Leylana said, "And how is Talina?"

I nearly bit my tongue. I broke off some of my bread roll

and listened intently to Ahran's answer. *Who was Talina? Please let it be his mother or some elderly female relative.* Although why it mattered so much, I wasn't sure.

"She is well," Ahran replied.

I realised I was holding my breath.

"Have you set a date for the wedding yet?"

I felt like I had just been punched in the stomach. It was worse than I feared. I felt a surge of anger towards him for not mentioning the fact that he had a fiancé, but then a small voice in my head questioned why he would. I didn't know why I was surprised that Ahran wasn't single. He was drop dead gorgeous and in the prime of his life, who wouldn't want to marry him?

"No Aunt, no date has been set yet. We have been waiting for the purchase of the farm to go through," Ahran replied.

I mimicked what he had just said in my head childishly. I was cross with myself for letting my attraction for him run away with me. Compared to the beautiful people of Ramia, I was short, with unruly hair and on the curvy side of slim, nothing like the svelte Elaya or the classical beauty that was Leylana. Talina was probably just as stunning as the other Ramian women I had met. Why would Ahran even give me a second glance?

I kept my eyes on my lunch. There was a pause in the conversation and I realised that Leylana had turned her attention to me. Had she just asked me a question?

"I'm sorry?"

Leylana repeated her question. "We are very keen to know what our little grandson is like. We just couldn't believe it when we found out that Tagan had a son." A shadow of sadness flickered across her face.

I tensed. Of course they would want to know what Toby was like, they were his grandparents. But they were also royal superhumans who lived in a beautiful parallel universe. I felt dismayed to think how excited Toby was going to be about all of this, what eight-year-old wouldn't be? How could I possibly compete?

"What are his interests? I expect he's a good sportsman, Tagan always excelled at sport," she gushed.

"Ley! Give the girl a chance to speak," the King said, gently reprimanding his wife. He leant towards me. "You will have to forgive my wife, she was desperate for grand-children and we thought that when we lost Tagan the chance of us ever having any had passed, so as you can imagine, ever since we found out about Toby it has caused great excitement." He was only just about containing his own.

My heart sank further.

The King paused. "My dear, have we offended you?" he asked, a concerned frown on his face.

"No, you haven't offended me," I replied. "It's just that I've had a lot to deal with over the last few days and now I face losing Toby no matter what I decide to do."

"What do you mean you will lose him?" The King sounded surprised.

In for a penny in for a pound. "Because if we stay at home there is every chance he will fall into Bazeera's clutches and if we come here you will want to keep him because he is your heir, which of course is the best thing for him anyway because he will be safer here..." I knew I was starting to babble, but I couldn't help it, my misery was affecting my ability to speak eloquently.

"You are right it is not safe for you to stay at home at the moment," the King said.

It didn't escape my notice that he made no attempt to allay my fears about them wanting Toby to stay here. My main concern was my nephew's safety, but what frightened me more was that he would prefer to stay here given the choice. And from what I had seen so far, he would be treated like the Prince he was. I sighed inwardly at my predicament. No matter which way I looked at it, I faced the very real prospect of losing him.

I glanced over at Leylana. Perhaps, I could appeal to the Queen's sensibilities. She was a mother, she would understand. Maybe we could come to an arrangement where we could share Toby, although I couldn't begin to think how this could work across two universes. The situation seemed impossible.

"Toby is an adorable little boy," I sighed, answering the Queen's earlier questions. "He is smart, funny, and very good at sport as it happens. He's got brown, curly hair and brown eyes." The Queen was quite literally on the edge of her seat, hanging on my every word.

Leylana bent down to pick up her bag and took out a slim leather wallet. She opened the case of what turned out to be a small electronic tablet. She tapped the screen and a 3D image of a young man wearing military fatigues sprang from the screen and hovered in front of us.

"Wow!" I exclaimed as I looked at the three-inch image. "That's incredible."

"It is our son."

Once I was over the initial shock of the unfamiliar technology I eyed the image of Tagan with interest. I had hated him with a vengeance for the last eight years and it was unsettling to see a handsome man, wearing military fatigues smiling up at me. He looked happy and relaxed as he leant back against a rock. "Toby is like his father," I said slowly, shaking my head at the likeness.

Leylana beamed, this obviously pleased her. She shook the tablet once and the image disappeared.

"I'm afraid I don't have a photo to show you of Toby, I've got a new phone and I haven't taken any yet," I said sheepishly.

The Queen didn't look overly disappointed. "No matter, we shall be meeting him soon. When do you think you will be back?" Leylana asked excitedly.

"As soon I can make the necessary arrangements," I said noncommittally.

The Queen positively effervesced.

"Ahran tells me you think it will take you a few days to make arrangements to leave Earth," the King said. "I'm afraid I don't think you have that much time. Bazeera knows of Toby's existence. I would urge you to go back, collect Toby and return as quickly as you can. I will make an office available so you can make any necessary phone calls from here and I would like to offer you recompense for the loss of revenue you will suffer as a result of closing your business for the duration of your stay."

The King spoke in such a way that I knew I simply

could not refuse, I would be a fool not to do as he was suggesting.

"You are very kind. I will collect Toby from school when we get back and return with him straight away." I raised my eyebrows questioningly at Ahran who nodded in agreement. In spite of my reservations about Toby's future, he would be safe and we would be living in the lap of luxury for the foreseeable future. It really would be no hardship.

"Good, well that settles it then." The King seemed relieved and Leylana visibly relaxed.

"We were sorry to hear of your friend's brutal attack," the King said, his tone turning grave. "If there is anything we can do that would help speed her recovery, please let us know."

"Thank you," I answered gratefully.

Grudgingly, I was beginning to like these people. Not only were they warm and welcoming, but they were also refined, caring, generous and protective. We continued to eat our lunch and I attempted to focus on mine and Toby's unusual and impromptu vacation rather than dwell on the less desirable aspects of the situation, such as the prospect of losing Toby and Ahran's relationship status.

I marvelled at how much the Ramians ate, even the willow-slim Leylana ate double the amount I ate. As someone who appreciated food, it was good to be among people who seemed to share my enthusiasm for it. Much of the following conversation was between Ahran and the King and about how business was going. Leylana chipped in from time to time. They both seemed to take an active role in the running of their kingdom, which sounded like it operated on an almost feudal basis. They clearly owned much of the land in the region and it was leased to tenants. These tenants operated within large cooperatives and Ahran was keen to hear how successful some of the more entrepreneurial tenants were faring as they trialled new technological methods of energy and food production. It struck me that this was a world of contrasts. A medieval system of kingship operating alongside technologically advanced methods of food production aligned with an ultra-modern lifestyle.

Ahran talked knowledgeably with Halsan and was clearly excited about his new venture. He was keen to pick the King's brains about the best way forward for some of his ideas. I was impressed. Ahran was obviously well-educated and had a sharp brain. I had learnt more in the last hour about him than I had in the last few days. And much to my dismay, I felt even more drawn to him.

I decided I would do whatever I had to do in the short term to protect Toby and then I would distance myself from Ahran as quickly as I could thereafter. Somehow, I would pick up the pieces of my life and try to forget that I had ever met him. What I hadn't figured out yet was how I could fashion a life that straddled two worlds.

Whilst their conversation flowed, Leylana and I chatted about Toby, what his interests were and what he enjoyed doing.

"And what was Toby's mother like?" Leylana asked as she sipped some fresh juice.

"Katie, was a sweet and gentle person." It didn't get any

easier talking about her. The extent to which I missed her had not diminished in the slightest over the last year. I swallowed. "She was clever, worked hard at school and was popular. We were very close. She was also a very good mother as it happens." I wanted them to know that she would have been a worthy daughter-in-law.

"What brought Tagan to Earth?" I asked. I had to smile inwardly at my use of the word. I had never referred to where I lived as *Earth*. Hatherley usually sufficed.

"Like lots of young people, he was keen to travel and wanted to experience a different culture."

I fought the urge to laugh. Most gap year students went to Thailand or South America, not another world entirely.

"Katie was devastated when Tagan left, it took her a long time to get over him disappearing without a trace." I couldn't help mentioning the fact that he had left so suddenly after Katie had fallen pregnant, I felt I owed it to my sister. I waited for Leylana's response.

"I'm sorry if your sister suffered as a result of Tagan coming home. He was a good person and he certainly would not have abandoned her if he had known she was carrying his child, but as you know our world is not perfect and we have our enemies. At the time, we were at war and Halsan wanted our son to return to help him strategically." She looked weary of the conflict. "Tagan had been a very successful Commander for the Strategic Operations division in our Special Force and came back to Dinara to help his former colleagues fight the threats to our kingdom."

I began to feel guilty about the uncharitable opinion I had held of Tagan for so long and I grudgingly accepted that his reason for leaving Katie and returning home was a laudable one.

A sad expression settled on Leylana's face. "Unfortunately, Tagan enjoyed life in the military and he found it hard to leave after he returned home. I always preferred it when he was working behind the lines, but he was committed to the men who worked under his leadership and he preferred to be with them, 'Where it mattered', he used to say." She said this with a little smile. "One night his unit was ambushed by Bazeera's forces, he and Ahran had gone back to save one of their soldiers who had been trapped. Tagan was killed in the cross-fire."

Ahran and the King had finished their conversation and were listening to what Leylana was telling me.

I glanced over at Ahran and his expression was troubled. How awful to witness your cousin's death? I also felt sorry for Leylana, I couldn't imagine how dreadful it must be to outlive your child.

"Once again, we face difficulties in our world," the King interjected. "Bazeera has become increasingly powerful and will not stop until she gets what she wants." He paused to take a sip of his drink. "But our Special Force is a formidable army and we have every confidence that we will defeat her."

"So you were in the Special Force with your cousin?" It wasn't sensible to find out any more about Ahran's life, but my question was out before I could stop it.

"I spent thirty years in it. Tagan and I spent the last few years in Reconnaissance together," he replied.

"What Ahran has not told you is that he and Tagan were

our top agents and they received the highest awards for their loyalty, commitment and bravery." Halsan's pride was obvious.

I was impressed. "What made you leave?" I asked

"Thirty years is long enough," he answered.

"I have no doubt he will be just as successful in his next venture," the King said, changing the subject, it was obviously a painful topic of conversation for them all.

Sulaan reappeared. "There is a phone call for you my Lord."

"I'll take it in my office."

The King wiped his mouth on his napkin and stood up. He turned to me. "Thank you for coming my dear, it was lovely to meet you at last. I will make sure preparations are made for your return. If you will all excuse me I have matters to attend to."

"Thank you for the lunch and thank you for everything you are doing for us," I said gratefully.

"Not at all, it's the least we can do." The King kissed his wife on the cheek and he returned to his office.

"We ought to get back if you want to visit your friend in hospital before Toby finishes school," Ahran suggested.

"Yes, okay." I had forgotten about the portal and I didn't relish the trip back through it.

Leylana stood up and Ahran respectfully followed suit, I took his lead and stood up too.

"Well Sophie, I cannot wait to meet my grandson, I won't be able to concentrate on a thing until you both return." She came around to my side of the table and gave me a hug. She looked over to Ahran. "Look after them both won't you?"

"Of course." He nodded.

The Queen left us and Ahran and I made our way back to the entrance. "If this building is built into the side of the mountain how come it is so light everywhere?" I asked, trying to make conversation to fill the awkward silence that had settled between us. Ahran had suddenly gone quiet. I hoped I hadn't upset him when I had asked about his time in the army. Tagan's death had obviously hit him hard.

"Fibre optics. Light is channelled through cables."

"Oh right," I said, nodding, although my mind was mostly focussed on the journey we were just about to make. "Is it a good idea going back through the portal having just eaten?" As much as I wanted to get back to see Audrey, I wasn't looking forward to losing my lunch.

"You might not find it as bad this time."

We left the palace through the front doors and walked down the front steps. The large wooden gates opened as we approached. We climbed the hill to the portal pretty much in silence. I used the time to digest the last hour or so. I had warmed to the King and Queen much more than I had thought I was going to and I was feeling less anxious than when I had arrived.

I was out of breath by the time we got to the top of the hill.

Ahran's breathing remained steady.

"Ready?" Ahran asked.

"No, can I just sit down for a bit and get my breath?" I

panted, knowing if we went now I would definitely throw up.

"Take your time," he said.

I sat down and Ahran came and sat next to me. He sat so close our arms were almost touching. I concentrated on a spot in the distance and tried not to be so conscious of him. For the last fifteen minutes it had felt like he was in my company under duress and now he had chosen to be so near to me. I couldn't keep up with him. I didn't want to move away, that would seem too obvious, maybe if I tried to remember my schoolgirl geography that would help me to take my mind off the distracting smell of him.

"Now, a hill that shape is it called a spur or a heel?"

"Sophie?"

"Mmmm," I turned to look at him only to find his face just inches away from mine.

All thoughts of geographical features vanished as I looked up into his face. Suddenly, all my good intentions disappeared and all I could think of now was how his lips would feel on mine. I searched his eyes, he looked conflicted and confused. For a few heart-stopping moments I thought he was about to move away, but he gently touched the side of my face instead. I didn't pull away nor did I give him any encouragement to continue even though the voice in my head screamed for his lips to touch mine. I knew somewhere in the back of my mind that there was a reason why he shouldn't kiss me, but for the life of me I couldn't remember what it was.

My heart slammed against my ribs and it was nothing to do with the hill we had just walked up. Something flickered in his eyes as if he had just resolved the conflict behind them and excruciatingly slowly, still with his hand on my jaw, his lips came towards mine, all the time his eyes daring me to stop him. I was lost in the drowning blue of his eyes and held in his spell with no hope of resisting him. His lips touched mine and my eyes closed automatically, my heart feeling like it was about to pound right out of my chest. For a few blissful seconds my mind was silent and I allowed the sensation of his kiss wash over me. My lips responded, parting beneath his as the intensity of our kiss increased. Ahran's body shifted and he pulled me towards him. His hand moved down the column of my throat and his thumb gently caressed the pounding pulse at the base of my neck. It was the hottest kiss I had ever experienced.

A groan came from deep in his throat and for some reason it made reality hit me like a slap in the face. I pulled away and sat back on my heels. We were both breathing heavily. We stared at one another for a few moments, the intensity of the kiss had surprised us both.

"We shouldn't have done that," I said breathlessly. I don't know why I had become the voice of reason all of a sudden because it certainly wasn't how I was feeling inside.

"I've wanted to do *that* ever since I laid eyes on you," he said without a trace of regret.

His words surprised me, there had been nothing about the way he had behaved towards me that had made me think he was attracted to me, in fact if anything his behaviour had made me think the exact opposite. My stupid misguided heart sang.

"If you had done it this morning, I probably wouldn't

have stopped you, but as I have recently learnt, you actually had no right to kiss me." It took a moment for him to realise what I meant.

"You mean Talina," he said flatly.

"Yes, *Talina*," I said, refraining from adding '*Duh*?!' on the end.

"Talina and I have been betrothed since we were children," he said as if it explained everything.

I couldn't help my surprise. "What, like an arranged marriage?" I asked, momentarily forgetting our little indiscretion.

"My parents and her parents are allies and our marriage will join together two powerful families."

"Do you love her?" It was suddenly very important I knew the answer.

Ahran hesitated. "I ..." he seemed to be searching for the right word, "Care about her," he replied.

He hadn't said *loved*, the traitorous little voice singsonged in my head.

"In Ramia, it is believed that our parents have our best interests at heart. Providing we like the person they have chosen for us it is believed love will grow and generally it does. My parent's parents did it for them as did my aunt and uncle's parents for them, they all have very successful loving relationships, it's how things are done here."

I thought about Ahran and Talina's love for one another growing and it made my gut twist.

"Well, let's pretend that didn't just happen then, shall we?" I said in as business-like a voice as I could muster. I stood up. I needed to step away and compose myself.

"The problem is, I don't want to forget it, I want to do it again," he said shamelessly, his eyes drilling into mine.

Even though my heart missed a beat at the thought of him wanting to kiss me again, I considered slapping him. "Well, you have just made it clear that this..." I said, gesturing wildly from me to him, "...is inappropriate because you are about to marry a woman you have been engaged to for..." *How old was he and how long ago was it since he was a child?* His kiss had befuddled my brain and I couldn't work it out. "Ugh," I said frustrated "God knows how long. I think we ought to just leave it there."

I strode off to the spot where we had appeared a couple of hours ago.

"Can we just get this over with?" I said, holding my hand out impatiently. The last thing I trusted myself to do was touch him, but I didn't want to fall into some inter-galactic abyss either. Holding his hand was the lesser of the two evils.

Ahran hesitated, but then walked over and took my hand in his. I tried to ignore the electrical pulse that passed between us. So *that* was what Katie was talking about. A fat lot of good it was going to do me now, I thought dismally. I held my breath as we walked through the portal together.

It was the same horrendous feeling as before, like I was hurtling towards the earth and my stomach churned violently in response. A few seconds later I stumbled out of the portal into my wood. If I hadn't been holding Ahran's hand I would have fallen flat on my face. I regained my balance and snatched my hand away from his, fighting the wave of nausea that was threatening to make me lose my lunch. I leant against a nearby tree and closed my eyes. I took a few deep breaths, more to fight the tears that were hovering behind my eyelids than the sickness I was feeling. I had just begun to feel more cheerful about everything when he had to go and kiss me. Of course, it couldn't just be any ordinary kiss. No, it had to be a heart-stopping, earth-shattering mess-with-your-head kind of kiss. Whether it had been extraordinary because he was superhuman, I had no idea, but what I did know was that there was a chemistry between us the likes of which I had never experienced before. The kisses I'd had with Marcus paled into insignificance compared to what we had just shared. The irony was that I had thought Marcus had kissed well until Ahran had to go and spoil everything.

Ahran waited for me to gather myself. "Are you okay?" he asked sympathetically, mistaking my turmoil for travel sickness.

"Yes, no thanks to you," I spat.

He didn't respond.

"Let's just go," I said, pushing myself away from the tree and started to head back in the direction of my house. Ahran followed a safe distance behind. I decided as I walked that I would ask Elaya to escort us back to Ramia. I needed to distance myself from Ahran as soon as possible.

As I reached out to open my back gate, my phone vibrated in my pocket. I pulled it out and looked at the caller display. It was Toby's school. I felt the blood drain from my face. *Oh Jesus! Toby!*

10

I put the phone to my ear. I knew something had happened, I could feel it in my bones.

"Miss McAllister?"

"Yes," I answered, my voice full of dread.

"This is Mr Harcroft, the headteacher at Hatherley primary school."

I knew exactly who it was. I had begun to feel like I was falling down a deep, black hole, far worse than the one I had just stepped out of. If the headteacher was phoning me, something was definitely wrong.

"I am not quite sure how to tell you this, but Toby has gone missing."

My legs buckled beneath me and I fell to my knees. Ahran was beside me in a heartbeat. He didn't need to ask, he'd heard what Mr Harcroft had just said.

I struggled to say anything and just about managed to repeat the word that had sliced through me like a knife. "Missing?"

"Yes, I'm afraid so," he confirmed. "He was in the playground after lunch and didn't return to his classroom after the afternoon bell, we think he may have wandered out of the school gates. I have informed the police and a number of my staff are out looking for him. He can't have gone far and I am sure we will have him back in no time." He was trying his hardest to sound reassuring.

Toby would never have just wondered off. Their search was futile. Toby would be in Ramia by now, God knows where, in the grasp of Bazeera. I dropped the phone.

Ahran retrieved it and said a few curt words to the Head teacher before hanging up. He knelt down opposite me and took my hands in his.

I stared at him unseeingly.

"We *will* find him," he said, looking into my eyes.

"You said Elaya would look after him," I said accusingly. I felt so numb I couldn't even summon a tear.

"I know and I'm sure she would have done everything she could have done to protect him. We need to talk to her and find out what happened." He pulled his phone out of his pocket and dialled her number.

She didn't answer. Ahran cursed in Ramian.

I sat on the ground paralysed by fear.

"We need to find her." I could tell by the look on his face he suspected something had happened to her too. I couldn't offer any words of comfort I was too disabled by my own grief.

Ahran offered his hand to help me up. "We haven't got time to waste."

He pulled me to my feet. I felt like I had become detached from my body and the only thing I was conscious of was how difficult it was to breathe. I walked robotically through my back garden and allowed Ahran to lead me around the front to his car. We drove to the school in silence and parked in the cul-de-sac outside. "You stay here for a minute. I'm just going to see if I can find Elaya."

I didn't argue and sat there, staring out of the window. I watched an elderly couple come out of their house. The lady had a shopping bag over her arm and the man helped her into the car. They reversed out of their drive chatting away to each other. A young mother pushed a toddler in a pushchair. She had a phone sandwiched between her chin and shoulder as she walked and she laughed at something the person on the other end had just said to her. Several cars passed by and a delivery van pulled up outside a house a few doors away from where I was. *How could everyone just be getting on with their lives when the bottom had just fallen out of mine?*

Where was Toby? Was he hurt? Who was he with? He was only eight. He would be so frightened. How had they taken him without anyone noticing? Would I ever see him again?

The questions kept coming and I didn't have an answer for a single one of them. My tears started to fall silently. I didn't notice Ahran return until he opened the door and got in.

His face was lined with concern. I knew it was bad news and my heart sank even further.

"I've found her. She's alive, but unconscious in a ditch a couple of fields away from the school. I didn't want to carry her back in case anyone saw me. I'll drive round there and pick her up. I will have to take her back to Ramia."

I grabbed his arm. "No, don't leave me!" The thought of him leaving threw me into a blind panic.

"You will have to go into the school; it will appear very strange if you don't. Why don't you call your friend so you've got somebody with you? I'll take Elaya back and I will come back for you as quickly as I can."

I nodded. I knew that what he said made sense. I was going to have to pretend I had no idea where Toby was until Ahran returned and then we could head back to Ramia and work out what we were going to do from there.

Ahran gently held my chin. "We will find him, I promise. Bazeera won't hurt him; he is worth more to her alive." I appreciated that Ahran was trying to make me feel better, but I struggled to share his optimism. I nodded weakly. I got out of the car and started to make my way into the school. I don't know how I was able to put one foot in front of the other. I looked back at Ahran and he gave me a weak smile, the worry was plain to see on his face. The car's engine roared to life and he sped off.

I walked towards the school reception. The sooner I got this charade out of the way the better. I dialled Bennie's number.

"Hi, Sophe."

The sound of my best friend's voice brought a fresh wave of tears.

"Toby's gone missing from school."

"Fuck! Where are you?"

"I'm just heading into the school now."

"I'll be right there." She hung up. Thank God Bennie was staying with her parents and not still in Africa.

I walked into the school reception and as soon as the receptionist saw me she came out and ushered me into the headteacher's office. There were a number of people in there with him; the deputy head, two police officers and the chairman of the school governors.

The Head approached me. "Miss McAllister, the police are doing a search of the area as we speak." The gravity of the situation meant that he did away with any preliminaries.

"What happened? Didn't anyone see anything? What about Adam, he and Toby are inseparable, didn't he see anything?" I fired my questions at him.

"We've just spoken to Adam. He said they had been playing armies at the back of the playground, Toby hid behind the bank and that was the last time Adam saw him."

"Wasn't there anyone on duty?" I asked, struggling to hide my anger.

"There were two members of staff out on the playground at lunchtime, but it is difficult for them to keep their eye on every child all of the time."

"Well, you need more staff on duty then! We put our children in your hands and you have a duty of care to protect them," I said, my voice rising an octave. I knew that there wasn't a lot the headteacher could have done but I took my fear and frustration out on him anyway.

"Miss McAllister, I can assure you we take our duty of care very seriously," he said, only managing to thinly veil his frustration at my suggestion that they had failed in their job.

"Well you obviously don't take it seriously enough!" I retorted taking a step towards him and stabbing the air with my finger.

"Miss McAllister I understand this is very distressing for you, as it is for all of us," the governor said, trying to placate me. "It isn't going to do Toby any good if we all get upset with one another. We need to concentrate on finding him as quickly as possible."

I would have been happy if he had left me to tear lumps out of the headteacher, but the governor's gently restraining arm prevented me from getting any closer.

There was a knock on the door.

"Come in," the Head instructed, clearly relieved by the distraction.

Bennie put her head around the door.

"Bennie!" I was so relieved to see her. I rushed over to her and gave her a hug.

She put her arms around me. "Any news?"

The police officer's radios had crackled to life a number of times since I had arrived, but nothing significant had been reported.

I closed my eyes and shook my head, tears spilling over onto my cheeks. Who was I fooling? Toby was long gone.

Bennie addressed the policemen. "Is there anything we can do?"

"We have officers combing the area and we have sent alerts to police forces in the surrounding areas. Is there anywhere that you can think of that Toby might have gone?"

"The only place he would go to is his friend Adam's, but I can't imagine he would have gone there because Adam is in school." I took a shuddery breath. "The only other place would have been my friend Audrey's, and she's in hospital at the moment." I knew I had to carry on with the pretence. All I could think about was getting back to Ramia and to Ahran and the King. They would have a plan, I was sure of it.

One of the police officers looked at his notebook. "Ah yes, Audrey Goodfellow. Am I right in thinking she was assaulted in your coffee shop yesterday afternoon?" I felt like slapping him. *Of course you are right! And that is all the more reason why I should be in Ramia!* I yelled in my head. "Yes, that's right," I replied.

"Do you think there could be any connection between the assault on Ms Goodfellow and Toby's disappearance?" *Yes, there's a bloody connection!* "I can't imagine what it would be?" I lied.

"Maybe there is somebody who has something against you Miss McAllister, a debtor or a jealous ex-boyfriend perhaps?"

It didn't take much for them to put two and two together and come up with five, it looked too much like a coincidence.

"I can't think of anyone," I said, shrugging. "Are you suggesting he has been kidnapped?" I asked, keeping up the pretence.

The headteacher looked aghast. It would not be good PR if it got out that one of his pupils had been kidnapped from the school playground during lunchtime under his teacher's noses.

"We just want to make sure we have considered all possibilities," the policeman said noncommittally.

I didn't have to pretend to look devastated by the suggestion that Toby had been kidnapped; I was already tearing myself into pieces wondering what had happened to him. I sobbed into my hands.

Bennie stepped in. "I think perhaps, I ought to take Sophie home."

"That's probably a good idea," the headteacher agreed, relieved I would be taken out of the picture.

One of the policemen spoke. "We have your details Miss McAllister, we will contact you immediately we hear anything."

I was relieved I could finally leave. I hoped I appeared too distressed to join in with the search. I nodded and Bennie and I walked out to her car.

"They'll find him Sophe, he can't have gone far."

I felt dreadful not being able to tell her what had really happened, but I knew I couldn't utter a word about it.

"Do you think he has been kidnapped by that woman Ahran warned you about?" Bennie asked once we were in the car.

I shrugged tearfully, the less Bennie knew the better.

We drove back to my house and I looked at my watch. How much longer would Ahran be? My stomach was in knots and I felt completely powerless. Every minute that went by was another minute Toby was being taken further and further away into a world he didn't know even existed.

The tears streamed down my face as I opened the front door and Mungo came bounding towards me. I knelt down and wrapped my arms around his neck. It was surprisingly comforting nestling my face into his thin coat. Somehow it made me feel closer to Toby. I sat back on my heels and looked into the dog's eyes. He looked quizzically back at me sensing something was wrong.

"Where is he Mung?" I asked quietly. I would have to find someone to look after him if I was going to return to Ramia.

Bennie followed me in.

I didn't want her to overhear my conversation with Sandie. "Can you put the kettle on? I'm just going upstairs to get changed." I had been crying steadily since we had left the school and I could sense that Bennie had no idea what to say or do to comfort me.

"Yes of course," she called after me.

I closed my bedroom door and dialled Sandie's number. I wiped my eyes with the back of my hand. "Hi Sandie, I've got another favour to ask." I tried to sound as bright as I could and hoped she hadn't heard about Toby's disappearance yet, it wouldn't be long before it was all over the village.

"Fire away," she prompted.

"We've got to go away for a couple of weeks and I wondered if you wouldn't mind having Mungo. I'd obviously pay you."

"Yeah, no problem. Where are you going?"

"Oh, I've just got a last-minute deal," I said, wincing at

the deceit as it rolled off my tongue. How quickly I was becoming accustomed to lying.

"Can you come and collect him tonight? I'll leave his food out and put the key in the usual place."

"Okay."

"Great, thanks very much." My finger hovered over the hang up button.

"Sophe…Sophie?"

"Yep?" I put the phone back to my ear. *Please don't ask any awkward questions.*

"What about the shop? You know and my wages?"

"Well, I'm going to close the shop temporarily, what with Audrey being so ill. I could do with a break. Don't worry about your wages, consider it a paid holiday." I knew as soon as Sandie found out about Toby she would wonder what the hell I was playing at, but I had to clear the way so that I could get to Ramia unimpeded.

"Thanks Sophe, that would be fantastic."

"Alright then Sandie, thanks again, see you when we get back," I said, praying that this would be sooner rather than later.

"Yeah bye Sophie, have a good time."

I hung up. If only we were going on holiday. I hated myself. Why hadn't I just taken Toby to the safety of King Halsan's palace when Ahran had first told me about Bazeera? I had been too wary of the wrong people. I angrily wiped my tears away. It was no good sitting here feeling sorry for myself. If Ahran didn't return soon I would go there myself, even if it meant travelling through the portal on my own.

I had to hurry before Bennie came up to find out if I was alright. I grabbed a holdall from under my bed and went through my drawers. Without too much thought I selected some clothes and stuffed them into the bag. I dashed into the bathroom and grabbed a spare toothbrush and some deodorant and threw them in on top.

"Sophe, are you alright?" Bennie called up the stairs.

"Yeah, I'm coming." I went back into my bedroom feeling frantic. How could I possibly pack for a trip that held so many uncertainties? I did a quick scan of the room to see if there was anything else I might need. My eyes came to rest on the photo of Katie and Toby on my bedside. It could be useful to have a picture of Toby, but there was also a part of me that felt I needed it with me, anything that would help me to feel close to them right now. I grabbed the photo frame and put it in the side pocket of my bag. As I passed Toby's room I paused briefly wondering if I should get anything together for him. No, it was better that I travelled light. I started down the stairs and changed my mind two steps down. I spun around and dashed back into his room. I grabbed his well-loved teddy and stuffed it in my bag. *If...*no, *when* we found him he would need it. I fought back more tears and pulled his door shut. My phone buzzed. Oh God, please let that be Ahran saying he's on his way.

To my relief, it was a text message from him.

Leave by the back door, go through your back gate and meet me in the wood. The police are on their way round at the front.

I had no time to waste. I ran downstairs and into the kitchen.

Bennie was sat at the table with her hands wrapped around her mug, looking distractedly out of the window.

"What's wrong?" she said when she saw my face.

"I've got to go Ben, I'm really sorry I haven't got time to explain," I said breathlessly.

"What's going on?" she asked, looking utterly confused.

"Please just stall the police. I will explain I promise." My voice was pleading and urgent.

"Okay," she said, looking concerned. "Be careful, won't you?" she added.

I hated doing this to her, but I had to, for her sake and for Toby's sake. It was better that she didn't know any more than she absolutely had to.

"Yes of course and thank you," I said, giving her a quick squeeze.

"I'm sorry, I've got to go." I left by the back door and sprinted to my back gate. I gingerly poked my head out to check that the coast was clear and then ran as fast as I could in the same direction Ahran and I had gone this morning. He was leaning against a tree as he spoke quietly into his phone. I ran down the track towards him. He looked up as I approached and put his phone in his pocket. Without even thinking, I threw my arms around his neck. I couldn't have been more pleased to see him. He wrapped his arms around me and briefly hugged me back. His arms were strong and reassuring and I drew what strength I could from him in that brief moment.

"Have you heard anything?" I asked.

He pulled away and gave a slight shake of his head. "Come on, let's get going before anyone sees us." He took my bag and grabbed my hand. We ran as fast as I could, but on more than one occasion I tripped or got snagged in a bramble, so he lifted me clean off the ground and carried me effortlessly towards the portal, moving much faster than I could have run.

"Hold on," he said.

I clasped my hands around his neck, screwing my eyes tight as he ran into the intergalactic gateway. There was that same sinking feeling although the nauseating sense of motion wasn't quite as bad as before, I felt safer in Ahran's arms.

I clung to him as we stepped into the light and warmth of Ramia and I buried my face in his chest to protect my eyes from the sun.

"Are you okay?" I felt the rumble of his voice. My mind flashed back to our kiss before we had left Ramia this afternoon and my stomach clenched at the memory.

"I think so."

Ahran handed me his sunglasses again, and I put them on. I needed him to put me down.

He made no move to let go.

"You can put me down now," I suggested as I cautiously opened my eyes and looked up into his face. I felt a little embarrassed in his arms. He hesitated before lowering my feet to the ground.

"Do you think you are going to be sick?"

"No, I'm okay."

His expression was doubtful.

We started to make our way down the hill. I still felt a little woozy from the change in atmosphere.

"I'm sorry. How is Elaya?" I'd forgotten all about her in my hurry to get here.

"Nothing too serious, she was lucky, just some bruising, she will heal quickly."

"Thank goodness for that!" I said, relieved that she wasn't in the same condition as Audrey.

11

How differently I felt coming here now, compared to how I had felt this morning. Then, I had been reluctant and full of trepidation, and now, I couldn't get here quick enough, my trepidation replaced by ice cold fear.

I glanced up at Ahran. My feelings for him had changed in the last couple of hours. After he had kissed me I had wanted to distance myself from him as far as I possibly could, now I wanted to stick to him like glue. This was no good for my own self-preservation, but I knew he was my best chance of finding Toby.

The big wooden gates opened slowly and Sulaan jogged down the front steps towards us as we entered the courtyard, his expression sombre.

"Ahran, Miss Sophie, the King and Queen are waiting for you in the drawing room."

He ushered us into the building and took us to a large room with comfortable chairs and a large screen on the wall.

Beneath it was a modern fire place. The King was pacing and talking to someone on his phone. Leylana was sat in one of the chairs staring out of the window twisting a hand-kerchief in her hands. When she heard us approaching she jumped up and came towards us, her eyes were red and puffy and devoid of any mascara. She opened her arms and hugged me tightly. Seeing her grief unleashed a sob from me and she responded with more of her own tears. For a few moments we cried together, unified in our misery.

"I just can't believe this has happened," Leylana said, wiping her eyes as she pulled away. "Just when we were getting so close to meeting Toby at last, that…that *hexrina* snatches him right from under our noses." I was a little taken aback by the venom in her voice, she had been so calm and poised at lunch.

"I thought he was safe enough whilst I made the arrangements for us to come and stay…" my voice trailed away.

"You must not blame yourself Sophie, we had no idea she would be so bold and snatch him at school, the woman is pure evil."

In her grief, she reverted to Ramian and spat out a flurry of words.

The King finished his phone call and walked towards me. I had expected him to shake my hand like before, but this time he leaned in and kissed my cheek. It was a tender gesture which brought a fresh rush of tears. I was so touched by their grief and it made me feel more confident that they wouldn't rest until Toby was found.

"My dear, I am so sorry this has happened. I should have

done more to protect him. Come and sit," he gestured to one of the large sofas. "I will explain what has happened so far and what our plan is." He looked towards Sulaan. "Can you arrange some tea for us all?"

Sulaan nodded and left the room.

I sat down. The Queen came and sat next to me taking my hand in her lap. I was grateful for the contact.

The King sat opposite and Ahran took the chair the Queen had just vacated.

"I have already sent out a number of my best agents to start searching for Toby." The King said, slipping into business mode. "It is highly unlikely that Bazeera's men will have taken him to her main residence, it's too obvious, but she has a number of other palaces dotted around her territory. My agents will start at each of these and see if they are able to pick up any trails."

Sulaan reappeared.

"Has anyone seen or heard anything yet?" I asked, hanging on the King's every word.

"No, nothing yet." The frustration was evident on his face. "The one thing we are counting on is that Bazeera won't harm Toby. She will want to use him to bargain with and we are expecting her to make contact with us soon, she won't waste any time trying to get what she wants."

I struggled to feel reassured by what the King had just said. The mere mention of Toby being harmed sent me into paroxysms of fear.

"Isn't there anything more we can do?" I asked, choking back my panic. I suddenly remembered the photo of Katie and Toby. I unzipped my bag and got it out. "I've got this, might it be helpful?" I handed it to the King.

"Yes, thank you." He looked at the photo with interest. The Queen got up to have a look at her grandson too. The King regarded the picture thoughtfully and Leylana started to cry quietly. He put his arm around her to comfort her.

"I'll have it copied and sent out to the relevant parties. Sulaan, would you take care of this?"

Sulaan bowed his head as he took the photo and went to do as the King had asked.

"My Lord, I am keen to take part in the search," Ahran said.

"Of course, I am counting on you Ahran, we need your skills," the King responded.

"I'm going with you," I said. There was no way I was staying behind twiddling my thumbs.

"Sophie, that's a bad idea, it could be dangerous, it's better that you stay here," Ahran replied in a tone that didn't encourage any argument.

I ignored it. "I can't stay here, I'll go mad. I want to go with you." I tried not to sound too hysterical. The thought of not doing anything and leaving it to everyone else was unbearable.

"*My Lord?*" Ahran gave Halsan an imploring look.

"Ahran's right. It is far too dangerous for you to go, it's much better that you stay here."

I continued undeterred. "With all due respect, he is my nephew and I have cared for him as if he were my own son over the last year, I cannot just stay here doing nothing. I'd rather die trying to find him than sit here helplessly."

The King looked at Ahran. "She has a right to take her part in the search, she will be safer with you than with anyone."

Ahran stood up and walked over to the window with his back to us as he ran his hand over his hair in frustration.

Frustrated or not I was damned if I was going to stay behind. "I could be of some help," I said, trying to keep the pleading edge out of my voice.

Ahran turned around to face me. "You could get us both killed," he said uncharitably.

I raised my chin stubbornly and suppressed the feelings of inferiority I felt next to these powerful superhumans. "I will do whatever it takes."

Ahran gave a humourless laugh. From the moment we had first met I had got the distinct impression he didn't have a very high opinion of my kind, it had been alright to kiss me when the mood had suited him, but it was clear that in this situation, he saw me as a liability.

"Ahran," the King said in conciliation, "Think of it this way, Toby is in a strange new world and is no doubt scared out of his wits, Sophie will be the first person he will want to see when he is rescued and you are the only person I would trust to take care of her."

I liked that he seemed certain Toby would be found and I could have hugged him for supporting me. I held my breath as I waited for Ahran's response. After what seemed like an eternity he raised his hands in a gesture of defeat. "If you insist my Lord." He couldn't say no to the King, but if the look on his face was anything to go by, he was furious.

I breathed a sigh of relief and tried to catch his eye to express my gratitude, but he refused to look in my direction.

A young man came in with a tray of tea and laid it out on the coffee table. I had never needed a cup of tea more than I needed one now. After serving the King and Queen the servant handed me a steaming cup. "Thank you," I said gratefully. I brought it to my lips. Its aroma was nothing like I was used to, it smelt creamy and spicy. I took a sip. It was sweet and sickly and made me want to heave.

I heard the sound of footsteps coming from the corridor. One set clicked with the distinctive sound of heels as they struck the marble floor.

"Miss Talina, my Lord," Sulaan said, entering the room and introducing the visitor.

Bloody hell! That was all I needed! I braced myself as I was about to meet Ahran's fiancé.

She was tall, and even taller in a very high pair of expensive looking nude heels. She was catwalk slim, with long, glossy, jet black hair and an olive complexion. She was immaculately turned out in dark camel coloured trousers and a cream, sleeveless linen blouse. Her make-up was flawless like it had been applied by a celebrity make-up artist and she was gorgeous in a glamorous, Hollywood kind of way. I could have happily punched her in the face.

"Talina, what a surprise!" The King said. It was with a certain sense of satisfaction that I noticed his jaw muscle flex with tension. He didn't seem overly pleased by her impromptu visit.

"My Lord," she responded and walked over to air kiss both his cheeks. "Forgive my intrusion, but Ahran called me to say he would be going away, I was in the area visiting one of my clients and thought it would be easier if I came here to see him before he went."

"No need to explain, it's nice to see you, although I am afraid we are all beside ourselves with worry," Leylana said as she stood up and gave Talina a hug.

"I am sorry to hear about your grandson. I am sure he will be fine. Ahran will find him in no time." I knew that she had meant to sound reassuring, but to my ears she sounded infuriatingly flippant. I disliked her immediately, although, to be fair, the woman had stood little chance of winning my friendship simply by virtue of who she was. I watched her with morbid fascination as she made her way over to Ahran and kissed him on the lips, which I thought was entirely inappropriate considering the company. I could feel myself bristling. So far she had completely ignored me.

"Darling, do you think you will be away long?" She asked as if he was going away on some business trip. She seemed completely oblivious to the lack of compassion she was showing.

"I've no idea how long it will take, we are all hoping it won't be too long for everyone's sake."

The King interrupted. "Talina, this is Sophie McAllister, our grandson's Aunt."

I stood up and reluctantly offered my hand. You never had a cattle prod to hand when you needed one. "Hello, pleased to meet you," I said without feeling.

Unsurprisingly, Talina gave me a limp handshake.

"I am desperately sorry to hear about your nephew, you must be distraught." Did she sound disingenuous just to my ears? *What the hell did Ahran see in her?* Apart from her phenomenal good looks.

"Yes," I replied. "Although I'll be happy when Ahran and I can get on and begin our search." For some reason I wanted her to know that I would be accompanying him.

"You are going with Ahran?" She raised a perfectly shaped eyebrow.

"Yes, I can't stay behind and do nothing," I replied.

"No, quite right, I would feel exactly the same," she said distractedly.

"Where do you think you will head first Ahran?" Leylana asked.

"Well, we'll head towards Chancuna, there is a known portal there which they may have used. We might be able to pick up a lead.

The King spoke to Sulaan and once again left to carry out the King's instructions.

I caught Talina glaring at me. Clearly the thought of me spending time with her fiancé did not sit well with her.

"Do you have to go so soon?" she asked as she rested a hand on Ahran's shoulder. She was like a female cat rubbing her scent over her mate and I had to look away.

"The sooner we leave the better," he responded, seemingly oblivious to her disapproval.

"Make sure you keep me informed won't you?" she said with a pout.

Ugh! The woman was unbearable.

"I'll walk you to your car," Ahran said.

He obviously wanted to say his goodbyes in private.

"Yes of course." She sounded a little disgruntled at being dismissed so quickly.

"Goodbye Sophie, it was nice meeting you, I know that Ahran will do his best to find your nephew." She offered me her limp hand again. I shook it noticing her perfectly manicured nails. *I bet she hadn't done a day's work in her life!* I thought about what my hands achieved in a day and knew that a French manicure wouldn't last five minutes.

"Goodbye, Talina." I tried to not sound relieved that she was leaving.

I turned away from the sight of Ahran's hand at the small of her back as they left the room.

The King was back on the phone and Leylana was listening intently to the conversation. I couldn't understand what was being discussed, but I wasn't cheered by the expression on his face.

"Is it bad news?" I asked, as he hung up.

"One moment," he said, raising his finger. He dialled his phone and briefly spoke again.

"There appears to have been portal activity just after Toby went missing at the furthest perimeter of Bazeera's territory. The region they are in, if indeed they are still there, is hostile, and mostly tropical, it isn't the easiest terrain to navigate around."

It sounded rather daunting. "How far away is it?"

The King thought about this for a moment. "About 150,000 kilometres."

I had no concept of how far this was, but I was pretty sure it was a *long* way.

"Can we travel there through a portal?" Surely with Ramian technology it wouldn't take that long.

"Unfortunately not, portal travel is only possible between universes and not within a universe, our atmosphere is too dense."

"Forgive my ignorance, but can't we just go back to Earth and re-enter through the portal that Bazeera's men took Toby through?"

"If only it was that simple," the King replied. "I strongly suspect Bazeera has closed that gateway by now and I cannot open a portal that is not in my territory."

The few rays of hope I had felt earlier started to fade.

"So how will we get there? Surely it will take forever."

"Well, you will have to fly to Zanzin and then take the train to either Borlaan or Histra, these areas are remote and there are no connecting flights."

Ahran returned from seeing Talina off and caught the last part of what the King had just said.

"So they've taken him to the other side of Morana." He didn't sound at all pleased to hear this.

"I am afraid so, but then Bazeera wasn't going to make it easy for us," the King said with a degree of resignation.

"No, I suppose not. Well, in that case we better start our journey. We'll head to the airport." He turned towards me, "Are you sure you want to do this Sophie?" Ahran asked, clearly hoping that I was having second thoughts. "It's going to be a long and gruelling journey across some hostile territory." He was trying his damnedest to put me off.

"Never been surer," I said, trying to sound more upbeat than I felt.

We all stood up to say our goodbyes. Leylana hugged me tightly. "The very best of luck and please be careful," she said as she pulled away still holding my arms. She gave me another quick hug. The King came over and put his hand on my shoulder.

"Goodbye my dear. All my best agents are out there looking for him and it should only be a matter of time before Toby is found."

I hoped more than anything he was right. And as if the situation wasn't bad enough, meeting Talina had added to my woes. I knew my hopes of her being a plain homely type had been wishful thinking. She turned out to be everything I feared, stunning and predatory. I resolved to myself that whilst this situation had thrown Ahran and myself together, I was going to have to rein in my attraction for him. I had to focus on the job of finding Toby and once he was safe we would get the hell out of here.

Sulaan came back into the drawing room and handed me back the photo of Katie and Toby. I felt sure that Katie would be doing exactly what I was about to do had she been here.

"Ready?" Ahran asked.

"As I'll ever be," I replied. He looked disappointed with my answer.

"A car is ready to take you to the airport," the King said. "Try to keep in touch when you can." He clapped Ahran on the back.

"Good luck," Leylana said as she hugged me and Ahran again, her eyes watering once more.

Sulaan handed Ahran a wallet of documents and we

made our way to the front of the palace where a car was waiting for us. It was unlike any car I had ever seen. It was silver with darkened windows and hovered about a foot off the ground. The passenger doors came out from the sides and slid back in one smooth motion as we approached. Ahran motioned for me to get in whilst he put the bags into the boot. I noticed that the car didn't move or sink as we got in. Ahran spoke. The doors shut and the vehicle obediently moved silently across the terrace and out through the wooden gates. I grabbed Ahran's arm involuntarily. It was the strangest feeling knowing that nobody was actually driving the car.

Ahran's expression softened for the first time in the last hour.

"You'll get used to it."

"But there isn't anyone at the controls. What about other traffic? And what happens if someone steps out in front of it?"

"It has an extremely intelligent sensor and anticipatory system, these things just don't crash."

I thought about the car crash that had killed my sister and wondered how long it would be before this kind of vehicle existed on Earth and how many lives it would save.

"When is our flight?"

"In about an hour and a half."

"Doesn't the King have his own plane?"

"He does, but it's not big enough for the distance we've got to fly, it's a long way even by Ramian standards. You can still change your mind Sophie."

I turned and faced him squarely. "Look, I know you

don't want me with you, you've made your feelings perfectly clear. But I can't stay behind, please understand that, so if we could just strike an amicable truce it will make it much easier for the both of us."

Ahran sighed and gazed out the window before turning back to me.

"You're right I don't want you with me."

That hurt.

"It's not safe. But my biggest fear is I don't trust myself around you," he said wearily.

My eyes snapped up to his.

"I want to kiss you again and see if it is as good as I remember," he confessed.

I drew in a shaky breath, his blue eyes were working their magic and it was a struggle to look away.

I was in trouble. I willed my brain to think rationally. "Well...we both know that what happened this morning was a mistake. We are adults and I'm sure we can restrain ourselves so that we can see this through without doing anything we would both regret." I congratulated myself. I sounded convincing even though every cell in my body strained towards him to see if what he was wondering was indeed true.

"I wish I could be so certain."

He was looking at my lips as if they were some kind of exquisite delicacy willing him to take a wickedly forbidden taste.

How was I going to stay away from him knowing that he wanted to kiss me as much as I wanted him to? *So much for trying to keep my distance.* I figured that being in the intimate confines of a car was a situation that needed to be avoided. The charge that hummed between us when we were this close was too difficult to resist.

He muttered something to himself in Ramian and looked away. Even though I didn't understand what he'd said it was obvious that for some unfathomable reason I affected him. On the one hand, it was exhilarating, but on the other, it filled me with utter dismay. The last few moments had just made this trip so much more dangerous and I contemplated whether I should turn back and let him go on his own after all.

12

W e came to a halt outside the airport.

"Come on, I need to get something to eat." His mood had chilled a few degrees.

The air was hot and dry when we got out of the car and I wished I'd worn something cooler, my jeans were clinging uncomfortably to my legs.

"How long is the flight?" I asked, feeling awkward after what had just happened between us.

"About 5 hours," he replied, slinging a bag over each shoulder.

"I can take my bag." If I wanted him to take me seriously I needed to show him I was up to this. He hesitated and shrugged as he handed it to me.

We made our way into the huge airport terminal.

"I don't have a passport or anything," I said struggling to keep up with his pace.

His face was expressionless. He had returned to being Mr Broody and it irritated me.

"You don't need one. Halsan has cleared you to travel," he said in a clipped voice.

It was busy inside the terminal. People were going about their business in the usual way. The only difference I could see between Ramians and humans, was that Ramians were taller, other than that I could have been in any international airport on Earth. I was also relieved to see that not every woman in Ramia was a goddess. I thanked the Lord for small mercies.

The girl at the check in desk fumbled her way through our bag check-in clearly flustered by Ahran. I watched her sympathetically. I understood how difficult it was to concentrate in his presence. When she had checked in our bags and they had been sucked up a chute behind her, she passed a scanner over the back of Ahran's neck and handed the paperwork back to him smiling shyly, her neck and cheeks flushed. Poor girl. *Can you imagine the effect his kiss has on you?*

Ahran took the papers and put them in his shirt pocket.

"Why did that girl scan the back of your neck?" I asked as we walked away from the desk.

"She was scanning my chip, the paperwork is for you."

I laughed. "What? You're chipped?!"

Ahran failed to see what was so funny. "Yes, we are chipped at birth. We don't have passports here our ID information is in the chip that's inserted into the back of our necks just after we are born."

"We only chip our pets at home," I laughed again at how ridiculous it sounded.

"We have no issues about identifying people here and it does away with the need for passports or ID," he said matter of factly.

I dwelled on this for a moment, maybe it wasn't as ridiculous as it sounded.

We went through a full body scanner and then we were free to enter the main concourse. I spied some clothes outlets on the far side. I really needed something cooler to wear.

"Have we got time for me to buy some lighter clothes?" I asked.

Ahran checked his watch. "Yes, you can do that whilst I get us something to eat. I'll meet you under that screen," he said, indicating towards an information screen near one of the shops.

"Okay, I'll see you in a bit." Suddenly I realised I had nothing to buy them with.

"Ahran!" I called after him and he turned around.

"I've got no money." I gave an apologetic shrug.

He raised an eyebrow as he took a card out of his wallet.

"Just hand this to the shop assistant."

"Thanks, I'll pay you back," I said sheepishly.

"Forget it."

I felt uncomfortable being indebted to him, but what choice did I have?

I made my way to the first of the shops and started looking through the rails. There were a couple of skirts and a pair of shorts that I thought might do. I draped them over my arm and began to make my way to the changing cubicles. For some reason, I felt like I was being watched. I entered one of the cubicles and peered through the gap at the edge of the curtain to see if my hunch was correct. I noticed a man with close cropped hair and dark clothes hovering near a waste bin. He glanced my way before slipping away and joining the throng of travellers. This wouldn't usually have been an extraordinary sight in a busy airport, but something about him struck me as odd, he was kind of aloof and in my experience most people in an airport had a purpose. I shook my head. Maybe I was just imagining it.

I hurriedly tried the skirts and shorts on. They were fine. I grabbed a pair of sandals as I made my way to the desk to pay. My eyes scanned the people around to see if I could see the guy in the dark clothes again.

Were we being followed? The thought made my skin prickle. I glanced over to the information board. There was no sign of Ahran. I handed the woman the card he had given me and once my purchase was complete, I went and stood by the screen as we had arranged. Suddenly, everyone in the immediate vicinity began to look suspicious. The minutes ticked by and still no sign of Ahran. I could feel the adrenaline starting to pump. What if he'd decided to go on his own after all?

And then I spotted him walking towards me with two baguettes in one hand and a couple of drinks in the other, his long legs eating up the ground as he approached me. My breath caught in my throat at the sight of him.

"I was beginning to wonder where you were," I said. Why did I sound like I had just walked up a flight of stairs? I chose not to tell him that I thought he'd deserted me.

"It took a while to be served. Shall we go over there and eat?" he said, pointing towards a pleasant seating area where real trees grew up through gaps in the marble floor.

We sat down and when I was confident no one could eavesdrop I leant across the table towards him. "I think we are being followed," I whispered.

"Hmm, I know," he replied taking a mouthful of his baguette.

"What do you mean you know? Why didn't you tell me?" I forgot to whisper and Ahran shot me a warning look.

"Because I didn't want to frighten you," he said quietly. "I noticed them both when we were at the check-in desk." I had to strain to hear what he said. He seemed to forget that I had to rely on my inferior hearing. "There are two of them?" I squeaked in horror.

He nodded, seemingly unperturbed by this.

I thought back to when the girl at the desk was checking our papers. I'd had no idea anyone was watching us. "What should we do?"

"Nothing, just carry on as normal." Ahran took another bite of his baguette.

I had lost my appetite. It was clear that acting normal was going to be a challenge for me. I already felt the urge to keep checking over my shoulder. "What do you think they are up to?" I asked, trying to sound as nonchalant as he had.

"They are tracking us and will be reporting back to Bazeera I expect," he said, after swallowing his mouthful.

"You don't seem too worried about this."

He shook his head slightly. "I'm not. We've just got to lose them."

"And how do we do that?"

"Not sure yet, I'll think of something."

I felt like I had inadvertently stepped into a Bond movie and the unhelpful voice in my head reminded me that people frequently got killed in those films. Now, I not only felt frightened for Toby, but also a good deal more concerned for my own safety.

"Should we still get on the plane?" I whispered, feeling completely unprepared for all of this.

"Yes, of course, it would take us forever to get to Zanzin any other way," he replied.

"But what if those men get on the plane with us?" The thought of being stuck on a plane knowing that there were two potential assassins watching our every move was unnerving to say the least.

"You ask a lot of questions don't you?" he said.

I detected a slight smile and shrugged. "It's not every day I find myself being followed."

"Fair point," he conceded. "Suicide bombing is not Bazeera's style, nor is public murder, so it's unlikely they will try anything."

She'd had the audacity to kidnap Toby in the cold light of day and from under everyone's noses, so I could be forgiven for not trusting his reassurance that she was the cautious type.

"Go back to the palace Sophie," Ahran said, drawing his own conclusions from my silence. "I can't promise we are not in danger and I would understand if you are having second thoughts." His expression was sympathetic and I almost weakened, but the thought of what Toby was going through strengthened my resolve. In some perverse way, being involved in his search, even if it meant risking my own life, seemed an appropriate penance for not taking the necessary precautions that would have prevented all of this from happening in the first place.

I raised my chin stubbornly. "I'm not going to change my mind, I have to do this."

Ahran's look was doubtful. It galvanised my resolve even more.

"You think I'm weak and pathetic, but I will prove to you that I am not," I said defiantly. Having got the distinct impression that Ahran didn't hold Sapiens in particularly high regard, I felt it was a good opportunity to champion my race. I may not have superhuman abilities, but I would do my upmost to show him I had other strengths. The only problem was, I wasn't sure what these were yet.

Ahran went to say something, but just shrugged his shoulders instead. "Well, don't say I didn't warn you. He wiped his mouth with a napkin. "We need to go."

He pointed to my untouched baguette. "You haven't eaten anything," he said, expressing his disapproval.

"I'm not hungry," I said, wrapping the baguette in a napkin and putting it in my bag. "I'll eat it on the plane." If I was going to show him I was up to what was ahead of us I couldn't afford to give him any reason to think I might be a burden to him.

We arrived at our gate in silence. As casually as I could

I scanned the queue for the guy in the dark clothes. He didn't appear to be here.

After a minute or two we were called to board. I took one last look behind me as we went through the boarding gate, everyone looked like legitimate passengers to me and I relaxed a fraction. We walked along the elevated walkway and boarded the plane.

I began to follow the rest of the passengers towards the main bulk of seats, but Ahran grabbed my arm. "Our seats are this way," he said, pointing towards the front of the aircraft.

"Oh, okay," I said and followed him. Our seats were in first class. I felt a frisson of excitement. I'd never been in first class before.

A female flight attendant standing at the doorway led us into the area that was reserved for the more affluent traveller. Her eyes raked over Ahran appreciatively and she gave him a million-watt smile. I would have to get used to the female attention he attracted. It hadn't taken me long to realise that even in Ramia he was exceptionally attractive.

She showed us to our seats.

"Do you want to sit by the window?" Ahran asked.

"Yes, thank you." The seats were as large as armchairs and I sunk into mine.

"Well, this is a new experience," I said, unable to hide my excitement. "I've never been in first class before." I grinned.

He smiled at me. "Enjoy it while it lasts, it's unlikely that all our travel will be as comfortable as this." He sat down next to me and I tried not to let his words dampen my first experience of luxury air travel.

I settled back into my seat, knowing that there was little we could do in the search for Toby until we arrived at our destination. Ahran showed me how to operate the T.V. glasses so I could watch the safety video and when it had finished, I took the glasses off and leant towards him. "I don't think anyone followed us on board," I whispered.

"You're right," he said, a smile tugging at his lips. "Although they have probably already reported back that we are heading to Zanzin." He seemed unruffled by this, but it caused my uneasiness to return.

Without warning he reached around my waist and clipped my seatbelt together. I froze, taken back by his sudden invasion of my personal space. I tried not to inhale his scent, but it was too late. It was citrus, sun, and Ahran. It made me feel light headed.

"You need that on. The take-off is fast," he said unapologetically.

I didn't reply. I wasn't confident I could manage any more than a whimper, so I just nodded instead. *What was wrong with me?* I'd turned into a quivering heap of hormones the moment he was in my air space. I'd never reacted like that to a man.

My attention was momentarily distracted from the Ahran effect when the plane started to taxi down the run way and began to pick up speed alarmingly. My eyes couldn't focus on anything outside and I clutched Ahran's arm before I was aware of what I was doing. The speed of the plane forced me back into my seat. I glanced up at him nervously and he took my hand in his. He began to trace circles with his thumb in the palm of my hand in an attempt to soothe me. My heart rate doubled.

The blurry landscape outside was now the least of my problems as the shockwaves of his touch chased up my arm. I swallowed, my mouth suddenly going dry. I was dimly aware that we were quickly gaining altitude and I leant back and closed my eyes. The trouble was, this seemed to intensify the effect his touch was having on me. God, he was only touching my hand and I reacted like this, imagine the effect of his touch on other parts of my body? My breath began to match my heartbeat. He had certainly succeeded in taking my mind off the speed. I opened my eyes and turned to look at him. His eyes were hooded and his pupils dilated. I withdrew my hand. Hand holding was another thing I had to add to the 'Ahran and Sophie List of Things to Avoid'.

"Thanks I feel better now we are actually in the air." Dammit, my voice sounded husky even to my own ears.

The sun was beginning to fade and the dimness in the plane made it feel more intimate. We were in our own private bay. I reached up and flicked the overhead light on in an attempt to kill the mood. We were cruising now, the engines were quiet and the ride was completely smooth.

I caught Ahran looking at me.

"Are you okay?" he asked, his eyes searching mine.

Not quite sure whether he was referring to my reaction to the speed or his touch, I plumped for the former. "It's amazing, you wouldn't think we were in the air at all."

His head was inclined towards me, his face expressionless, but there was a softness in his eyes. *Oh hell!* It was so much easier when he was being prickly.

"Well, we've got five hours to kill. Tell me more about yourself."

His directness surprised me. "I'm not sure we should get to know each other any better," I replied.

He chuckled. "We are going to be in each other's company for a while, it's going to be difficult to remain strangers," he argued.

There was a hint of a challenge in his eyes. Okay, if he could keep his emotions in check so could I. Couldn't I?

"What do you want to know?" I asked.

"Who was your first crush?"

I arched an eyebrow at him. I pummelled down the feelings this stirred in me and tried to summon a light-heartedness of my own.

"A boy called James Gardiner who lived down my road."

"Did you ever do anything about it?" he quizzed.

"No, he barely knew I existed. He was five years older than me and I was too shy to pluck up the courage to speak to him," I confessed.

"His loss."

I smiled philosophically. "That's what I like to think, although he is a successful corporate lawyer now with a three million pound house, a wife and four children."

"Sounds like a lucky escape," he said good-humouredly.

I laughed. "Who was yours?" I asked, tucking my ankle under my bottom so I could face him. I was beginning to enjoy myself.

"Petrula Lassiva."

I tried to hide my smirk. She sounded like some seventies Eurovision Song contestant.

"What?" he said, trying to sound offended, but couldn't prevent a smile from creeping across his own features.

"Nothing. So, who was she?"

"She was…is," he corrected, "A very beautiful movie star in Ramia, most men have a crush on her."

I pictured a sultry film star dressed in a floaty Kaftan, seductively draped over a chaise.

"Have you ever met her?" I asked.

"No," he laughed, as if it was the most ridiculous suggestion ever. "Petrula is a goddess among women, she rarely lets mortal men near her."

He had absolutely no idea that there was nothing remotely mortal about him. I sent up a little silent prayer and thanked the lord that they hadn't met. Petrula wouldn't have been able to resist him any more than the rest of us.

I started to relax. We were on our way to find Toby and I was happy about that. There was nothing more we could do other than kill time and try and bring our association back onto a more even keel.

"So judging by your conversation with Halsan earlier you've bought a farm? You don't seem like the farmer type; all flat caps and sheep dogs," I teased.

He chuckled. "Cows are more my thing, sheep have a habit of dying."

"Do you come from a farming background?" I asked intrigued.

He laughed at his own private joke. "No, my father is a

politician and my mother is the King's sister, although she found it her calling to become a teacher," he explained.

I nodded encouragingly.

"I did a business degree," he continued, "And then a veterinarian degree, but I've always been interested in farming in a sustainable, animal centred way. Farming has a much better reputation here than it has on Earth, Ramians value their local food producers much more. Here, we understand what damage cheap food, transported thousands of miles does to the planet."

The Ramian ethos was impressive. "Your people seem to have really got it sussed when it comes to looking after their world."

"It is one of the fundamental building blocks of our society."

I reflected on what he said for a moment.

"So where do you think we've gone wrong?" I asked interested to get his take on the failings of mankind.

"It's simple. Greed," he declared.

"Aren't Ramians greedy?" I queried.

"Yes, but not at the expense of the world they live in, maybe it's because we live longer and live to see the effects of our actions. That's where Sapiens go wrong. They think that whatever happens in a hundred years' time is irrelevant to them, they seem to care little about how their actions might affect their ascendants."

I knew that everything he said was depressingly true and didn't want to dwell on how we were wrecking our planet, so I changed the subject. "Where is your farm?"

"It's about an hour's drive from the palace."

"So is Talina looking forward to becoming a farmer's wife?" It came out before I had a chance to filter. I couldn't quite imagine the immaculately turned out Talina slugging around in wellies.

Ahran hesitated. "Talina is more of a city girl."

"That's going to make married life difficult for her isn't it?" I knew I should stop, but I couldn't help myself, it was like I had turned into a rubbernecker morbidly watching the outcome of a car crash.

He shrugged in a way that didn't encourage any further probing. As far as I could see, it was a recipe for disaster, or was I just hoping that was the case?

"How about you? What has your life been like?" Ahran said, expertly changing the subject. I had to chuckle at his turn of phrase. Most of the time he spoke English like a native, but every now and then what he said didn't sound quite right.

"It's not that interesting, although I suppose that's changed in the last week." I grimaced. "I grew up in Hatherley, did an English Literature degree at UCL. Before Katie died I had a marketing job in London, but after her death it was kind of a relief to have a good reason to go back home. I no longer had to prove myself in the city.

"Why did you work in London if you hated it so much?" Ahran asked.

"I really wanted to be a writer and after temping at a PR firm after my degree they offered me a permanent position. I couldn't turn it down. I had student loans and rent to pay and so my writing career never really got off the ground." I shrugged.

"Do you miss anything about city life?"

"I was never a high flyer. Even before Katie's death, I couldn't keep up with the lifestyle and looked forward to my weekends back home too much." I took a sip of the drink the overly attentive flight attendant had just given us. "I like green. Green trees, green fields. You don't get much of that in London. Going back to Hatherley was like putting an oxygen mask on." I paused. "I keep in touch with a couple of friends there and visit once or twice a year and that seems to satisfy any yearning I have for a faster pace of life." I looked across at him. "How about you, have you ever lived in the city?" I asked

"Yes, although our cities aren't like yours," he pointed out. "After I completed my military service, I studied in Dortaan for my business degree. It's one of the largest cities in Dinara but it is very beautiful with lots of open green spaces. It was no hardship living there. Then I did veterinary at Harla."

"You have to do military service here?" I asked.

"Yes, everyone has to do it for at least three years at some point between the ages of thirty and seventy."

"Really? What, even women?"

He nodded. "Women aren't expected to get married or start a family until they have been in the army, navy or air force. It's very much frowned upon if they do and their families are liable for a heavy fine."

"God, that sounds archaic. I thought Ramia was a progressive place."

"It is, but it helps to reduce the number of girls having babies too young."

"And increases the number of back street abortions," I snorted.

Ahran looked philosophical. "Maybe."

I was beginning to get the impression that Ramia wasn't as perfect as I had first thought.

"And after your military service you did *two* degrees?" I raised my eyebrows

"I am a little older than you," he said with a wry twist of his lips.

"Even so, they're demanding degrees."

He actually looked slightly embarrassed, it wasn't a look I was familiar with, he always seemed so self-assured. "It's not unusual to do more than one degree here," he explained.

"So why did you go back into the army and not go into business or become a vet?"

"Because I liked it and I was good at it," he said unashamedly. "It was dangerous and exciting. I'd had a restrained upbringing and the army provided me with boundaries that I was used to and the freedom to take risks, and I suppose, the opportunity to go a bit crazy at times."

I raised my eyebrows willing him to expand. I couldn't imagine Ahran going crazy. He seemed so in control, restrained even. "Go on," I encouraged.

"Maybe I'll tell you another time. It's not good for me to share my deepest darkest secrets with you," he said with a wicked smile. "Didn't you say we shouldn't get to know each other too well?" he said, throwing my earlier comment back at me.

Dammit, I was dying to know.

"Didn't you have a particularly happy childhood then?"

I asked, picking up on his comment about having a restrained upbringing.

He paused for a moment. "Let's just say my father was very controlling in a 'hands off' kind of way." He didn't elaborate any further.

I wasn't quite sure what he meant, but I shelved it for the time being. I couldn't help it, I was being drawn in, the more he told me, the more I wanted to know. It was a dangerous game to play.

"Why the Special Force?" I asked

He took a sip of his drink. "I impressed them enough to be offered a position. To be asked is a great honour and I wasn't ready to go home."

"And that's where you worked alongside Tagan?"

"Yes, from time to time. We were on a Special Force covert mission when he was killed." A dark shadow swept across his face. It was plain to see that the memories were still painful. I wanted to reach out and comfort him, to reach up and stroke away the troubled look on his face, but all of a sudden he seemed closed off.

After a moment or two he continued, his dark expression carefully replaced by a mask of indifference. "Tagan liked the strategic side of things whereas I always preferred reconnaissance."

"That sounds dangerous," I said.

"It was, but at the time I needed it."

I couldn't help thinking that his life must have been pretty rough if he was prepared to put it on the line every day. I wondered what had happened to make him feel like that.

"You enjoyed risking your life?" I asked.

"I did for a long time. The Special Force took me to places I had never been before. It was fast paced and exciting, but the reality of what I was putting myself through hit home when Tagan was killed."

He seemed to have better control over his emotions this time and I only saw the briefest flicker of pain in his eyes before he moved on. "I have always loved the countryside and wanted to use my degrees so I decided to buy a farm and when one came up in the location I was after, I bought it. I had come to the end of my contracted period and was ready to say goodbye to the military.

"Do you miss it?"

"Sometimes, but I grew tired of being rootless. I have different priorities now."

The thought of Ahran and Talina putting down roots together didn't sit well with me. Since when had Ahran's future started to matter so much? Had it been when he had kissed me? Or when I had met Talina? Or had it been when I first laid eyes on him standing under my porch? Much to my dismay, I realised it was probably the latter.

The flight attendant interrupted our conversation and handed us steaming hot plates of some sort of casserole and rice. She poured us both a glass of wine and I took a mouthful of the meaty dish in front of me. It was delicious and nothing like the aeroplane food I had ever tasted. It was also preferable to the sweaty baguette I had stuffed in my bag.

I spent the time we ate thinking about what Ahran had told me about his life and I admired his drive to branch out and do something he felt passionate about. I couldn't think of anything better than living in beautiful countryside, building a business based on something you felt strongly about *and* doing it with someone you loved. *Did Talina share his passion?* From what I had seen of Talina the only thing that she seemed passionate about was herself.

I looked over at Ahran's handsome profile. I wondered what it would be like to share my life with him. I shook my head slightly, what was I thinking? I hardly knew the guy, not to mention that he was engaged to another woman *and* from an entirely different universe. He wasn't technically even the same species. The idea of me and Ahran ever being together was so utterly ridiculous it was laughable. I needed to stop these silly daydreams and focus.

"You've gone very quiet. No more questions?" he asked, sipping his wine.

I reached for my glass and took a large gulp, it was sweet and warming. I welcomed its soothing effect as it hit my stomach.

"Not for the moment," I said as breezily as I could.

"What about you Sophie, are you happy?" he asked, keeping his eyes trained on me.

It struck me as a slightly odd question. "Well, I would have preferred that Toby had not been kidnapped by aliens," I said with a frown.

Ahran's lips twisted into a humourless smile. "We all wish *that* hadn't happened, but I mean before the recent turn of events. Were you happy?"

I blew out my cheeks as I thought back to my life before Toby had been kidnapped. "It's been a really tough year.

Losing Katie was one of the most difficult things I have ever had to deal with. She wasn't just my sister she was my best friend." I took another sip of wine. "Our mother never really got over the death of our father when we were young and even though Katie was only three years older than me it was her I always turned to. The bond we had continued into adulthood."

I looked up at Ahran with tears in my eyes and was met with his own look of anguish. Was he thinking about Tagan again? I guessed he knew what it was like to lose someone he'd loved.

He started to say something, but faltered. "I'm sorry," he said eventually. "From the brief glimpse I've had of your life it seems like you have coped well."

I smiled and swallowed back the tears.

"Toby is a great little boy, I am lucky to have had him."

"*Have him*," Ahran corrected. "We *will* get him back Sophie."

I so desperately wanted to believe him, but at this moment in time Toby seemed so far away.

"You don't think they are being cruel to him, do you?"

"He is an innocent and children are highly regarded in Ramia. There is no reason why they should be cruel to him. Toby is Bazeera's ticket to getting what she wants and she wouldn't compromise her chances."

Ahran's words offered me some comfort. I gazed back into his eyes, struck by the sincerity I saw there. He really was trying to reassure me. I wanted to believe him, but I was so far out of my comfort zone in this strange place that I hardly knew what to think.

His hand was resting on top of the tray in front of him and I wanted to slide my hand into his to draw on some of his strength, but I fought the urge.

"Thank you." It was all I could muster as tears threatened. Tears not just for Toby, but for myself and the awkward, difficult and dangerous situation I had found myself in.

Whilst we ate dessert I tried to rein in my emotions. I yawned as our trays were cleared away.

"You ought to try and get some sleep," Ahran advised.

I nodded, feeling weak with exhaustion. "I can quite safely say that today goes down as one of the worst days of my life and that's saying something. I've had some pretty bad ones," I said, giving him a weak smile.

He smiled back sympathetically.

"You're right. I think I will try and get some sleep," I said, retrieving the headphones from the pocket on the side of my chair, before reaching down for the blanket that was stowed under my seat. I reached up and switched the overhead light off.

"Night," I said, pulling the blanket over me. I picked up the T.V. glasses. "How do I work these again?"

"Here," he said, as he put them on me. I managed to not inhale as he did it this time. I also pushed myself back into the seat to avoid any contact with him. I was knackered, my defences were down and there was no telling what my body would do in response to his touch.

"Goodnight Sophie," he said quietly.

For a long time, I stared at the images, not taking in the movie. How was I ever going to get through this? I feared for Toby and wondered how he was coping away from me and home. I didn't know how we were even going to begin to find him. I was also pretty concerned that my growing attraction for Ahran could only end in tears.

After some time the gabble of Ramian dialogue flowing through the earpieces receded into the background and I surrendered to the creeping fingers of sleep.

"WAKE UP SOPHIE," Ahran said as he nudged my arm. "We are just about to land."

I had assumed the foetal position in my chair, I was no longer wearing the T.V. glasses and my left arm had gone dead with the weight of my head. I sat up a little disorientated and stretched when I realised where I was.

"That was quick," I said croakily.

"It was for you, you slept for most of it."

"You didn't sleep?"

He shook his head.

"Can't you sleep on planes?"

"Something like that," he said evasively.

Apart from the massive deceleration the landing was smooth and we were ushered off the plane by our flight attendant. It wouldn't have surprised me at all if she had pressed a piece of paper into Ahran's hand with her phone number on it.

We left the plane and made our way to the arrivals lounge. It was the middle of the night and apart from the passengers that had been on our plane, the place was deserted. It wasn't long before our luggage appeared down a chute and onto the carousel. We went through security and made our way through the airport.

"I'm just going to nip to the ladies, I won't be a minute," I said as I spotted what was literally the universal sign for the toilet to our left.

"Okay, no problem." Ahran pulled his phone out of his pocket and leant up against the wall outside the ladies. "I'll just wait here," he said distractedly.

I walked into the loos. There was a woman with a sleepy child washing their hands at the basins and I smiled at them as they left. Somebody entered the cubicle next to me. When I had finished I went to the basins and washed my hands. I caught sight of my reflection in the mirror, I was pale, my hair needed a good brush and the little make-up I had put on earlier had worn off.

I scrabbled around in my handbag for a brush and hair band. The person who had been in the cubicle next to mine came out and I briefly made eye contact with her before I felt the blow between my shoulder blades.

She hit me with such force that it catapulted my upper body forward causing my head to smack against the glass whilst my abdomen collided with the sink unit. Pain seared through my head and I let out a whimper as I slid to the floor.

Disorientated, I felt her hands take a grip around my neck. I used all the strength I had to claw at her fingers, but my attempt to lessen her grasp was futile and my vision began to cascade into a multitude of colours under her lethal hold. My chest felt like it was about to explode. I gasped for breath and came to the sickening conclusion that it would only be a matter of seconds before my world went blank.

I could feel myself drifting. The hands around my throat were too strong and I had nothing left to fight with. My arms fell loosely to my sides as I gave into the burning feeling in my throat and lungs. Two images flashed in my mind, one was of Toby and the other was of Ahran, and then I lost consciousness.

13

"Sophie, can you hear me? Open your eyes," a male voice demanded.

Air was being forced into my lungs in between pumping thrusts to my chest. My head was pounding and it felt like a stock car had driven right into my pelvis. I attempted to draw in the breath that was making its unrelenting way into my lungs, but the sensation against my dry throat only caused me to splutter and cough.

"Gretcha garlena," said the now familiar and welcome voice.

My eyes fluttered open and I took a couple of painful breaths unaided. "What happened?" I croaked, struggling to understand why I was lying on the floor of what looked like a public toilet and why I was in so much pain.

"You were attacked," Ahran replied, his face full of concern.

I attempted to sit up, but a bolt of pain shot through my head and I fell back onto the floor.

"Hey, steady, take your time. You've got a nasty cut on your forehead."

My arm felt heavy as I touched my head, it was wet and sticky and I stared uncomprehendingly at the blood that now coated my fingers.

Slowly it came back. I remembered brushing my hair, a woman behind me, the blow to my back and then not much more after that.

My lungs and throat burned.

"Have you got any water?"

"Yes, let me help you sit up." I tried to assist, but my strength had all but deserted me. "Easy," Ahran said, "I'll lift you."

I felt as weak as a new-born and lay heavily in his arms as he gently eased me into an upright position against his chest.

"Here have some of this," he said, pressing a bottle to my lips. The cool water soothed my parched throat. I drew in some steadying breaths and felt slightly better in spite of the pain coursing through my head.

"Where is she?" I asked as panic began to kick in.

Ahran tilted his head towards the form lying on the floor just a few feet from us.

I gasped. She was as still as a stone.

"Oh my God! Is she dead?" I knew the answer as soon as I noticed her open, vacant eyes.

"She would have killed you." Ahran's lips formed a grim line. He was applying pressure to the cut above my eye.

"Ouch! That hurts," I winced.

"I'm just trying to stem the bleeding, you need to have this looked at," he said with a frown. "If I support you, do you think you can stand up?"

"I think so." I was creeped out by the dead woman lying only a few feet away from me and was only too happy to give what he was suggesting a try.

Ahran's arms cradled me as I summoned all my strength to prepare myself to stand. I was on my feet in no time having put very little effort in on my part. "Ah my head!" I cried out in pain.

Concern carved itself into every line of Ahran's face. "I've got you." He took my weight effortlessly. "Do you think you'll be okay if I sit you over there for a moment?" He pointed towards a row of chairs that lined the wall. "I need to hide the body."

My eyes widened, but I nodded in agreement. He carried me over and lowered me carefully onto one of the seats.

"Here." He handed me the bottle of water and I took another sip.

He went over to the dead woman, hooked a hand under her arm and dragged her as easily as if she had been a ragdoll over to the janitor's cupboard. With his free hand, he pulled out a penknife concealed under his trouser leg and extracted one of its arms with his teeth. *How on earth had he got that through security?* He unpicked the lock in one deft movement. The door swung open and he bundled the body into the cupboard carrying his task out with emotionless efficiency. He shut the door and used the penknife to lock it again.

I closed my eyes at the image of the woman slumped in

the cupboard. The only other time I had seen a dead body was when I'd had the unenviable task of identifying my sister at the hospital. The image forced a tearless sob from my throat.

Ahran was back at my side in the blink of an eye.

"Are you alright?"

I nodded even though I felt anything but.

When he was satisfied I wasn't going to pass out, he went over to the sink and dampened some paper towels. He knelt down in front of me and set about cleaning me up. It hurt, but his close proximity helped to keep my mind off the pain. "There, that looks better," he said as he dabbed at my face one last time.

"You need to change your top there's blood all over it."

I looked down at my favourite pink sweater, the front of it was now red with my blood. "There's another top in my bag."

Ahran left me sitting on the chair and went to get our bags.

"Here," he said dropping my bag in front of me.

"Thanks." I leant forward and unzipped it. The pain caused by the sudden movement made me suck in a breath. I replaced my blood-soaked sweater with a navy hoody and stuffed my stained sweater in my bag.

"We need to leave. We're lucky no-one has come in here. Are you ready?"

"Where are we going?"

"You need to see a doctor."

"I'll be fine," I said, trying to reassure him. I didn't want to make a fuss, this was exactly the sort of thing he had meant when he had warned me that our trip would be dangerous and I had just inadvertently proven that I shouldn't be making it with him.

"We're not going anywhere until someone has looked at that cut," he said, pointing to my head wound. "It's still bleeding."

He was right. The warm trickle of blood hadn't stopped. I rearranged the damp paper towels and applied more pressure. "You'll need to put your hood up so we can get out of here without drawing too much attention to ourselves."

He put his rucksack on his back and swung my bag over his left shoulder so he could support me with his right arm.

I went through the motions of walking, but knew that without Ahran I would have crumpled into a heap on the floor. It felt like I'd been hit by a train. My back hurt, my neck hurt, my hips hurt and my head continued to throb. I glanced back at the door of the cleaning cupboard as we left and felt sorry for the poor unsuspecting cleaning person who would get a nasty shock in the morning. My gaze skimmed over the crack in the mirror and I could only feel relieved that I was leaving this skirmish alive.

We walked an indirect route through the terminal and I looked up at Ahran questioningly. He pointed to the minute CCTV cameras fixed to strategic points around the airport. "We need to avoid those."

"Oh." I wouldn't have even noticed them.

I tried to act like every other traveller who had not nearly been strangled to death and we managed to leave without raising any suspicions. Ahran hailed a hover cab and we glided off into the night. I laid my head back on the seat and tried to avoid replaying the events of the last hour in my mind.

Ahran sat quietly brooding next to me. I couldn't think of anything to say that would make the situation any better so I opted to say nothing.

I looked out of the window. There were a couple of other cars on the road and like ours they glided silently along. It was kind of eerie. The buildings were no more than four stories high, modern looking and largely made of glass. The streets were clean and well lit and there were lots of trees. A great deal of thought had obviously gone into the planning of the beautifully planted seated areas which helped to minimise the overall impact of the buildings. I now understood what Ahran meant when he said that living in a Ramian city was no hardship. Even though it was urban, it was leafy and there was a sense of space.

Eventually we pulled up outside a nondescript building down a side street. It looked like a small shop. The windows had frosted glass and a light glowed from inside. Ahran touched his fingertips to a pad in front of us and the door glided open. He helped me out of the car and I eyed the shop front. It was the only building in the street with its lights on. "Is this the doctor's?" I asked.

"Yes." He spoke into the intercom at the door. Within a matter of seconds the door opened and a young woman greeted us who, despite the late hour, looked alert and efficient in her fitted white uniform.

We stepped inside and it smelt of hospitals. The nurse motioned for us to take a seat on one of the two, white leather sofas and left through a door in the wall opposite.

The only other piece of furniture in the room was a clear Perspex coffee table with a large bowl of exotic looking fruit sitting on top, the splash of colour it provided was in stark contrast to the plain white walls and furniture.

I sat there feeling like a naughty child. "I'm sorry," I said feebly.

Ahran arched an eyebrow at me.

What did that mean?

Before I could ask him the nurse reappeared. She spoke in Ramian and we followed her into one of the inner rooms where the doctor was waiting for us. He was an older looking man with silvery grey hair.

Ahran said a few words and the doctor nodded. The nurse lowered the couch into its horizontal position and I laid down so the doctor could examine my head. He shone a torch into my eyes and cast his eye over the wound. He indicated for me to open my mouth and he took something off the stainless steel tray the nurse was holding. He spoke and Ahran translated. "He's giving you something to help with the pain."

The doctor laid a small square of rice paper on my tongue. To my amazement, the pain in my head, neck, back and pelvis dissolved away in a matter of seconds.

"Wow! That's some pain killer," I said.

"It should last for twenty-four hours," Ahran explained.

The nurse placed a pair of over-sized goggles over my eyes and I closed them waiting for the prick of the needle that would administer the local anaesthetic, but all I felt was a tingling sensation where the wound was.

The doctor spoke.

"You can sit up now," Ahran said, relaying the doctor's instructions.

I sat up feeling a hundred times better than when I had come in. The nurse removed the glasses and handed me a mirror. I looked at the doctor's work. The wound had been cleaned and there was a fine pink scar where the cut had been, I could hardly believe that it had healed already.

"Good God! It's almost gone, what did he do?" I said as I gingerly touched the small welt and examined it more closely in the mirror.

"He treated it with a laser and has applied some anti-scarring gel. You should hardly notice it in a couple of days' time."

"That's amazing," I marvelled as I looked at it from different angles.

I smiled at the doctor and thanked him. He smiled and nodded.

As we left the place that performed tiny miracles, in spite of my ordeal and the lateness of the hour, I felt surprisingly alert and buoyant. How was it possible that I felt even better than *before* I'd been attacked?

"How are you feeling?" Ahran asked.

"Remarkably well actually."

"That will be the drugs the doctor gave you."

"What was it? Cocaine?"

Ahran laughed. "Not cocaine. The painkiller the doctor gave you would have contained a mood enhancer, the idea is that if you feel emotionally strong you will heal quicker."

I nodded slowly. *Clever.*

We walked down the darkened street to the main road

at the end and although I no longer needed Ahran's support he insisted on holding my hand, in case I felt faint, apparently. Whilst this was a banned activity in my book, in my enhanced state of mind, I chose to go with it. He had slowed his pace so that I didn't have to trot to keep up.

Back at the airport I'd had a glimpse of Ahran the soldier, cold and implacable. He had dispatched my attacker's body without a second thought. But with me, he had been attentive and caring. I was probably reading far too much into it, either that or it was something to do with the drugs I had just been given, but it seemed like a change had come over him. He'd gone from acting like I was an annoyance, an irritation that he couldn't swat away fast enough, to someone he could tolerate, feel protective over even. My close shave at the airport had confirmed that we were indeed being followed by people who were out to kill us, but to my greater peril all I wanted to do now was melt into Ahran's side and let him shield me from whatever threat we faced. Of course, it wasn't right, I was supposed to be distancing myself from him, but the more distance I tried to create the closer I wanted to be.

We walked towards the main street. I did my best to silence the spiteful voice in my head reminding me that whilst Ahran had spent the last hour being my knight in shining armour Toby remained a hostage and no doubt scared out of his wits. It occurred to me that if Ahran hadn't been babysitting me he could have been closer to rescuing Toby. I disengaged our hands, but Ahran just put his arm around my shoulders and pulled me closer.

I looked up at him and his expression challenged me to pull away.

"The closer you stay to me the better; I'd rather not risk your safety again."

"I shouldn't have come," I said.

He gave me a squeeze. "I'd be lonely if you weren't here." I gave him a weak smile.

We walked in silence for a few minutes. The air was cool and I could feel the heat of his body next to mine. I struggled to concentrate on the simple task of putting one foot in front of the other. "Where are we going now?" I asked as Ahran hailed down another hover cab that was vacantly cruising down the street.

"To a hotel to get some sleep and then in the morning we push on."

The cab stopped at the curb and we climbed in. The car pulled away smoothly and we made our way back down the street towards the nearest hotel. It turned out to be a no frills affair with a self-service check-in just on the edge of town.

We finally entered our room and I eyed the large bed nervously. How on earth was I going to get any sleep sharing a bed with him?

I groaned inwardly.

"I'll sleep on the couch," he offered, sensing my uneasiness.

"Don't be ridiculous, the bed is huge," I said as brightly as I could. "Do you mind if I use the bathroom first though?" I was desperate for a shower.

"Go ahead," he said as he sat down on the bed and leant against the headboard, stretching his long legs out in front of him. I couldn't help but notice the way the denim of his jeans pulled taut across his thighs. Feeling flustered, I began to rifle through my bag and realised that in my hurry to pack I hadn't put any nightclothes in. I would just have to wear knickers and a t-shirt. I grabbed my toothbrush and heard the canned laughter that suddenly blurted from the T.V. as I shut the bathroom door behind me.

It had been a traumatic and exhausting day.

I turned the water on and climbed into the shower, my thoughts turning to Toby. Where was he? How were they treating him? It was his first night away from home with complete strangers in a strange world and he didn't even have his teddy to help him sleep. My heart hung heavy in my chest and I began to cry. I slowly washed my hair and soaped my body as I sobbed. I stood there for a long time my tears mingling with the running water. When they finally began to subside, I got out and wrapped myself in one of the fluffy towels from the heated towel rail.

I cleaned my teeth and towel dried my hair before brushing it and letting it fall in damp waves over my shoulders. I put on a fresh t-shirt and clean underwear and glanced at myself in the mirror. At least the heat of the shower had brought some colour to my cheeks. I unlocked the bathroom door and Ahran looked up as I came out.

Dammit! He was still awake. I was hoping he might have fallen asleep.

"Are you okay?" he asked

"Yes, I'm fine," I said self-consciously. I felt like sprinting to the bed and diving under the covers, but I made myself walk at a normal pace, all the time aware of Ahran's eyes on me.

"I am *shattered*." I was feeling awkward and this came out slightly more exaggerated than I had planned. My attempts at acting like I was unaffected by our sleeping arrangements were failing dismally.

"Is the television bothering you?"

"No, not at all."

He shifted over so I had more space. Now that I was lying next to him there didn't seem to be nearly as much room as I had first thought.

I took a sip of water from the bottle I'd got from the vending machine in the foyer earlier.

"Night then," I said, wriggling down under the covers.

"Goodnight."

I struggled to get to sleep. Maybe this had something to do with lying in a strange bed, in a strange universe. But probably it had more to do with the fact that Ahran was lying next to me.

I GRADUALLY CAME TO, aware that I was lying on my side, my back nestled into a large, warm sleeping form and an arm draped heavily over my hip. My first instinct was to move away, but I allowed myself a few moments longer, it felt so good to have skin to skin contact with someone. I lay there and welcomed the feel of Ahran's warm body knowing I should move away, but not quite able to do it. I froze when he moved and pressed his thigh up against the back of mine. The contact made my stomach clench and my drowsiness vanish. I tried to put some distance between us, but his arm wrapped around my waist holding me in place.

"Don't move," he said. "This feels good." *How long had he been awake?*

"Which is exactly why I should move," I replied, taking hold of his wrist and using all my willpower to lift his arm up and slide away from him.

I sat up. He raised himself up onto one elbow and I did my best to ignore his spectacular shoulders and chest.

"You did that on purpose," I accused, and self-consciously pulled the sheets up to my chin.

"And who can blame me when I've just woken up next to a beautiful woman who is all warm and sleepy? I challenge any man to resist," he said with a wicked smile. I tried to ignore the fact that he had just called me *beautiful*.

"Ahran, *please*," I said in exasperation.

"Please what?" he asked with a devilish glint in his eye.

Was it just me trying to do the honourable thing? "Ugh!" I jumped out of bed and headed for the bathroom, putting as much distance between us as the room allowed. I heard him chuckle behind me and it made me angry. He should be concentrating on finding Toby not trying to seduce me. I felt even angrier at myself for reacting to his touch like I had. Wasn't it only yesterday I had met his fiancé? I washed my face and brushed my teeth ferociously. I really was going to have to set some boundaries because all of a sudden, he didn't seem to have any.

I spat out the toothpaste and examined the barely notice-able scar on my forehead. I rubbed my hand over the dull ache in my abdomen wondering what sort of night Toby had had. If only he knew we were on our way. I brushed my hair and put it up into a ponytail, it was likely to be warm outside and I wanted it up off my neck.

I came out of the bathroom and Ahran was standing in just his close-fitting boxers with his back to me tapping something into his phone. I tore my eyes away from his tight backside and grabbed my jeans and bra before diving back into the bathroom. I proceeded to silently counsel myself. *Okay, I haven't had sex in a while. He is an extremely attractive man. Any woman would react in the same way.* I was going to have to be stronger. If Ahran tried anything like that again I would set him straight once and for all. He had a fiancé waiting for him back home and in case he had forgotten, he had a job to do. Once I was dressed and my resolve had strengthened I went back into the bedroom.

"I'm going to have a shower," he said turning towards me, "And then we ought to get going. We'll pick something up to eat on the way."

"Okay," I said, picking up the controller and switching on the television just so I didn't have to look at him still in his boxers.

Whilst he was in the bathroom I flicked through the channels. Ramian T.V. wasn't a lot different from television at home as far as I could see; music channels, shopping channels, a morning chat show. Same stuff just different planet. I quickly skipped through the news channels just on the off chance that there was a news story about a woman found dead in an airport cleaning cupboard. After ten minutes I felt satisfied that no such story seemed to feature. I switched over to a music channel and absentmindedly watched a long haired brunette crawl seductively along a beach as I worried whether they were feeding Toby properly. Just as two overly enthusiastic presenters were about to sky dive off a cliff, Ahran came out dressed in black jeans and a khaki shirt with the sleeves rolled up.

"Ready to go?"

"Yep," I said, tearing my eyes away from him. I clicked off the television, stood up and picked up my bag. Ahran slung his over his shoulder and we headed down to reception. He pressed his fingertip to a pad on the wall and the inner door clicked to let us out.

"If someone opened the door couldn't we just sneak out without paying?" I mused.

He shook his head. "No, they have an image of my finger print from our check-in last night, my account is automatically debited if we don't manually check out.

"Oh, right and by the way, I will pay you back," I promised.

"Don't worry about it, the King is paying all our expenses."

A hover cab was waiting for us outside, Ahran had obviously called it whilst I was in the bathroom.

"Where are we going now?"

"To hire a car," he replied.

"Is that the quickest way for us to travel?" I asked, doubting the rationale behind his decision. Surely it would take us forever to get to Morana by road?

"No, but I received intelligence this morning that

Bazeera's agents are all over the airports and it's better that we avoid public transport for the time being."

I had a flashback of hands around my throat and was forced to agree with him.

After a short journey, we stepped out onto the pavement. It was already warm and there wasn't a cloud to mar the brilliant blue of the sky. Under any other circumstances, I would be enjoying the warmer climate, but I already felt hot in jeans and regretted my decision not to put my new shorts on. My dress choice had been driven entirely by vanity; I hadn't shaved my legs for a week. Maybe I'd be able to borrow Ahran's razor without him knowing.

We walked into the car hire place.

A well-groomed woman who looked to be in her early forties in Earth years was sat at the desk and she looked up as we walked in. She gave me a cursory glance, but her gaze rested on Ahran. She smiled and perceptibly straightened in her chair.

I rolled my eyes.

He flashed her a dazzling smile and I watched the movement of her throat as she swallowed. Ahran spoke to her in Ramian and she gushed her response. They exchanged a few more words and she checked a computer screen embedded in her desk. The woman tapped the screen and spoke to Ahran. He thanked her and she touched her hair self-consciously. *Yet another female falls for the looks and charm of Mr Elessar.*

"We need to go to their underground car park to collect the car," Ahran said, totally oblivious to the woman's attempts to get him to notice her.

I swapped my bag onto my other shoulder and followed him into the lift.

"Here, let me take your bag," he offered.

"No, I'm fine thanks," I said, hitching it further onto my shoulder. I would show him I could do this.

He smiled. Another private joke obviously.

The lift doors opened onto a well-lit underground car park and a young lad approached us. He greeted us and we followed him to our hire car which turned out to be sleek and nondescript. The boy gave us a thorough rundown of how the car worked. Ahran was remarkably patient with him considering he had probably been familiar with these cars since before the lad was born. He even asked him a question or two. The boy walked away with his chest puffed out like a little bird, satisfied that he had yet another happy customer.

We put our bags in the boot and got into the car. Ahran's fingers flew over the keypad on the dashboard. Unlike the cabs I had been in so far, this car had a half steering wheel, the kind you see in sports cars.

"We should be able to get to Rosrua before nightfall."

I nodded even though I had no idea where this was.

"Are you hungry?"

"Starving," I replied. We hadn't eaten since the meal on the plane.

"We'll stop and grab something before we leave Zanzin."

We travelled for about ten minutes through the streets of the town. The impression I'd got of the place last night shifted slightly. It was just as modern looking, but in the light the sense of space and tranquillity was enhanced by the greenery and the colour of the planting schemes. There were people going about their business just as they would in any bustling town back home, but everything seemed more organised somehow. The town lacked the usual chaos of the morning rush hour. There were no beeping horns, no delivery lorries blocking the right of way of the oncoming traffic and there didn't appear to be any traffic lights. The traffic flowed smoothly and silently.

"Are all your towns like this?" I asked, breaking the silence between us.

"Pretty much."

"It seems so organised and less random than back home."

"There are very strict planning regulations which are designed to keep built up areas as uncongested as possible," Ahran replied.

"It's very quiet, there aren't the usual sirens or delivery vans blocking the roads," I pointed out.

"That's because all vehicles are automatically programmed to give way to emergency vehicles and all shops have underground delivery bays."

"Everything is kind of perfect here, isn't it?" I said, trying not to sound sarcastic.

"We try to live as harmoniously as possible. Our technology is more advanced than on Earth, which means we are able to organise things to allow as little chaos as possible. But I wouldn't say everything is perfect. There is conflict between states, we still have a crime rate and things go wrong from time to time."

It was hard to imagine anyone disrupting the peace and the natural order of things here.

"Although we do have better systems of surveillance and identification, which means it's more difficult to get away with committing a crime."

"It sounds like '1984'."

Ahran looked puzzled.

"You know, '1984', Big Brother is watching you," I said with feigned menace.

He looked blank and I realised we had our cultural differences. "It's a well-known novel on Earth depicting a society in which people's lives are controlled by the state, their every move watched," I explained.

Ahran appeared unmoved. "Surveillance and traceability are facts of life here. We don't give it a second thought."

I'd forgotten that everyone here was chipped. I'm not sure how I felt about it. Was it better for everyone's safety that people were so easily identifiable or was it a step too far?

The landscape was beginning to change and we were moving into what looked more like suburbia. The order and organisation of the city were echoed in the residential areas. Like many of the other buildings I'd seen here, people's homes were modern and mostly single storey. Ahran explained that this was because they had less visual impact. Houses and roads were organised in a grid-like pattern, but the landscape was not ugly, in fact far from it, it was very beautiful in a structured kind of way. There were plenty of trees and the gardens were all well-cared for.

"People seem to take a pride in their gardens," I

observed, my thoughts turning to the odd garden back in Hatherley where the owners had allowed them to become overgrown and unsightly.

"Gardening is a national pastime here. It's part of our culture to take care of the spaces we live in. The government offers reduced housing rates for people who take care of their properties, although it isn't really necessary because there is a certain amount of social pressure to look after your plot within the neighbourhood."

"We could do with more of that back home," I reflected. "What was it like where you were brought up?"

"I grew up in the city. My father worked long hours and would sometimes stay out all night so it was important we lived close to where he worked."

I detected a note of bitterness in his voice.

"You didn't like living there?"

"No, I didn't mind it, what I objected to was having a workaholic for a father."

I got the distinct impression I'd hit a raw nerve. It wasn't the first time Ahran had appeared tetchy over the subject of his father. I looked at his face and his expression was deadpan.

"I'm sorry, I didn't mean to pry."

"You weren't prying. My father was a pretty lousy father," he said with a frown.

I felt decidedly uncomfortable.

"Come to think of it he was also a pretty lousy husband to my mother. She didn't have it easy. She worked part-time as a teacher and then spent the rest of her time trying to make up for my father's lack of interest in family life."

I nodded. He was beginning to open up and I didn't want to say anything that would prevent him from carrying on.

"He never seemed to be able to find any time in his busy schedule to spend time with his children," he said.

"If it's any consolation, I lost my dad when I was six so I never really knew what it was like to have a dad either," I said, trying to show my support.

"At least your father had a good excuse," he said with a wry smile.

"Do you get on with your father now?" I asked.

"We have a... *formal* relationship," he said with a degree of condemnation. "It's not as if we can even reminisce together because we don't have a history to reminisce about. I don't enjoy his company. He makes me feel like I am being interviewed the whole time." He paused. "To be honest it was a relief when I left home to go to college, at least I wasn't constantly being reminded of his short-comings."

I was sure there were times when Toby had daydreamed about what it would be like to have a father. From the little I had learnt about Tagan it sounded like he might have been a better father than Ahran's had been. Maybe, when this horrible episode was over and Toby was safely out of Bazeera's clutches, Toby would be able to build a relationship with his father's cousin, at least then he might not grow up feeling the bitterness of never having a good male role model like Ahran obviously did.

"Do you get on better with your mother?"

"Yes my mother and I have a good relationship, I am

lucky, some people don't get on with either of their parents, and of course I have Elaya. She is not only my sister, but I count her as a friend. She has always been there for me."

I pictured Ahran's striking sister and began to understand how Ahran must have felt when he had found her beaten and lying in a ditch near Toby's school.

"Have you heard from her?"

"I spoke to her yesterday, she is feeling much better. Don't be fooled by Elaya's feminine exterior, she is tougher than she looks."

I was relieved to hear that she was on the mend. I'd only met her briefly, but having just learnt that she had been there for her brother, who had clearly suffered as a result of their father's disinterest in his children, made me warm to her more.

"You are very lucky to have your sister," I said wistfully.

"Okay, now I feel awkward," Ahran replied, looking more than a little uncomfortable himself. I smiled letting him off the hook.

"It's been a year since Katie died and I still fantasize about her walking through the door as if the accident had been some kind of sick joke."

Ahran looked troubled. "The loss of someone you love is hard to come to terms with, but it does get easier as time passes," he said after a little while.

"Thanks, that's good to know."

I stared out of the window. We were travelling through more open countryside now. The landscape was flat and vast and I could see for miles. In the distance was a mountain range jabbing the cerulean blue sky. Everywhere was green and lush and there were herds of animals; sheep and cows dotted over the landscape in whichever direction I looked. From my level vantage point I could see the odd homestead. I figured each farm must be very large.

"Is your land like this?" I asked, changing the subject. I wondered how long it would be before I started to feel more able to talk about my sister. It was still so painful.

"My land isn't quite as flat, but it is just as green."

"I'd like to see it," I said without thinking. *What was I saying?* Visiting Ahran's home was a bad idea.

"I'd like to show you it," he said quietly, something about his tone made me turn towards him.

My eyes searched his face. He seemed a little unsettled by what he had just said himself.

"It's a very peaceful place," he continued quickly. "There is a river that runs along the southern boundary which teems with wildlife. At this time of the year, the fledglings are venturing from their nests, it's fascinating to watch." I was moved by his obvious love of the countryside and before I could stop myself, I pictured us lying lazily on the bank of the river, watching the comings and goings of the riverside birds. I closed my eyes to erase the image.

"Are you okay?"

"Yes, no, it's nothing," I said wearily. I was weary from worrying about Toby, weary from the stressful and frightening situation I had found myself in and weary from fighting my feelings for him.

We stopped to get some food and then I spent the next few hours trying to busy my mind with other things. I hadn't contacted poor Audrey since Toby had been kidnapped, and I felt guilty for not being there for her. I wondered whether she had regained consciousness and what the doctor's conclusions were about the effects of her stroke. I vowed to phone the hospital as soon as I could. Maybe, I'd even get to speak to her. The thought of hearing Audrey's calm, reassuring voice lightened my mood. I wondered what Bennie had told the police. It can't have been easy explaining my sudden disappearance. I was pretty sure I owed her *big time*. My life back on Earth seemed a million miles away, and my heart grew heavy as I realised it probably was a million miles away. I would make it up to them both somehow, but for now, I was stuck in this place and even as beautiful as it was I wished more than anything that I was back living my uneventful life with Toby, contemplating a future with Marcus, never having even heard of Ramia.

14

Several hours later we stopped for a comfort break and just as we were about to get back into the car Ahran's phone rang. I struggled to make sense of the conversation and mindlessly made tracks in the dirt with the toe of my pump whilst I waited for him to finish and translate.

"Well?"

"There's been a sighting of a boy who fits Toby's description about an hour from here."

"You are kidding?!"

Ahran shook his head. "Intel is sending pictures." Just as he said this, his phone bleeped. Ahran opened the message and looked at it. "It could be him," he said, passing me the phone.

There were three CCTV pictures, two of which were fairly blurry, but one had better clarity and showed the profile of a boy who did indeed look like Toby. I felt a frisson of excitement tinged with hope. "It certainly looks like him!"

"Let's go and find out," he said, holding open the passenger door.

We drove in relative silence, facing the prospect that by some miracle we could be close to Toby. My heart beat rapidly in anticipation whilst I tried to tell myself not to get too excited, it could be a false alarm. I looked at the picture of the boy on Ahran's phone several times and the more I looked at it, the more I was convinced it was Toby.

"Can't you go any faster?" I asked, slightly irritated by the speed at which we were travelling at. I knew full well that Ahran was perfectly capable of driving like a bat out of hell. "I'm going as fast as I dare, they have strict speeding laws in this state, we can't risk being stopped, they would automatically impound the car and ask questions later. The traffic police are renowned for being *vascissii.*

"*Vascissii?*" I asked, not understanding the term.

"Yes, they do what they want and are not afraid to use force."

"Oh, I see," I said, satisfied I now understood, but sat back in my seat frustrated nevertheless.

After seventy-three minutes and twenty interminable seconds we arrived at the town where Toby had been spotted. Ahran pulled into a parking lot near the main street.

"What do we do now?" I asked, not sure where we should begin.

"Have you still got that photograph of Toby?"

I nodded and reached for my bag.

"Let's use that and start asking around."

"Isn't there a quicker way?"

"Do you have any other suggestions?"

I was desperate to help in some way, to be of *some* use, but my knowledge on how to carry out a kidnap search was distinctly lacking. My frustration was getting the better of me and I realised how unprepared I was for all of this.

"Er, no," I said, forced to show my hand.

Ahran nodded as if to say, '*As I suspected*' and got out of the car.

Feeling way out of my depth, I retrieved the photo frame I had hastily seized from my bedroom the day before and joined him on the pavement.

"So where do we start?" I asked, taking a deep breath and looking up and down the pleasant street. It was too late to have cold feet now. Like in the other towns I had seen so far, people were going about their business in a calm and orderly manner.

"I have the location of the cameras that caught the footage of Toby. We start there."

We walked down the high street and Ahran pointed out the first camera. We went into the double-fronted shop that was behind Toby in one of the CCTV stills and Ahran showed the picture to one of the ladies working inside. After a brief examination she shook her head and called over another woman, who disappointingly did pretty much the same thing.

"Nothing here, let's move on," Ahran said, turning around.

After entering numerous shops nearby and getting the

same response, I began to feel more and more despondent. "Now what?"

"Let's try the market over there," Ahran said, pointing to a small street market selling fresh produce. "Market stall owners usually know who their regular customers are, as well as those who are from out of town."

The first stallholder we approached was a portly-looking man selling an array of fresh fish. Ahran spoke to him and showed him Toby's picture. To my surprise, he nodded and spoke quickly. I listened intently, and whilst I didn't understand a word he said, I was encouraged by the way he said it.

"Well?" I asked as Ahran thanked the man and turned away.

"He said he recognises him; he was here yesterday with a woman. He'd had a brief chat with the woman whilst she was buying some fish and she told him they were new to the area and had just moved into a smallholding just outside of town. He said the boy was very shy, it was almost as if he was scared to say anything."

"Oh my God!" Poor Toby! He must be so frightened. "Do you think the woman was Bazeera?"

Ahran threw his head back and laughed.

"What's so funny?" I said, struggling to see anything amusing about our situation.

"I can't quite see Bazeera buying fresh fish at a street market." He laughed again, my suggestion really tickling him. "You don't understand. Bazeera never gets her hands dirty. Nor do I think she has ever visited a street market.

The less she has to do with *commoners*," he said, "The better as far as she is concerned."

"Oh right." I was not at all happy about Toby having anything to do with this woman. "So it was one of the kidnappers?"

Ahran shook his head. "Unlikely. He's probably been passed on several times by now. More difficult to trace that way. They will be keeping him in some safehouse no doubt. If the boy in the CCTV pictures is Toby, then maybe the place the man at the fish stall spoke of is one of these."

I looked at him in dismay. There was nothing about the word 'safehouse' that reassured me.

"Don't worry, we'll check it out and if he's there we will find him."

I nodded reluctantly. We had been searching for Toby for less than a day and already I felt emotionally drained. Before we left the market, Ahran bought a loaf of bread and insisted on having it wrapped, which I thought was a little odd. I guess he wanted to keep it fresh for our journey ahead.

We reached the car and headed out of town.

"Do you know where you're going?" I asked, looking across the vast landscape.

"Shouldn't be too difficult to find, these out of the way places don't have a complicated infrastructure. It's usually one road in and one road out."

We drove for a little while longer. "From what the fishmonger said, I think it's down here," he said, pointing to the left hand turn we were approaching.

We turned off the main road, past a post box and onto a

AMELIA FORD

dusty dirt track. The landscape was very flat and it was easy to see the house through the heat haze at the end, although it was some distance from the road.

Either side of the track, crops grew and the ears of corn swayed gently in the breeze. It was very warm outside, but cool in the car and I rubbed my bare arms in anticipation as we approached the house.

"They can't fail to have seen us coming," I said, concerned that we were leaving ourselves exposed and wondered whether Ahran was being a bit careless. If Toby was being held here, it was unlikely that we would receive a warm reception. How were we to protect ourselves? "Are you sure about this?" I asked.

"I'm not about to pose myself as any kind of threat. I'm just your average delivery man." Suddenly, I understood why he had insisted on having the loaf so well wrapped. It was a prop in his courier ruse.

"Now get down," he said, gesturing with his hand. "I'm doing this one on my own."

I crouched down in the footwell of the passenger seat as he instructed and we drove the last mile before pulling up in front of the house. I felt him hesitate. "That's weird."

"What?" I said, not able to get any kind of visual from my hiding place.

"There are all sorts of animals in cages in the front yard."

"Really?" I said, poking my head up over the dashboard, my curiosity getting the better of me. Sure enough there were a variety of different sized cages with numerous different animals inside. Suddenly a brown, curly-haired boy came into view.

"Get down!" Ahran warned.

"Toby!" I cried and before I had even registered what Ahran had said, I was out of the car and running towards the boy. He didn't look up, instead he bent down to pick up a large tortoise.

Ahran caught up with me, just as a woman appeared on the deck.

I stopped dead in my tracks as the boy turned towards us. Something wasn't right. He was taller than Toby and his features didn't quite fit the imprint of Toby's face in my mind.

Any optimism I had been feeling drained out of me. *It wasn't him.* Suddenly, I felt extraordinarily weak and it took all my effort to prevent myself from slumping to the ground in a hopeless heap.

In the next moment, the woman was running towards Ahran, flinging her arms around his neck and kissing him, in between a flurry of words.

I subconsciously shook my head, trying to make sense of the situation which was rapidly going awry. Who was this boy who looked so much like Toby and who was this woman who seemed to know Ahran? A little too well for my liking. I felt a range of emotions mingle with my crushing disappointment.

"Sorry," Ahran said, turning towards me as if he had suddenly remembered I was here. "Sophie, this is a very good friend of mine, Anya Larkal. Anya, this is Sophie McAllister"

The woman detached herself from Ahran and stepped towards me with her hand outstretched. "Good to meet you," she said, taking Ahran's cue and switching to English, whilst looking intrigued as to who I was.

"We are on the trail of the King and Queen's grandson, he has been kidnapped and Sophie is the boy's Aunt," Ahran explained.

I found myself staring at Anya, who seemed to possess an almost celestial beauty. She was tall and willowy with long blonde hair down to her waist.

"I'm so sorry to hear this," she said in a lyrical voice.

During our introductions, the boy had joined his mother, a conclusion I had come to after noticing his striking resemblance to this beautiful woman, with the exception of his colouring. She put her arm around his shoulders; drawing him a little closer as she received this news.

"Tagan had a child?" she asked, the level of her interest increasing.

Ahran nodded.

Whilst I was trying to come to terms with the fact that our search for Toby was not over, I could feel myself becoming increasingly drawn to this woman. There was something about her; her voice maybe or something about her presence that seemed to lure you in.

She raised her eyebrows, "With Nuella?"

Ahran shook his head and Anya nodded wide-eyed. "I see," she said, glancing at me as she began to draw her own conclusions about Tagan's fidelity.

I felt a prickle of jealousy on behalf of my sister. I didn't have a clue who Nuella was, an old girlfriend or fiancé perhaps? But whoever it was, it was becoming increasingly obvious that nobody here knew of my sister. I struggled to believe what the Queen had said about Tagan being an honourable person, it just served as further confirmation that my sister had been nothing more than extra-curricular activity for him.

"Come, come inside. Let's have a drink. Are you hungry?"

Ahran hesitated as if we hadn't just eaten.

"That is a stupid question," Anya said, correcting herself and not giving him a chance to answer. "Of course you are hungry." She winked at Ahran, which caused an uncomfortable sensation in the pit of my stomach and left me questioning the status of their relationship. After Ahran's behaviour this morning and now witnessing his exchange with Anya, I began to wonder whether he had the same fidelity issues as his cousin. Although, if he'd had a fling with Anya I could hardly blame him, she was quite mesmerising.

"I made some bread this morning and I have some ham, some tomatoes and some *chiklea*," she sang as she swept up the garden path.

"Don't ever do that again," Ahran warned under his breath as we followed on, breaking the spell the alluring Anya seemed to have cast on me.

"Do what?" I asked.

"Disobey my instructions, you could have got us both killed."

I knew he was referring to my error of judgement which had caused me to run from the car against his instructions. I was about to argue, but knew I had no choice other than to eat some humble pie. "I'm sorry." He gave me a smileless nod, acknowledging my apology, but not showing any outward sign of forgiveness.

"Take a seat on the deck, I'll bring it out to you," Anya said and disappeared into the house to get our refreshments.

I sat on the porch swing and took in my surroundings, feeling a little punch drunk by it all.

Ahran perched on the wooden railings opposite. It was a small, cedar-clad homestead with a covered deck and steps leading down into a garden. There was a large out-building to the left of the house and the whole plot was shaded by Eucalyptus and other heat loving trees. The grass was surprisingly green, considering the climate, and there were more cages than I had first realised. There were all manner of animals and my eyes widened as I caught sight of a small lion in one of them. Uninterested in the events of the last few minutes, he sat there in the respite of the shade with his eyes half-closed and his tail curling and uncurling rhythmically in contentment. There was a racoon-like creature in another cage and what looked to be a pelican in another. It was as if we had stepped into the pages of George Durrell's *My Family and Other Animals*, although the cages were much smaller than I thought anyone who had any care for their welfare would be happy about. This surprised me, Anya seemed so kind and gentle.

The boy, who had been feeding the ducks came up onto the deck and began to swing idly on the post at the top of the steps, shamelessly staring at us.

I smiled at him, but he just cocked his head to the side

and continued to stare. He did look a lot like Toby, but up close he was not only taller, he was slimmer in the face and slighter of frame.

Ahran spoke to him, but the boy shrugged and signed with his free hand.

"Dansun is deaf," Anya said, joining us on the deck carrying a tray of food and a jug of something ice-cooled. Ahran jumped up and took the tray from her in a gentle-manly manner, freeing her up to pull over a small table from the other side of the deck. "He's been totally deaf from birth, he lacks the part of the brain responsible for hearing. Do you sign?" she asked, as she poured some of the clear liquid into the glasses, the ice dropping noisily as she did so. This, of course explained why the fishmonger in the town had thought the boy was unresponsive and scared. He wasn't shy and scared, he was stone-deaf.

"A little," I said. "Not that I expect he'd understand the sign language I know."

I was a little rusty, but asked him his name using the signing I was familiar with. I'd learnt a bit when I had volunteered with a deaf charity as a teenager. Dansun looked puzzled at first and then the penny dropped. He signed his response and asked me who I was. I understood most of what he signed even though there was the odd gesture that we made that the other didn't understand.

We continued our little silent conversation and Anya smiled. "Well, I can see you two are getting on just fine."

"So, what brings you here and what's with the zoo?" Ahran asked.

"I'm working for an animal organisation, rescuing and

rehabilitating sick and injured wild animals. They've posted me here to set up a clinic."

"Do the animals live in these cages?" I asked.

"No, not at all. These are their transportation crates, I've got people coming tomorrow to build proper enclosures."

This explained the small cages.

"They are converting that shed over there into a small surgery," she said, pointing to the outbuilding I had noticed earlier.

Ahran nodded as if none of this came as any surprise. "Anya is an exceptionally good vet and is well-known for taking in waifs and strays," Ahran said affectionately.

It was difficult to watch how Ahran looked at Anya and to hear the admiration in his voice, but it was easier to understand how Anya's manner would soothe the most pained wild creature or any hot-blooded Ramian male for that matter. Her style was slightly Bohemian and nothing like the poised and well-healed Talina, but there was very definitely an unearthly quality about her as if she was about to sprout large, soft-feathered wings.

"Were you two at college together?" I asked.

Anya nodded and a look passed between them that suggested there was more to it than that.

"Yes, and lovers," she said guilelessly, surprising me with her candidness and unfortunately confirming my suspicions. "Until he broke my heart."

She didn't appear to look too heart-broken, if anything she seemed rather amused.

"You have a cheek *Tutscha*," Ahran replied. "If I

remember correctly it was you who waltzed off with a healer you met on one of your mercy missions."

"I cannot deny it," she said with a chuckle.

"Are you still with him?" Ahran asked.

She nodded. "Tylor is the father of my child, but he has a strong need to take care of the sick, particularly those who don't have access to modern healthcare, and he is away a lot. I am very proud of what he does." In spite of her words, I detected a note of sadness in her voice.

I struggled to understand who the needy sick were that she was referring to. As far as I could see Ramians had everything they needed, even in these out of the way places.

"Can he not work closer to home?" I asked, feeling the need to comfort her and ease her pain in whatever way I could.

She smiled. "Tylor is not a medical man in the way you understand it, he has a special gift that enables him to heal those without the use of conventional medicine. He is not one of us."

"What Anya is saying, is that her man is from a tribe we call the Hidden People," Ahran said, in response to what must have been my puzzled expression.

"Who are the Hidden People?" I asked.

"We have a native people here in Ramia, much like the Aborigines, or Native Indians you have on Earth. They live in the remote areas of this land and rarely come in contact with the rest of the population."

"I see." I felt like I had a better grasp of Anya's circumstance although it made me want to comfort her even more. How could anyone walk away from her?

"Can you not travel with him?" I asked.

She shook her head. "Our son needs a more settled home and I have my life's work here," she said, gesturing to our surroundings. The important thing is that we are here for the times he is able to return."

I admired her strength and resilience. I wasn't sure I could have done the same in her situation, if I loved the guy, I would have probably followed him around wherever he went. I glanced at Ahran, but quickly looked away.

What was wrong with me? Was it something to do with Ramians? Not only could I feel myself being increasingly drawn to Ahran, but I could also feel myself developing a school-girl crush on the beautiful Anya. There was definitely a quality about these people, but it was hard to put my finger on what it was. Some had it more than others. Talina, not so much, but Leylana, the King, Ahran, Anya, they all had something about them that drew you in, something that was difficult to resist.

"Shall we eat?" Anya said, breaking my train of thought.

I took a slice of the ham she offered, a spoonful of *chiklea* which looked like some form of chunky coleslaw, and a piece of bread. I really wasn't that hungry, but Ahran proceeded to tuck in.

"Have you known Ahran long?" Anya asked.

"Er, no. We've actually not long met," I replied slightly awkwardly. Even though their lives had gone separate ways, I got the impression she was still very fond of Ahran and there was a certain protectiveness in the way she asked the question, as if she was judging whether I was a suitable acquaintance.

"Until a few days ago, I had no idea Ramia existed or that Toby was anything other than a normal, human boy." Even though I was here and everything that Ahran had told me about Toby's heritage had been substantiated, it was still difficult to believe that any of this was happening.

"So Tagan met your sister on Earth?"

"Yes. Although, I'm not sure my sister knew anything about who he was or where he was from."

She nodded. "You have to watch these soldier boys, they have a reputation of being able to charm the larks and the lapwings *and* the ladies into bed."

I knew she was teasing, but her words aligned with what I already thought of Tagan and what I had begun to suspect of Ahran. "Yes, I kind of got that impression." I did my very best not to look at him.

"Hey, you are condemning us even before we've had a chance to defend ourselves," he said, doing his best to sound wounded.

Anya smiled at him and gently touched his cheek. "What woman could resist this face?"

I dropped my gaze to the food on my plate and silenced the voice in my head before it could say, *not you!*

"Has Ahran told you anything about his college days?"

I shook my head, knowing I really shouldn't learn any more about Ahran, but desperately wanting to hear everything she could tell me about him.

"We had fun, didn't we?" Anya said.

"You were as wild as I was," Ahran replied.

Anya smiled and nodded sagely. "We were all stretching our wings."

"Some of us more than others," Ahran said, raising an eyebrow at Anya. "Remember that night skinny dipping in the River Lo-Lo with Hania, Tallas and Sorrol? I believe it was you who suggested the best way to see the Tewla fish is naked and by moonlight. I'm not sure I remember seeing that in any of our textbooks."

"I think you may have just had different editions," Anya said with a barely contained smile.

Ahran chuckled and I struggled to keep my mind from wondering what Ahran looked like skinny dipping in the moonlight.

"We were high on life. We had no cares at that time, youth should be spent skinny dipping in the moonlight," Anya said.

"Your father wasn't a well-respected, government lawyer and brother-in-law to the King."

"Oh no! Did it get into the press?" I asked.

"Did it get into the press Anya?" Ahran asked, sounding like he knew full well what the answer to the question was.

"Pictures of Ahran's naked bottom were plastered everywhere," she laughed. "My favourite headline was, she paused as she thought of the translation, *'Third in line to the throne bears all.'*

I clasped my hand over my mouth in shock. "Oh God! Seriously?"

She nodded, whilst Ahran looked bashfully amused.

"It wasn't the first time he'd been in the press. I think *'Ahran, The College Years'*, kept much of the Dinaran paparazzi employed for the duration of his degrees. As far as they were concerned it was a sad day when he joined the

Elite Force and much of that behaviour had to be curbed for the sake of the nation's security."

"That's hilarious," I said, shaking my head and chuckling.

"Or the time when Ahran impersonated one of our generously busted surgical lecturers..." The memories of their college years obviously coming thick and fast to Anya now, "Who happened to be absent one day and the whole fifteen-minute performance of him carrying out a hysterical mockery of her lab rat dissection with two balloons stuffed down his t-shirt, caught on film and sent to her."

I laughed out loud. "Really?"

"I still don't know who did it," Ahran said, shaking his head and sounding suitably bemused."

"It was Roekl," Anya said guiltily.

"You knew?!" He was clearly surprised by Anya's admission.

"As much as I disliked the guy, I knew that if you had found out it was him, there was no telling what you might do and you were already on your last warning with the Dean."

Ahran nodded, with resignation. "Yeah, you are probably right. I wasn't known for my level-headedness in those days."

"What would you have done?" I asked.

He shrugged. "Taught him a lesson. Roekl was such a douchebag, he had it coming to him."

"Which is precisely what I thought," Anya said. "But don't hold it against him. I heard that he had witnessed his father slit his mother's throat when he was a child."

"*Jesus!*" I said, wrinkling my nose.

"You never know what someone has been through. Sometimes they aren't accountable for the things they do," Anya said, her voice full of forgiveness for their unfortunate fellow student.

"I knew there was something odd about him," Ahran said. "I wonder what he is doing now?"

"According to Sorrol, he never did anything with his veterinary degree and after his military service became a counsellor for people suffering from domestic violence."

"I guess some people can turn themselves around," Ahran said, sounding a little surprised. "I'm not the hot-headed idiot I used to be."

Anya placed her hand on his knee. "You weren't bad Ahran, a clown sometimes, but your heart was always in the right place."

Anya gave him a gentle look of admiration, the kind of look that passes between two people who have a history and who matter to each other. It made me draw a breath. Their lives had gone separate ways, but they still shared a strong connection. They may have been lovers once, but more than that, they were allies and I recognised this. I may have lost my sister, my closest ally, but I did have my friends and I knew I would do anything to protect them. I felt such a pang for Audrey and Bennie at that moment that I nearly demanded Ahran give me his phone just so I could tell them how much they meant to me. I looked in his direction, maybe it was the absence of my dearest friends, maybe it was the madness of the situation I was in or maybe it was the tenderness I had witnessed between Anya and Ahran, but I was envious. Envious that they were here together, loyal allies sharing their memories of a past together. But most of all, and it was this that made me realise that I was losing my battle to stay detached, I was envious that she had shared it with Ahran.

"Sorry, were you talking to me?" I said, becoming aware that Anya had said something and was waiting for my response.

She smiled softly as if she had read my thoughts.

"I'm giving you a bad impression of Ahran," she said and I wondered why she felt the need to champion his cause. Could she tell I was beginning to feel something for him?

Who was I kidding? Of course she could. I had already established that there was something different about Anya. Maybe she could indeed read minds, or maybe she had the ability to hone in on the emotions of the people around her, whatever it was I had the distinct impressions she knew exactly how I was feeling.

"Ahran saved my life once."

I nearly put my finger to my mouth to silence what she was about to say next, I really didn't want to hear any more stories about him, let alone one where he was the hero.

"A group of us decided to go camping in the mountains. We thought it would be fun to hunt for our food and live for a few days without the trappings of modern life."

Ahran snorted as if he knew exactly which story she was about to tell.

"Stupidly, I headed into a wooded area in search of edible mushrooms. I don't know what I was thinking because I knew it was mating season for some of our larger predatory animals, we had only just completed a module on it in college," Anya said, sounding disappointed with her naïve younger self. "Sure enough, a large, male, mountain lion had come down from higher mountain territory, away from his usual solitary existence in search for a mate and there I was happily collecting *cantharellus cibarius* in his mating ground."

She popped a tomato into her mouth. "I smelt him before I heard him, and slowly turned to find he was no more than a few metres away from where I was kneeling."

My eyes widened, thoughts of Ahran having been momentarily superseded by concern for Anya's plight. "What did you do?"

She laughed. "Nothing that any sane person would have done, I got up and took a step closer. I can remember his eyes so clearly. They weren't the blank eyes of an aggressive killer, but beautiful, intelligent, amber eyes of a magnificent animal with untold stories hidden behind them."

I frowned at her carelessness, but understood her sentiment.

Ahran shook his head in dismay. "Little did she know that she was about to have her throat ripped out."

Anya nodded. "Yes, Ahran is right, but in that life-defining moment, it was that beautiful, wild creature that made me realise what I wanted to do with my life."

"She didn't speak to me for a week," Ahran said.

I turned to him. "Why?"

"Because I broke its neck."

My eyes shot back to Anya. She was nodding, obviously having come to terms with the events of that day. "Ahran is right, it would have killed me, it was thin and no doubt I would have been lunch if Ahran hadn't jumped on it's back and killed it."

"What? With your bare hands?" I said, turning back to Ahran, not quite believing what I was hearing.

He didn't deny it and just shrugged.

"Bloody hell!" I spent a moment glancing from one to the other wondering whether they were having a big joke at my expense, but then I realised they were telling the truth. Clearly that sort of thing is perfectly possible when you were super-human. I nearly dropped my face into my hands questioning what the hell I was doing here in a place where people kidnapped innocent children from other worlds and men wrestled lions to the ground. I couldn't have been more happy that Anya lived to tell the tale, but it only served to highlight the enormous gulf between myself and these people, and more specifically me and Ahran.

We must have spent over an hour with Anya and her son, before it was time for us to move on. I found it a rather unsettling experience. I had learnt more about Ahran than was sensible and I had witnessed an obvious affection between him and Anya. I didn't question why I felt it so uncomfortable to witness, although I completely understood why Ahran was drawn to her, hell, I felt it too. I admired the sacrifice she was making for her son and it reminded me of the reason why I was here. Even though Toby was not my son, he was my closest living relative and I knew I would do anything to protect him. Meeting Anya had also made me consider whether Toby had the same mysterious quality that I had recognised in some of the other Ramians I had met. On reflection, Toby did possess it to some degree. I thought the way I felt about him was because he was my nephew, the son of my beloved sister, but now I began to wonder whether there wasn't more to it than that. He was after all, half Ramian. But whatever it was, Anya possessed it in bucketfuls, and much to my consternation, so did Ahran.

15

"It's me chick," Bennie replied.

I opened the door. *See, there was nothing to worry about.* Bennie stood on my doorstep with a Chinese takeaway in one hand and a bottle of wine in the other.

"The wanderer returns bearing gifts of alcohol and bucket loads of MSG," she said, holding out her arms. I had never been more pleased to see her.

"Come in its freezing," I said with a grin, shutting the door behind her and giving her a hug.

"Steady on girl, you'll break a rib," she said breathlessly.

Bennie was a stunner. She had sleek, shiny, jet black hair cut into a blunt bob. Her recent trip away had given her a golden tan which made her blue eyes almost luminescent. She looked just like a Russian Bond girl.

"You look fantastic," I said as I took the food and bottle from her.

"You look pasty," said Bennie, less generously.

"Thanks love, I can always rely on you for a compliment," I said with a chuckle.

"You know me Sophe, I say it how it is. What's the matter?"

I loved Bennie. She was great at reading people and especially good at reading me. She never skirted around the issue she just got straight to the point. This approach worked for me, I wasn't big on small talk.

"Oh, I've just been working hard and it was the anniversary of Katie's death at the weekend." I wanted to add that mine and Toby's lives were possibly in danger, but I was going to have to build myself up to that.

"I did try and call you on Sunday," Bennie said apologetically, "But the phone at the ranch we were staying at was on the blink and then I had to catch my flight. Well, you know how it is," she said, seeking my forgiveness.

I understood and I certainly didn't hold it against her. "Don't worry hun, I know it's not easy when you're in the middle of nowhere. Let's eat before this gets cold." She followed me into the kitchen and I got the plates out of the oven. Bennie started to dish out the food.

It smelt fantastic, MSG or no MSG, Chinese food was my favourite. I put the wine Bennie had brought in the fridge and took out the bottle I'd put in there earlier.

"Shall we eat it in the lounge in front of the fire?" I suggested, pouring us both a glass. I knew I didn't have to stand on ceremony with Ben, eating off our laps was standard practice.

"Yes please, it's taking me a little while to adjust to the change in climate," she replied with a shiver. "It's supposed to be the rainy season in Kenya, but it was unseasonably hot and dry."

"That's global warming for you," I said with a wry smile.

I balanced the prawn crackers on my plate and carried my wine in the other hand. I had already pushed the sofa nearer to the log burner and we both perched on the edge of our seats balancing our plates on our knees. Not surprisingly Mungo made an appearance at the smell of the food.

"Mungo, mind my drink." I put my hand down to shield the wine glass by my foot but he took no notice. It wasn't the wine he was interested in and before I could stop him he stole a prawn cracker from the bowl I'd put on the floor.

"In your bed!" I growled and he reluctantly obliged. As far as he was concerned it had been worth the risk. He skulked off, his tongue smacking at his lips.

"Mungo still looking after his figure I see," Bennie said as she twirled some noodles around her fork. I nodded and rolled my eyes. I'd have answered if I hadn't just put a forkful of rice in my mouth. I swallowed. "How was your trip?"

"Yeah good, the lion cubs were adorable. I love filming them, they seem to know how to play to the cameras. We got some really good footage." Bennie loved her job.

"Doesn't it ever worry you, being so close to lions that one could rip your throat out as soon as look at you, especially when they've got young?"

"I don't really think about it, I'm too busy trying to get the right shot, besides we always have rangers with tranquilizer guns at the ready," she explained.

"I don't think I could do it," I confessed sipping my wine. "I feel uneasy at the lion enclosure at the zoo, somehow the fencing never seems robust enough."

She laughed. "You worry too much. How's the shop going?"

My life seemed mundane in comparison, although the recent turn of events had brought some unwelcome excitement. I willed myself to tell Bennie about Ahran's visit, but bottled it at the last minute. "The shop's doing well even the locals are catching onto the idea of the Panini."

Bennie chuckled. "I bet you haven't converted Mrs Groombridge."

"You're right, I haven't," I replied. "She continues to eye them with nothing but suspicion. She'd never stray from a toasted teacake and a cup of strong tea." I bit into a prawn ball. "Have you heard anything from Matt?"

Matthew Waterhouse was one of the producers Bennie sometimes worked with. He was also her occasional bed partner. I knew she was in love with him, but he was an arrogant arse living the playboy lifestyle that life in the media offered him. As far as I could see, he didn't view Bennie as anything more than a willing body. She was far too good for him and it always amazed me that someone so strong and beautiful as Bennie had such a weakness for someone like Matt 'git features' Waterhouse. I knew she was hoping I wasn't going to ask her about him, she was fully aware that he was her Achilles heel, but I figured if I gave her a hard time often enough she might come to her senses.

"He might have been there," she replied vaguely, and by

the look on her face I knew she had done more than just film lion cubs with him.

"*Bennie!*" I cried in frustration.

"I know, I know so send me to rehab. I just can't help myself, he's got the most glorious ..." she hesitated and I winced at what was coming next. She gave me a sideways look, "Arse." Bennie could sometimes be rather too graphic about her sex life and the mental image of my best friend doing bedroom gymnastics was not one I liked to dwell on.

"And how's the charismatic Dr Hampton?" she said sarcastically.

"Touché! I said, raising my glass of wine at her and gave her a crooked smile. "He's not that bad, I don't know what your problem is with him. He's nice looking, he's got a pretty good sense of humour and good prospects."

"That's *exactly* it! You keep telling me he's got good prospects, which tells me that he's obviously not lighting your fire in the sack," she concluded.

"Um, I'm not exactly sure what he is like in the bedroom yet," I added a little sheepishly.

"You mean you haven't slept with him?" Her voice rising several octaves. "*How long* have you been seeing him?"

"It's only been three months."

"Three months! For God's sake Sophe, what are you waiting for? You've got to try before you buy love, and if the goods don't hit the spot you move on."

Sometimes she could be really annoying. "We don't all shag every guy we meet," I said, defending myself.

"Ouch!" Bennie responded good-naturedly. She could take it as well as dish it out.

"You've never been short of male attention," she declared. "Just look at yourself. Those big innocent green eyes, the slightly mad, but utterly gorgeous blonde hair and a figure that most men can only dream about getting their hands on. Get out there and have some fun! Even better, come and spend a weekend with me I'll find you someone more interesting than Dr Boring."

I put my plate down on the floor by the side of the sofa.

"He's not boring! He's funny and a good kisser. In fact, for your information, I have decided to take our relationship to the next level, it's about time I moved my life on." I sat deeper into the sofa and curled my legs beneath me. "I feel like my life has stood still over the last year whilst I've been dealing with Katie's death, but Sunday was definitely a turning point for me. I finally feel like I want to get on with the job of living and start to build a future for Toby and me."

"Do you know what Sophe? That's the best thing I've heard all week." She put her plate down and picked up her glass of wine. "I've watched you over the last year knowing that you were grieving and hurting, feeling like I wasn't being much help. It's so good to hear that you are coming out the other end."

"You have helped, just by being my friend." I leaned over and gave her a hug. She squeezed me back.

Bennie wasn't into big displays of emotion and she pulled away looking a touch embarrassed. "Want more wine?"

"Is the Pope Catholic?"

She refilled our glasses. "Speaking of Toby, how is that gorgeous little boy?"

I knew the time had come for me to tell Bennie about the mysterious Ahran Elessar and so I took a deep breath. "Oh he's fine. For an eight-year-old he's so mature and sensible, sometimes I feel like he's looking after *me*."

"I think you underestimate how much he has learnt from you Sophe."

"He's doing really well, bless him." I hesitated. "Although, I had some rather disturbing news yesterday."

Bennie took a sip of wine. "Go on."

"This guy turned up at the shop asking for me," I began.

She raised her eyebrows. "What did he want?"

"I wasn't there, Audrey spoke to him. He said he would come back at lunchtime, but didn't show. When I got home he was waiting for me."

"Was he hot?"

I pictured Ahran in my mind and my heart picked up tempo. I couldn't decide whether it was because I was attracted to him or because of the worrying news he had told me. To my dismay I realised it was probably both. "Yeah, he was absolutely gorgeous," I sighed.

Bennie leant forward. "And?"

"Well, it wasn't like that."

She looked disappointed. "So what did he want then?"

I picked my words carefully, knowing I was at risk of sounding like a complete loon.

"He told me that Toby's father was some kind of foreign prince and heir to a massive fortune, but that he was dead and Toby was the next rightful heir." I looked at my friend willing her not to think that I had gone crazy.

"Wow Sophe! What are we talking? Millions?"

I gave her an exasperated look. Trust her to think about the money. "The fortune is only half the story because he also said that some mad, power hungry woman has a vendetta against Toby's father for killing her son."

"Shit!" Bennie exclaimed.

"That's not the end of it," I continued. "This guy seems to think she wants to get hold of Toby to wreak her revenge and use him as a bargaining tool to get her hands on Toby's father's wealth." It still sounded completely insane to me and I expected her to laugh in my face.

She didn't. In fact, she didn't say anything for a while.

"It's crazy isn't it?" I said, willing her to agree with me and to tell me to get a grip. But much to my disappointment she didn't do either of those things.

"Well, maybe there is something in it. Why else would he make up a story like that?"

"So you think he could be telling the truth?"

"I don't know, what did he say his name was?"

"Ahran Elessar."

"And who is he in relation to Toby's father?

"He's his cousin. He wants me and Toby to stay with his family until they've got rid of this woman."

"What?! Are they gangsters or something?" Bennie asked.

"That's what I thought, but apparently not."

"What did he say Toby's father's name was?"

"Tagan Halsan."

"Have you googled it?" she asked.

"No," I confessed.

"Sophie! That would have been the first thing I'd have done. Get your laptop," she instructed. "If he is who this Ahran says he is, there should be some record somewhere, like on some international royal rich list." *So simple, why hadn't I thought of that?*

I jumped up to get my computer. I could feel the adrenaline starting to pump. It seemed to take an age for it to boot up. Finally, the distinctive search engine loaded and the cursor flashed impatiently. I stared at it motionlessly, unable to type anything as I thought more seriously about the danger Toby could be in.

"Give it to me," Bennie said, taking the computer and putting it on her own lap.

She quickly typed in *Taygan Halson* and after a few seconds it reported that nothing had been found, but suggested a different spelling. Bennie looked at me.

"Try the other spelling," I said, looking over her shoulder.

Only a few random threads came up with either Tagan or Halsan, but nothing with both names. I felt deflated but relieved at the same time. "Well, I suppose that proves it was a piss take."

"Not necessarily, it might not show up if he's from a different country. Where did you say he was from?"

"Um, I'm not sure." Suddenly I realised how remiss I had been, I hadn't asked even though it was pretty crucial considering he had asked me and Toby to stay with his family.

"Sophie!"

"I had been too worried about the implications of what he was suggesting to think rationally. He's got an accent," I added unhelpfully. "Oh and he left me a phone to call him on if I felt we were in any kind of danger." I felt relieved I had something to offer.

"And have you phoned it to see if it checks out?" she asked

"Well, no, I haven't felt in any danger yet," I replied defensively.

"So you didn't call it anyway?" Bennie asked.

"No." I was starting to feel cross with myself and frustrated that Bennie was highlighting each one of my mistakes.

"Sophie!" Bennie said, making no attempt to hide her disapproval.

"Where's the phone?" she asked

"In the kitchen."

"Well, let's ring it."

"Are you sure that's a good idea?" Suddenly, I felt like the world's biggest coward.

Bennie cocked her head and shot me a, *'You-are-kidding?'* look.

"Okaay, I'll get it," I said, giving in.

I retrieved the phone and handed it to her.

"You should make the call," Bennie suggested, handing it back to me.

I stared at her as panic began to set in.

"Okay, *I'll* do it," she said with exaggerated patience.

"And that is why you are my friend," I said, handing

Bennie the phone and feeling relieved I wouldn't have to make the call after all.

Bennie touched the screen and dialled the first of the two numbers saved on the phone.

Ahran picked up after the third ring. Bennie put him on loud speaker.

"Sophie? Is everything alright?" His deep voice filled the room.

Bennie raised an eyebrow and gave a half smile of appreciation. I frowned at her, but more cross at myself for the way the sound of his voice was making me feel, in spite of the seriousness of the situation.

I looked at Bennie and nodded, encouraging her to answer. "Oh hello, it's not Sophie. I am a friend of hers, my name is Cordelia Blythe-Smith. Could I ask to whom I am speaking?" she asked in her best telephone voice. I stifled a snigger. She never usually spoke like that.

"Ahran Elessar. Are Sophie and the boy okay?" His voice gave me goose bumps. At least it was Ahran. To my dismay it all seemed to be stacking up.

"She's right here you can ask her yourself."

I looked at her in horror and shook my head violently.

"Sophie?" she prompted. I could have quite cheerfully strangled her.

I cleared my throat. "Oh hello Ahran, it's Sophie." I glared at Bennie.

"Is everything alright?" he asked.

"Yes everything is fine." I hesitated as I wracked my brain as to what to say next. "I was just wondering ...er...whether you had got some evidence for me yet, you know...proof about our,..er, predicament." I said falteringly and rolled my eyes, it was such a lame reason to phone him.

Bennie was trying to whisper something to me, but I couldn't make out what she was saying and listen to Ahran at the same time.

"I will be with you tomorrow evening as promised and I shall bring something with me then. Have you thought any more about my proposition?"

The thought of him being here again was oddly comforting.

"We can talk about that when you get here," I said, playing for more time. Bennie was still flapping at my elbow.

"Okay, I'll see you then." And before I could say goodbye he hung up.

"Ah!" Bennie said in frustration. "You donut! You didn't ask where he and his family were from. That's what I was trying to tell you! God Sophe, you'd never make a spy."

"I didn't know what you were saying, you were making me feel flustered." I was annoyed with myself for being such an idiot and not asking.

"Oh well, he's coming tomorrow I can ask him then, anyway the phone checks out," I said triumphantly.

"If he is as sexy as his voice, I'm happy to take Toby and go and stay with him myself," Bennie offered.

I scowled at her. "This is no joking matter. Toby's life is potentially in danger."

"I know, I was only kidding," Bennie said, raising her hands in defence.

I was hit by a sudden wave of hopelessness and dropped

my face into my hands. "What am I going to do Ben?" I'd only just felt like I was getting my life back on track and now *this*.

"If this mad woman is for real then the important thing is to keep you and Toby safe. If Ahran and his family are offering you protection then maybe you should consider it... Or you could just go to the police."

I thought about this for a moment. "If I went to the police what would I tell them? I've got nothing to prove that what Ahran has told me is true, they'd just laugh in my face."

"Admittedly, they probably wouldn't do anything until something had actually happened," Bennie agreed.

We both fell silent for a moment.

"You could hire a bodyguard?"

"Like I'm made of money," I said sarcastically.

"Then your only option is to go and stay with his family."

I threw myself back onto the cushions of the sofa in despair. "And we're back to where we started."

"What about Toby's school, his friends, my business?" I said despairingly.

"Well, the first thing you need to do is find out where Ahran lives, it might not be that far away," she said with a degree of optimism.

"How many other royal families do you know other than the Windsors in this country? It's got to be somewhere abroad."

"Well, think of it this way, it might be somewhere hot with a beach where you can work on your tan."

I had to admit somewhere warm did have an appeal. It had to be somewhere hot judging by Ahran's golden skin.

"I suppose we could go for a little while and hope that the threat of Bazeera passes quickly. We could do with a holiday."

"Attagirl!" Bennie said encouragingly. "You never know you might have a good time."

"Maybe Audrey wouldn't mind running the shop for a while," I said distractedly, beginning to think through the practicalities before stopping myself. "I can't believe I'm even contemplating this."

"Can you afford not to?"

"I don't want to put Toby at risk when I have the option of protecting him."

"Well, there's your answer."

"I need proof. I'm not going to just run off with some stranger without being sure that what he says is the truth. He might be some serial killer and the next time you see us is when our bodies are being unearthed from some remote wood on the BBC news."

Bennie grimaced.

"It happens, Ben."

"So what proof do you think he'll come up with?" she asked.

"I have no idea," I said, shrugging my shoulders.

16

We hit the road, heading for a motel that Anya had suggested would be a good pitstop. I must have fallen asleep, because it was dark when I woke up. I stretched and tilted my head from side to side to try and ease out the crick in my neck.

"Did you have a good sleep? Ahran asked.

I rubbed the back of my neck and took a deep breath in an attempt to shore up my crumbling defences before I looked across at him.

"Yes, just a bit stiff. Have I been asleep long?" His handsomeness was not diminished in any way by the poor light. In fact, the dimness within the car heightened my other senses and I became all too aware of him. *Just focus on what you are here for Sophie.* I opened the window to get some fresh air.

"About an hour and half," he replied. "Do you want to hear some good news?"

I detected a note of optimism in his voice and it snagged my attention.

"I could do with some good news right now," I muttered. "What is it?"

"Whilst you were asleep I had a phone call from Halsan, one of his agents reported a sighting matching the description of Toby."

After the last false lead, I struggled to summon the same optimism. "Okay. Where?"

"Near Terrina. It's still a long way, but it's the only thing we have to go on at the moment."

"Let's head there then," I said flatly, wondering whether we were just about to go on another wild goose chase.

"There is a night train leaving at eleven from the next town, it will take us straight into Terrina. We've got a few hours to kill so I suggest we stop at the motel Anya mentioned and get some food and freshen up."

"Sounds like a plan," I said a little more brightly. I felt relieved I wouldn't be spending another night in a hotel with him, somehow sleeping on a train didn't seem quite so bad and at least we would be in separate bunks.

We travelled the few remaining kilometres to the motel and I began to feel more optimistic. Before, it had felt like we'd been travelling blindly, but now we had somewhere definite to head to.

We arrived at the motel which was more dated than some of the other buildings I had seen in Ramia, but it was neat with colourful planters outside. We parked in front of a single-story block with a row of numbered doors. Ahran got out of the car and I quickly re-did my ponytail. He got our bags out of the boot and I joined him in the well-lit car park. How was he still able to look so devastatingly good after most of the day stuck in a car?

"Shall we eat first?" he asked.

"Good idea, I'm starving."

He took my hand in his. I wasn't prepared for the sudden contact and a charge of current shot up my arm making my knees unstable. If only I didn't feel *that*, if only my body didn't react to him like it did. He would be so much easier to resist. I felt angry at myself for being so weak and then I felt angry towards him. You would never know he was engaged to be married, he was *far* too tactile. I didn't want to create a scene in the car park but I did slip my hand away from his.

I've just got to get through the next few days, I've just got to get through the next few days, I chanted silently as we walked towards the small diner situated next to the motel.

The warm glow of the restaurant was inviting and the delicious smell of home cooking made my stomach rumble as we walked through the door. A jolly looking middle-aged man approached us and spoke in Ramian to Ahran. Apart from the height, I wondered what it was about me that indicated I wasn't Ramian.

The waiter showed us to our table and we sat down. There was no menu on the table or anything hi-tech just an ordinary chalk board attached to the wall with what I presumed was the menu written on it. I squinted at the indecipherable script; there wasn't one letter I recognised. The waiter left us to make our decisions.

"Let me translate," Ahran said, reading the blank look on my face.

He ran through an appetising list of meals. Most I recognised, although he had to explain a few things I'd never heard of. I finally settled on a chicken dish with a creamy sauce served with fresh vegetables and crispy potatoes. My mouth watered at the prospect.

The waiter reappeared and Ahran reeled off our order to him. The waiter smiled pleasantly, poured us some water from the jug on the table and went into the kitchen. There was another couple and two families already eating their meals and talking quietly amongst themselves.

I leant in slightly.

"You must be hungry. You haven't eaten since this morning," I said. From what I had observed so far he had a massive appetite.

"You're right I could eat a hippopotamus."

I smiled at his choice of big things to eat. It must have been something in the translation.

I looked into his lovely eyes. It would be so easy to reach out and touch him.

"So, have any of the King's agents come up with anything else?" I asked by way of distraction.

"No, nothing." He hesitated and took a sip of water. "I wasn't going to tell you this, but I think you should know… two of his agents have been killed." He paused. "We need to be vigilant. Bazeera does not want us to find Toby and she's doing everything she can to make sure we don't." He took a sip of his water. "But we have another lead and hopefully this time it will take us to him."

The journey ahead of us still seemed impossible, and with the unwelcome piece of information about the King's agents, the danger we were in was undeniable.

"I suppose finding him is one thing, but actually getting to him without anyone getting hurt is another matter altogether," I said, voicing my fears.

"You leave getting him to me. You aren't going anywhere near where they are holding him." There was a warning look in his eyes.

"I'm coming with you," I said, standing my ground.

"Sophie, I am telling you now, you are not." There was a razor-sharp edge to his voice and some of the people in the restaurant glanced in our direction. They quickly turned back to their meals when I met their eyes. "Be reasonable," he said more quietly. "This is how I used to earn my living. I'm not putting your life at risk any more than it already is."

I wanted nothing more than for Toby to be found and brought back safely, but the thought of Ahran putting himself in considerable danger was a difficult pill to swallow.

"Well, shall we just see where he is first?" I wasn't prepared to give in just yet.

"Has anyone ever told you that you are stubborn?" he asked, his anger dissipating.

"I am not stubborn," I said stubbornly.

He raised an eyebrow at me.

"I just know… my own…mind," I faltered.

He beamed his heart-stopping smile knowing that I had just dug myself into a hole. I had trouble breathing. I had a hard time doing even the simplest things when he smiled at me like that.

"Are you aware that you do that?" I said without thinking.

"Do what?"

Oh God, what had I started?

He waited for me to continue.

I took a deep breath. "You have a way of smiling that makes it very difficult for a woman to think straight. You did it to the poor girl at the airport check-in, the flight attendant on the plane and the woman at the hire car desk. They didn't stand a chance."

"I had no idea," he confessed. "And does it have the same effect on you?" he asked, leaning in further. He still had that glint in his eyes, but some of his light-heartedness had disappeared.

I hesitated, should I lie or just tell him the truth? To be honest it would be a relief to just tell him how he made me feel, but I knew that would just be plain madness.

"Yes," I said simply. There was no need to give him an exhaustive update on the pitiable state of my emotions.

"Very interesting," he said. "Is there anything else I do that has an effect on you?" he asked, his tone lowering. I began to feel like a cornered animal. I knew I shouldn't have started this. "It doesn't matter," I said, hoping that he might just drop it, but judging by the expression on his face, I knew I was about to be disappointed. Suddenly, I had a better understanding of what small defenceless fish feel like when they're being circled by a large predatory shark.

He picked up my hand and started to rub circles with his thumb in my palm.

"I know that you are not immune to this," he tormented.

"Don't!" I warned as I withdrew my hand into my lap. I struggled to ignore the increase in tempo of my heartbeat, which was not helped by the realisation that he could probably hear it.

I looked up into his eyes expecting to see a hint of playfulness, but he returned my look with such intensity that it made my breath catch in my throat. Fortunately, I was rescued by the waiter who offered us some bread rolls. I slumped back into my chair. I felt light-headed and was grateful for the few seconds of respite the waiter serving us afforded me. Ahran's eyes didn't leave me which made it even more difficult to establish any kind of regular breathing pattern. I tore my eyes away from his. I needed to distance myself from him. I asked the waiter where the Ladies loo was. He didn't understand and Ahran had to translate. It struck me just how reliant on him I was. The waiter pointed to a door on the other side of the diner.

"Excuse me," I said, scraping my chair back and standing up. I threw my napkin on the table and made my escape to the ladies' restroom.

I braced myself against the sink and sucked in some deep breaths. I could feel tears prickling my eyes. I rubbed my hand across them angrily. *Damn him!* I may be emotionally vulnerable, but I was damned if I was going to let him play me for a love sick fool. I leant over the sink and splashed some cold water on my face and patted it dry with a paper towel. I pulled my hair band out, scraped my hair back and tied it tighter than it was before. It was time to put an end to his flirtations, other women may fall at his feet, but I was not about to be the next in line. I took a deep breath and squared my shoulders feeling more resolute.

Ahran was staring out of the window, but looked my way as I approached. I felt his eyes search my face.

"Have I upset you?"

"What makes you think that?" I said as I sat down without making eye contact. I placed my napkin back across my lap.

"You look like you've been crying."

No other man would have noticed.

"Oh..I..er..just had a sneezing fit in the Ladies," I lied. I felt stronger knowing what I wanted to say and I didn't want him to distract me from saying it.

I dared to meet his eyes. "Look Ahran, I really appreciate what you are doing for me, you know, looking for Toby, but the only reason I'm here is because I couldn't bear to stay behind and not do anything." I had his attention and so ploughed on. "As far as I am concerned our relationship is purely a practical one, we are here to get a job done, to find Toby, and once that is done I shall return to Hatherley and you will return to Talina and your farm. In the meantime, I'd really appreciate it if you would keep your distance. I'm not in the market for a casual relationship and certainly not with a man who is engaged to be married to another woman. I'm just not that sort of person."

Now that I had said it, it hadn't sounded quite like I had imagined in my head. Had I read too much into his gestures? I just sounded like I was completely over-reacting, after all, what *had* he done other than hold my hand on a couple of occasions? Ahran didn't say anything and the expression on his face was unreadable.

So, I blathered on. "Apart from all of that, I hardly think that getting involved with someone from a completely different universe is a good foundation for a long and meaningful relationship."

He remained silent.

"I mean, how would that work? It would bring a whole new meaning to 'long distance relationship'. I laughed nervously. "Anyway, you are engaged and I am in a relationship, end of story." I had added that last bit for effect, although I knew, and so probably did he, that the lack of any contact with Marcus over the last few days meant that there was no real relationship to speak of. I no longer felt angry, just really silly. Ahran hadn't said a word during the whole of my toe-curling soliloquy and his expression was icy.

"Well, I am very sorry if I have offended you in any way. I'll make a note to remind myself to keep my distance the next time you are being strangled." He was angry. He didn't raise his voice, in fact it was barely audible, which made me realise just how furious he was.

"You know that's not what I meant. I meant that when you hold my hand or give me those smouldering looks." I blew my breath out in frustration. "Oh, just forget I said anything." This of course was completely impossible because I had said it and now it was out there sitting between us like a huge iceberg, which, had one been there in reality, would have been a few degrees warmer than Ahran was being at the moment.

Bugger, bugger, bugger! That had not gone at all how I had planned.

The waiter came and brought our meals and we spent the remainder of our time in the diner barely saying a word to one another. I stole the odd glance at Ahran who looked stony faced and I regretted opening my big mouth. I knew now that the only reason I had asked him to keep his distance was because I didn't trust myself every time he came near me. I had sounded like an ungrateful bitch. He hadn't wanted me to come in the first place, I had forced myself on this trip and so far I had been nothing but a hindrance.

I contemplated returning to Dinara, but I knew I couldn't go back on my own. I didn't speak a word of the language nor did I have a clue where I was. If I wanted to go back Ahran would have to accompany me. I could feel hot tears stinging my eyes and I blinked them away quickly. The last thing I needed to do right now was cry.

If I could have tasted the food, I was pretty sure it would have been delicious, but I struggled to get much of it down. Ahran ordered a pudding and I just settled for a coffee, not wanting to prolong the awkward situation I had so cleverly engineered for myself. It was a relief when Ahran paid the bill and we headed back out to the reception to check in.

After Ahran had given the necessary details to the teenage girl on the desk and she had given us our key card, we headed to our room which was about half way down the block we had parked outside. Ahran slid the card through the card reader on the door and it clicked open.

During the time it had taken us to get our key and find

our room I had vowed that I would do my level best to be more useful. I wasn't quite sure what I was going to be able to do yet, but I would think of something, if only to assuage my guilt. Ahran had barely said anything since my regrettable diatribe in the diner and I sat on the bed wishing I was anywhere but here.

"I am going out, keep the door locked and don't open it to anyone," he said in a tone that dared me to argue. I had no idea where he was going, but nodded my agreement anyway. He opened the door and left.

I threw myself back on the bed feeling relieved. I had succeeded in making the situation unbearable. With hindsight, I much preferred the tactile Ahran to the cold stony faced Ahran, even if it meant I had to fight my feelings for him the whole time. I closed my eyes and took a few deep breaths. I would have given *anything* to have been back home with Toby and for none of this to be happening.

The door clicked, and my heart skipped a beat. I sat up too quickly and it was a moment before I realised it was Ahran.

"That was quick."

He had a bag I didn't recognise in his hand. He came and sat down on the edge of the bed. I had to move over to avoid touching him. To my horror, he reached into the bag and pulled out a gun.

"What's that for?" I asked, as if it wasn't obvious.

"I think it would be sensible if we were better armed."

"What do you mean *we*, I've never held a gun in my life!" I said, all awkwardness vanishing with the shock of his suggestion.

"These aren't ordinary guns and they are very easy to use."

"*Use?* I have no intention of using one," I said, shaking my head adamantly and staring at him as if he had lost his marbles.

He ignored me and continued.

"They are laser guns. The first shot stuns the target for a few minutes, if a second shot is fired within that time, then it kills."

It was Ahran the soldier talking now and he was so cool, he may as well have been describing the local scenery. I reminded myself that he was a trained killer and that he himself could be pretty dangerous. Who knows how many people he had killed in his career? But the thought of *me* killing someone with one of these guns just made me feel sick. I couldn't imagine how he had got hold of them, we were in the middle of nowhere.

"Where did you get them from?"

"The waiter in the diner."

I snorted. I was having a hard time picturing the pleasant waiter in the diner as some kind of small arms dealer. "You are kidding?"

"These people are pretty vulnerable out here and they have to protect themselves somehow. Here, take this," he said, passing me one of the guns. I reluctantly took it and let it dangle impotently in my right hand. I hardly wanted to acknowledge I was holding it, let alone accept I might have to use it.

"It fires like any other firearm, you just pull the trigger," he said, ignoring my lack of enthusiasm. When I made no move to do anything with it, he sighed and knelt up on the bed behind me, putting his arms around my sides. He took hold of the gun still in my hand, placed his forefinger over mine on the trigger and pointed it towards the wall on the far side of the room.

I struggled to concentrate.

"Your aim doesn't have to be that accurate, as long as you hit the target somewhere it will stun them." His finger squeezed mine and we pulled the trigger together. There was no sound just a blue flash and then a scorch mark on the wall. The sudden bright light made me jump.

"Jesus!"

Whether I was responding to having just fired the gun or to his hot breath on my neck as a result of him putting himself at my eye level, I wasn't sure.

He seemed to hesitate before pulling away and quickly got off the bed. I suppose I was grateful for this, he was obviously respecting my wishes after our conversation in the diner. Was he worried that I would misinterpret every little gesture he made towards me? *Nice one Sophie! You really know how to make a bad situation worse.*

I laid the gun on the bedside table, not wishing to hold it any longer than I had to.

"With a bit of luck I won't need to do that again."

"Let's hope not, but I want you to keep it with you at all times, okay?"

"I am sure that won't be necessary."

"*Sophie!*" he growled.

"Okay, okay I will keep it with me at all times," I said, knowing that I wasn't in a strong position to argue.

"Do you want to have a shower first? We've got an hour before we have to leave to catch the train," he asked.

"No, you go ahead I'm just going to stretch out here," I said as I hitched further up onto the bed and swung my legs up. I needed a few minutes respite.

"Alright, I won't be long."

He went into the bathroom, but didn't fully close the door and I could hear him getting undressed before switching the shower on. I rolled over and groaned.

After a minute or two, I felt for the remote control and turned on the radio channel on the T.V. I switched off the light and laid there for a minute or two as I listened to the impassioned opera that filled the room. *How appropriate?!* It matched my mood perfectly. I rolled over onto my back and stared at the ceiling, trying to clear my mind. I reminded myself that it didn't matter how I felt, what mattered was that we got to Toby and rescued him as quickly as possible.

Suddenly, my eye was caught by a shadowy figure passing our window. I sat up to get a better look. I felt a distinct sense of unease which increased dramatically when I saw the handle on the door turn as whoever it was, tried to get in. I weighed up my options a) This person had inno-cently got the wrong room and would soon realise that their card key wasn't working b) This person could be after us in which case I should go into the bathroom and alert Ahran c) This person could be after us and I could pick up the gun on the night stand and shoot the bastard.

My eyes darted to the gun on the bedside table. Before I

had really given it much thought I jumped up, grabbed it and flattened my back against the wall by the door. My heart pounded as the person trying to get in, succeeded. The door opened slowly. I held the gun in both hands with my finger on the trigger, just as Ahran had showed me. The door opened wider and I held my breath worried that it would touch me and reveal my hiding place. Fortunately, it stopped millimetres away from my toes and the dark figure slipped silently into the room. My cover remained. In the light from the bathroom, the man was as tall as Ahran, but not quite as broad. He was inching towards the bathroom door, his right arm extended and I could make out the outline of a gun in his hand. My heart was beating so hard I was terrified he would hear it, but the opera was still blaring out of the television and his attention was totally focussed on the bathroom.

This definitely wasn't a case of someone getting the wrong room.

He took a step away from me and I had the perfect opportunity to shoot him in the back.

I hesitated, but reminding myself that it would only stun him, I concentrated on stilling my shaking hand and slowly pulled the trigger. I jumped at the flash of blue light and watched him crumple to the floor.

I dropped the gun.

"It's all yours," Ahran said over the music as he came out of the bathroom. He was wearing his jeans, but his chest was bare and he was rubbing his hair with a towel.

He nearly tripped over the body lying on the floor and let out an expletive.

"Sophie?" I could hear the alarm in his voice as his eyes searched for me in the darkened room.

"I'm over here," I replied. I was rooted to the spot staring at our intruder. The way he had landed was almost comic, like he was doing an impression of a face down starfish.

Ahran switched the lamp on by the bed and turned the television off. He glanced from me to the body on the floor and back to me again.

"He had a gun. I shot him," I said, dazed.

"How many times?" he asked coolly.

"Just once," I replied, still unable to move.

I knew what he was about to do as soon as he stepped towards me and I didn't make any attempt to stop him. He picked up the gun, aimed it at the body and fired a second shot. The man's body jolted perceptibly. I thought I might pass out. Gingerly, I felt my way along the wall and then the nightstand and slumped onto the bed.

With the gun still poised in his hand Ahran went to the open doorway and looked out. When he was satisfied the coast was clear he shut the door and came and sat next to me. "Did he hurt you?" he said, his eyes searching my face.

I exhaled through pursed lips. "No, he didn't have a chance."

"Good girl," he said, his relief evident. He pulled me to his chest.

I didn't protest and closed my eyes, thankful he was there. All too quickly he pulled away.

"We should get out of here, there could be others."

He opened his bag and pulled out a sweater. I tried not

to notice the play of muscles across his chest as he put it on. It wasn't Ahran who needed to be told to keep his distance; it was me who needed a stern talking to.

"How did he know we were here?" I asked, beginning to recover from the shock of what had just happened.

He shrugged. "Maybe the car we hired had a tracking device and somehow they tapped into it."

I stared at him shocked.

"Come on, grab your bag, we need to go," he said, zipping up his own bag.

He handed me the other gun, I just stared blankly at it. He sighed and reached around me, I thought he was about to hug me again, but instead he pushed the gun into the waist band at the back of my jeans. He slung our bags over his shoulder and picked up the other gun.

"How are we going to leave if the car we hired is being traced?"

He tapped the end of his nose with his gun, rather foolishly in my opinion, and grabbed my hand. He gently pushed me behind him and edged out of the door to survey the car park.

It was disconcerting to think that there could be others lurking outside and it triggered a surge of adrenaline that shot to my fingertips.

Ahran surveyed the car park. He was very still and his head was cocked. He was clearly using all his highly evolved senses to see if it was safe for us to venture out. I tried to stay as still as I could and even held my breath so it wouldn't interfere with his surveillance. He seemed satisfied that there was no immediate threat and we edged out of our motel room.

I narrowed my eyes at the traitorous hire car as we passed it. A few spaces down was a motorbike just like the ones on Earth. "It's a motorbike!" I whispered, feeling ridiculously pleased that here was a vehicle I was familiar with, its two wheels planted firmly on the ground. I immediately felt a pang of homesickness.

"It's an import, you don't see many of them and you have to have a special licence," he explained as we stood by the sleek, black Kawasaki ZX-14R. I didn't know a Kawasaki from a Robin Reliant, but it's make and model was helpfully emblazoned down the side in silver lettering.

"It's one of the most powerful bikes you have on Earth, but it's considered more of a classic here." Ahran crouched down and fiddled with something on the bike. I heard a click.

Suddenly it occurred to me that Ahran was intending to use it as our escape vehicle. "I'm not getting on that!" I said in a forced whisper.

Ahran ignored me and straddled the bike, organising our bags in front of him. He held out his hand to me.

"Would you rather stay here?" he asked, nodding towards our room where another would-be assassin lay dead.

"We can't just steal it," I said through my teeth. "And we don't have any helmets."

Ahran shrugged. The engine came to life and he revved it to drown out my protests. With his other hand, he cupped his ear and shook his head demonstrating he could no longer hear me.

I sighed, he'd made his point and I reluctantly climbed on the bike behind him. I'd never been on a motorbike before. I tightened my grip around his waist as we spun out of the car park. The motorbike quickly ate up the ground, putting distance between us and the motel. I looked back over my shoulder to see a man standing in the car park waving his arms frantically. I couldn't help but feel bad that we had just stolen his bike.

I hugged myself closely to Ahran's back as the air whipped my face. I closed my eyes feeling scared and exhilarated all at the same time.

17

We were going so fast I had to close my eyes. I clamped myself to Ahran not just for my own safety, but because I had a legitimate reason to hold onto him. The air was cool, but the heat radiating from him was enough to keep me warm. As I rested my cheek against his back, I imprinted the feel of him into my memory, knowing that when I was back home and alone at night I could draw on memories like this and relive the feel of his body, the warmth of him, his hard stomach muscles under my finger tips and the complete sense of security I felt despite the fact that our lives couldn't be more in danger.

It wasn't too long before the surrounding area became more built up so we were forced to slow down as we wound our way through the streets. It was late and the traffic was light. The train station eventually came into view. We had completed our journey without being followed and I was beginning to feel more at ease. Ahran parked outside the station and switched off the engine.

I sat back and immediately mourned the feel of him.

"Jump off. We've got a train to catch."

I climbed off the back and he put the bike's resting arm down and climbed off himself. He took hold of my hand, ignoring everything I had said to him in the diner, and we walked into the station together. I just didn't have the strength to protest anymore.

Our train was due to depart in twenty minutes so we bought our tickets, grabbed a coffee and sat as inconspicuously as we could in the corner of the station cafe. We spoke once or twice, but I knew Ahran's attention was really on everyone who entered and left as he assessed their threat potential. Thankfully, everyone seemed to just be going about their business, not in the least bit interested in who we were.

An announcement came over the personal address system presumably announcing the imminent arrival of our train. I looked out of the window and watched its approach. Like most of the other modes of transport here, it hovered a couple of feet off the ground and travelled virtually soundlessly. The front of the train was seriously aerodynamic and I would have happily bet a year's takings that it was faster than any train I had ever been on.

"That's our train. Ready?" Ahran said.

I nodded and drained the last of my coffee.

We made our way onto the platform. The train doors opened and we climbed on board. It smelt of warm newness. I had been on sleeper trains one summer when I'd travelled around Europe as a student, but none of them had been as sleek or as nice as this.

We moved through the train and found our cabin. Ahran pushed the door open and ushered me in. I caught him glancing up and down the corridor before following me in. Our room for the night was compact with two bunks down one side, although they were wider and longer than the ones I had any experience of. On the other side of the cabin were two shallow armchairs and a door which led into an even more compact en-suite. I finished my inspection of our facilities and re-joined Ahran in the confines of our cabin.

"It's a bit cramped, but the bunks are actually more comfortable than they look," he said.

"It's far more luxurious than any sleeper I've ever been on and it certainly beats having to share with sweaty, middle-aged, Italians who snore," I confirmed.

Ahran laughed. "Well, fortunately for you I'm none of those things, and I don't think I snore."

I smiled and sat down on the bottom bunk. I was expecting to find it as hard as a board but it was surprisingly soft. I swung my feet up onto the bunk and laid back. "I see what you mean, this is more comfortable than my bed at home." I felt a sudden wave of tiredness. It had been another long and traumatic day. I stifled a yawn.

"Do you want the top or bottom bunk?" Ahran asked.

I sat up and rested on my elbows. "It would probably make sense if I have the top bunk, although I'm warning you now, I do have a tendency to fall out, or at least I did when I was a kid."

"Did you?" he laughed. "That explains a lot." He came and sat down on the edge of my bunk.

"Hey!" I said, giving him a light punch on his bicep. It was as hard as granite. I liked his banter and I was pleased an easier atmosphere had returned between us. He gave me a crooked smile in response and it made my insides feel fluttery.

"I'll sleep on the top bunk, we can't have you falling out."

I wanted to say I would be perfectly alright, but his smile and proximity were making it difficult for me to find enough breath to protest. I managed a nod. I had hoped that the more time I spent with him the more immune I might become to his smile, but it just got worse. And as if he was deliberately fanning the flames, he reached out and tucked a stray strand of hair that had come loose from my pony tail.

"I know," he said, raising his hand before I could protest, "That was an illegal gesture." He didn't sound in the least bit apologetic, but looked into my eyes to gauge my reaction. I couldn't move away even if I wanted to. He hesitated for a brief moment and then ran the back of his hand down my cheek. My eyes shut of their own accord and I savoured the feel of his skin against mine as his touch burned a trail down the side of my face.

"In spite of what you said in the diner, your body tells me something completely different when I am near you." His voice was no more than a husky whisper.

"Ahran," I said in a small, choked voice.

"Your skin is so soft."

Had he heard me? He needed to stop because I was absolutely powerless to stop him.

His face came closer to mine, his eyes focussing on my lips. My heart began to race as I anticipated the moment our lips would meet. I tilted my chin up and his lips touched mine.

It was a tender kiss and it made my heart ache. He pulled away, his eyes searching mine.

The last thing I wanted him to do now was stop. I wanted to feel the full force of his kiss, I was desperate for it and I couldn't stop myself from leaning towards him, this time touching my lips to his. He didn't move, and for a second I thought I had daydreamed the last few moments, but when I opened my eyes his were closed, his expression caught somewhere between pleasure and torment. What did he expect? It was a dangerous game he was playing.

He groaned. His mouth was far more urgent this time and our lips opened simultaneously, our tongues hungrily searching each other's. The heat that had begun in my abdomen started to course through my veins. My poor misguided heart soared and for the first time I didn't care. I was kissing him as passionately as he was kissing me.

There was a rap on the door and we both ignored it, nothing else seemed important.

The rap came again, more sharply this time. Whoever it was, they weren't prepared to be ignored. We pulled away from each other breathlessly.

Ahran stood up slightly flustered and narrowly missed hitting his head on the bunk above.

My eyes were level with his groin and his obvious arousal. I was secretly thrilled that I had this effect on him.

"I think you better get the door," he said a little sheepishly. "It will be the guard checking our tickets."

"Oh, okay," I said, slipping off the bed and feeling more than a little wobbly myself. "Where are they?"

"Here," he said, reaching into his bag and passing them to me.

I opened the door to the guard who was waiting patiently. He scanned our tickets on an electronic tablet in his hands. When he had finished he nodded and handed them back to me before moving on to the next cabin. I closed the door.

Pausing to collect myself, I turned around to Ahran, not quite sure what to say after what had just happened. I cleared my throat. "Once again, *that* should not have happened." I was beginning to sound like a stuck record.

"I can't help it Sophie, I want to kiss you. I want *you*." Before I had time to protest he raised his hands defensively. "I know it is wrong, for God's sake I've been trying to fight it, but that's the way it is. There's too much chemistry between us, I know it and you know it."

"But we can't...*I can't*." It was all I could do to stop myself from going to him and carrying on from where we had left off.

"If it's about Toby, I understand. If you want to wait until we've found him and he's safely back home, I respect that."

He really did think we were inevitable. "It's Toby,

Talina, the fact that we aren't even from the same planet," I said, feeling exasperated. "There's a long list."

"I admit, it's not an ideal situation, but I'm done battling with it. I want to kiss you, hold you, make love to you."

His words sent a warm shiver down my spine, but I remained firm. "I don't want to be just another notch on your bedpost Ahran."

He looked shocked. "You would never be that."

"Wouldn't I? You might be used to having other women, but I'm not used to being an 'other' woman."

"You think I am in the habit of doing this?" He sounded angry.

"I don't know Ahran, are you?"

He ran his hand through his hair and contemplated his answer. "There have been other women," he admitted reluctantly, "But this is different."

That was exactly what I didn't want to hear. Wasn't he betrothed to Talina? How could I possibly maintain any self-respect, entering into a physical relationship with him knowing that I was just another woman in a long line of women he had cheated on Talina with? I actually felt sorry for her, something I never thought I would feel.

"It's no different Ahran. It's sex and I refuse to be just another warm body in your bed." I wasn't quite sure where I found the strength to challenge him because there was a big part of me that wanted to jump on him and rip his clothes off, but the flash forward of me sitting at home, alone, my self-respect and heart in tatters, was enough to fuel my resistance. "So, let's just forget it shall we?" I said with a defiant tilt of my chin. On the outside I looked like a woman fully in control of her emotions, but on the inside I was falling to pieces.

"Well, you seem to have got it all worked out." His tone was acerbic.

"It's called self-preservation Ahran," I said, my resolve strengthening.

"It seems to me that you are scared of letting anyone get too close," he accused.

The accuracy of his assessment caught me off-guard and I faltered. "You don't know anything about me," I said defensively.

"I know more than you think," he declared. "There hasn't been anyone significant in your life for a while, not because you don't attract men, you do, look at you, I defy any man in this world, or yours, who would not want you lying next to him, but you are scared stiff that if you let them get too close they will let you down."

I opened my mouth to speak, but closed it again without saying a word.

"You've not slept with the poor guy you have been stringing along, what's his name? Mark…Marcus," he said, answering his own question. "Because you are afraid that if you do, you will have to give more of yourself and that frightens you."

"That's none of your Goddamn business."

"I'm right though, aren't I?" he said triumphantly.

"How dare you?!" I hissed.

"You've only got one life Sophie, it's no good worrying about the 'what if's' every time you meet someone new because before you know it, your life will have passed you

AMELIA FORD

by. You're not the only one who has experienced loss, we all have and we've all had to deal with it and get on with the job of living, we're not the ones dead and buried."

I gasped. I could feel tears stinging my eyes. "What have you got to be proud of?" I said, lashing out. "You're an emotionless killer." I was on dangerous ground, but I wanted to wound him like I felt he had just wounded me. "You've spent your life taking your anger at your father out on anyone who gets in your way rather than actually standing up to him and telling him how let down you feel."

He looked like I had just slapped him in the face, and then the emotionless mask he used whenever I got too close, slipped conveniently into place.

"That's enough," he said firmly.

"Oh! It's alright for you to say what you think, but when someone hits the mark where you're concerned, suddenly it's not okay? What are you afraid of Ahran?"

"I said. That's enough!"

I knew I had gone too far, but then so had he.

"We are both tired I think we should get some sleep," he said in a tight voice.

He was right. We weren't achieving anything by tearing lumps out of one another, but just to make my point I word-lessly picked up my bag, went into the en-suite and tried to slam the door behind me like a petulant teenager. Unfortunately, it had a slam resistant stay on it which completely spoilt the effect.

I put my face in my hands and groaned. Oh God, what had I said? I had thrown everything he had done to save our lives back in his face. *Sophie, you are an idiot!* He, on the other hand, had summarised my life in one foul, perceptive swoop. He had got the measure of me in such a short time it unnerved me, especially when he seemed such an enigma at times.

I washed my face, brushed my teeth and took off my jeans, folding them neatly before putting them in my bag. I took my time, reluctant to face him again. Taking a deep breath, I went back into the cabin. The light was off and he was lying on the top bunk although I didn't think he was asleep. I climbed into the bottom bunk without saying anything. Hopefully a good night's sleep would clear the air.

We must have been travelling at some speed, and yet the only indication we were travelling at all, was the slight sway of the train as it traced its way across the landscape. I lay there for a long time, playing our conversation over and over in my head. I felt bad about what I had said about him and his father, but I suspected I was right. As for me, what he had said was exactly how I had behaved over the last few years. I was so terrified of losing people that I no longer let anyone get close. He was right, there were no guarantees in life and it was about time I took a few risks. That's what living was about wasn't it? And if I didn't, there was every chance I'd end up a lonely old woman, full of regrets because I had never let anyone get close enough to share my life with. What was it Bennie always said? You had to kiss a few frogs before you found 'Mr Let's See How It Goes And Work On It'. She didn't believe in princes or Mr Right. I still wasn't sure getting together with Ahran was a risk I was prepared to take though, it would be like jumping out of a plane with no parachute. Some risks were just beyond reckless.

I pulled the sheets up around my neck and my mind drifted to our kiss. That was the one sticking point. I was *so* attracted to him, when I was near him it was like I was being sucked into his very own force field and I was power-less to resist. Maybe I *should* go to bed with him? Perhaps it would exorcise the power he had over me. It didn't have to mean anything. Bennie seemed to be able to do it without falling apart afterwards.

They were brave words, but could I just walk away? I rolled over in frustration. Toby had to be my priority and whatever I decided to do about Ahran had to come second to my reason for being here. It was Toby's second night away from home with people he didn't know in a land he never knew even existed and here was me wondering whether or not to jump into bed with Ahran. I felt pretty despicable.

I closed my eyes. "Hang in there buddy, we are on our way," I mouthed. I had never believed in God, most of the things that had happened in my life had been enough proof that he didn't exist. But if he did and he had any ounce of remorse for the loss I had suffered over the years and the pain it had caused, maybe he would make an exception and protect Toby. I figured it would be a good way of making amends.

I could hear Ahran's steady breathing and I envied him being able to sleep. I tossed and turned and eventually fell into a fitful sleep. Just as I was climbing up a crumbling rock face and watching the rocks fall a hundred feet to the ground I was woken by someone banging on the door.

Ahran jumped deftly to his feet, awake and alert in a split second.

"What is it?" I said, sleep-dazed.

"Not sure."

He opened the door to the same guard who had checked our tickets earlier. They exchanged a few words. He shut the door and turned back to me, I couldn't see his face in the dark, but his voice conveyed his concern.

"Get dressed."

"Why? What is it?" I asked.

"Apparently, there is some kind of emergency and the train is stopping at the next station."

"Oh," I said, sitting up and switching the reading light on at the head of my bed.

"I'm going to see if I can find out more. Get dressed and don't open the door to anyone," he warned. Without another word he slipped out of the cabin.

I got out of bed and put my jeans and a sweater on. The days were warm here, but the nights felt decidedly cool. I went into the bathroom, brushed my hair and put it into a ponytail. I went back into the cabin and sat in one of the armchairs and awaited Ahran's return. By way of a distraction, I touched the small screen embedded in the wall next to my seat. It sprang to life and began to run a promotional film about travelling on a train like this and all the picturesque places you could visit.

Within a couple of minutes Ahran was back.

"Anything?"

"I've just walked the length of the train and I couldn't see or hear anything that might be considered an emergency. Something isn't right and I have a suspicion the reason we are stopping might have something to do with us."

His words sent a cold shiver down my spine.

"We need to get off," he said.

"At the next station?"

"No, we need to get off *before* we get to the next station."

"But the train is still moving." He wasn't making any sense.

"I know, don't worry, it will be fine."

"Please tell me you are not thinking about jumping off the train whilst it's still moving?" I couldn't see anything out of the window, it was pitch black, but I could sense we were still travelling at speed. The thought filled me with horror.

"The train will start to decelerate some way before the station and we will jump off before we get there."

"But that's madness!" I protested.

"We'll jump together and I'll shield you from the impact."

"And how are you going to do that?" I asked doubtfully.

"You've just got to trust me."

"Is this our only option?"

"I can't think of a better one. I am pretty sure Bazeera's agents are waiting for us at the next station."

I weighed up our options. Jumping off a moving train or getting off at the next station into the waiting arms of a handful of lethal killers? I had to admit that jumping seemed to be our only option.

"The train is slowing and we need to go," he said, slipping into soldier mode.

I was scared half to death, but what other choice did we have?

We left our cabin and headed down the corridor, I thought we were heading to the doors, but Ahran pulled me into the communal toilet and shower room instead. I looked at him, my eyes full of questions. He shut the door behind us.

"We can't use the doors because they'll know they have been forced, we are going to have to jump out of the window."

This idea was getting worse by the minute.

I looked at the frosted glass. It was quite large, big enough for an adult to climb through, but it was completely sealed.

"How are we going to jump out of it, if it doesn't open?"

"Leave that to me," he replied.

I could tell that the train was slowing, we must have been nearing the station and we were running out of time.

"Stand to the side."

I did as he said.

He took a few deep breaths and then swung his leg up and kicked the window in one swift, controlled movement. There was a loud crack and the window shattered, but stayed in place. He kicked it squarely in the middle for a second time. The glass popped out of its frame in one piece and fell into the night. I stared at him wide-eyed.

"I'm going to lift you up. You will need to sit with your legs dangling out, don't worry I won't let you fall. I am going to straddle you, I'll count to three and then we'll jump together, okay?"

"No, not okay. Do you really think this is a good idea?"

"I am strong enough to take the impact and I will shield you from the ground. The worst you'll feel is winded." I was glad that one of us was convinced it was going to be okay.

I reluctantly moved in front of him and he placed his hands on my waist. My pulse quickened. Did my desire for him have no boundaries? How reckless was my body to still be affected by his touch when we were about to throw ourselves out of the window of a moving train?

In one deft movement Ahran swung me up and through the window until I was sitting on the window frame. I clutched the top of the frame in panic. Before I knew it, he was balanced on the window frame with his legs either side of me. I struggled to keep my legs still as the wind whistled past.

I felt his mouth close to my ear. The train was virtually silent, but the noise of the wind buffeted in my ears.

"Okay, tuck your head into your chest." He had one arm around my waist and was gripping the top of the window frame with his other hand.

I tucked my head down as far as I could, too frozen by fear to argue.

"One."

Against my better judgement, I let go and Ahran held me tightly to him. I closed my eyes. This came close to being the most scared I had ever been in my life, surely we were jumping to our deaths?

"Two."

I swallowed and sent up a silent prayer.

"Three."

I felt the thrust of his hips as he pushed us away from the window frame and I let out a soundless scream, the kind of scream you do in a terrifying dream. We flew through the air and for a moment I felt weightless. Ahran tucked my head further into my chest and wrapped himself around me. I was completely cocooned by his large muscular body.

We hit the ground, the impact forcing the breath out of me as if I had been hit by the train we had just jumped out of. Like clothes in a tumble dryer, we began to roll over and over through the undergrowth and after what seemed like an eternity we finally stopped. I laid there not moving, frightened that every bone in my body had been broken. I was lying on my right side and Ahran was still holding me with his body curved against my back, his knees crooked into the back of mine.

"Sophie?" His voice was urgent.

I wasn't quite able to speak.

"Are you alright?"

I detected a note of panic.

I forced myself to answer. "I don't know," I croaked. My lungs felt like they were stuck together. "I… can't…breathe."

"Just relax and breathe in slowly."

I'd been winded before, but this was something else. I felt like I had been crushed by a ten tonne truck. I tried to do as he said and relaxed, I could feel the panic rising as I struggled to drag the air into my lungs.

"Go up onto all fours, you might find it easier."

I did as he suggested, although every muscle protested. It did feel better, there didn't seem to be quite so much pressure on my chest. Gradually, I took one shaky breath and then another. I ached from head to toe, but the sheer fact that I was able to move meant that my initial assessment had been incorrect. All bones were intact.

Ahran gently rubbed my back.

"How about you? Are you okay?" I said, rocking back onto my heels.

I turned to look at him, terrified that he might be hurt. It was difficult to make out his face in the dark.

"I am fine, I am sure I'll have the odd bruise, but nothing that won't heal."

I put my arms around his neck and hugged him. He gently put his arms around me and hugged me back.

"We've got to stop having these near-death moments," I said, pulling away. "That has got to be the craziest thing I have ever done. How is it that neither of us are hurt?" I laughed incredulously.

"You really need to start trusting me more." I could hear his smile rather than see it. It was the first time I'd really been aware of his superhuman strength.

"Do you think you can stand up?" he said as he got to his feet.

"Yes, I think so," I said, reaching for his hand. "Ah!" I said, wincing as I stood up.

"What is it?" he asked anxiously.

"My shoulder hurts."

"Whereabouts? Here, let me have a feel," he said as began tracing the muscles of my shoulder blade with his thumb.

"Ouch! *There*."

He stabbed his thumbs either side of where it hurt.

"Ahran!" I was a little taken aback by how hard he had pressed, didn't he realise how painful it was?

"Now circle your shoulder. It should start to feel a little easier."

I circled it a few times and he was right. "What did you just do?"

"Pressure points."

"Pressure points?"

"You just needed to release the tension between the two pressure points, your muscle had gone into spasm."

I circled it another couple of times expecting it to hurt, but the pain had eased considerably.

"Oh right, thanks." He really was a one-man survival machine.

"Sophie, I have to hand it to you, you are one brave Sapien. You walk away from being strangled without as much as a backward glance, you shoot a trained killer without hesitation and then you jump off a train with little complaint. I don't know of many Ramians who would have coped with what you've put up with over the last couple of days."

I didn't like to admit how good it felt to hear the admiration in his voice.

"I'm no ordinary Sapien," I said flippantly.

He laughed. "No, you are certainly not ordinary." Something in his tone made my stomach flutter.

"Okay, so what do we do now?" I asked, suddenly feeling embarrassed.

"We walk."

"I had a feeling you might say that. Have you any idea where we are?" I asked as we began to pick our way through the undergrowth.

"No, not a clue."

"Don't you have some kind of inbuilt navigation system? What kind of superhuman are you?" I teased. I wasn't sure why I felt so jolly all of a sudden. Maybe it was because I had just survived another brush with death, maybe it was because for the time being we were safe, no one was following us and no one knew where we were, or maybe it was because I had just earned Ahran's respect.

We walked through undergrowth in a wooded area and it was almost impossible to see where I was putting my feet. I stumbled a number of times, and Ahran's arm came out and caught me every time. I couldn't tell how long we had been walking, but it seemed like we were moving deeper into the wood rather than towards civilisation.

"I'm not sure how much farther I can walk," I said, stumbling for the umpteenth time. I felt absolutely exhausted, all I wanted to do was climb into bed, but I had no idea how far away bed was.

"You are doing really well Sophie. Try, to keep going a bit longer. I am hoping we might come across a farm so we can bed down in a barn for the night."

This wasn't quite what I had in mind. The wood seemed

to be thinning out and it looked as if there was a more open space ahead of us.

"I can smell sheep. With a bit of luck we might come across a lambing hut," he speculated.

I sniffed the air, but all I could smell was a feint earthy smell as our feet disturbed the undergrowth. I tried to picture what a lambing hut might look like; it must be where sheep gave birth. I think I might have preferred to sleep out under the stars.

"There!" Ahran said, making me jump.

"What is it?"

"A lambing hut."

I strained my eyes in the darkness, but couldn't see beyond more than a few paces.

"I'll have to take your word for it," I said dryly.

We walked for a few more minutes and then I was just about able to make out the outline of a small building. His night vision was so much better than mine.

Was there anything he didn't do better?

The lambing hut wasn't quite what I was expecting. It was the size of a large garden shed and had curtains at the window. Why on earth would sheep need curtains?

"Do sheep really give birth in these huts?"

Ahran chuckled. "No, of course they don't. These huts are for the shepherds. When sheep are lambing it's necessary to keep a close eye on them. We like our animals to give birth as naturally as possible and because our climate is mild we don't bring them indoors to lamb. The shepherd sleeps in a lambing hut so he can inspect his flock at intervals during the night."

"Oh," I said, laughing at my own ignorance.

We approached the hut and I stumbled up the steps which were steeper than I thought. Ahran lifted the latch and the door swung open. It looked like we had somewhere to spend the night after all.

"We aren't too far away from lambing season and these huts are usually pretty well-equipped." Ahran felt his way around the room.

"Aha! This is what I was looking for."

I strained my eyes to try and see what it was he had found. I couldn't see anything, but heard him winding something up instead and then suddenly a light filled the room.

"A wind-up lamp!" I exclaimed as my eyes adjusted to the light.

"Once I've got this going," he said, "I'll light the fire."

"There's a fire?" I was starting to feel chilly and wrapped my arms around myself, the thought of a warming fire made me shiver with anticipation.

"Yes, there's a small log burning stove over there," he said, cocking his head towards a small pot bellied stove.

He finished winding the lamp and put it on a small table where it glowed happily and then turned his attention to the stove . There was a neat pile of logs stacked next to it, as if someone had been expecting us. Whilst he set about building a fire, my gaze travelled around the room and rested on the bed at the end. It wasn't a double, but it was wider than a single and big enough to accommodate a Ramian. It was going to be snug with both of us in there, but the thought of a night snuggled up to Ahran was comforting if a little scary. I had to admit I was too exhausted to worry about sharing a bed with him tonight.

"Do you think there might be some bedding anywhere?" I said, walking over to the bare and uninviting mattress.

"Have a look underneath, there might be some blankets there," Ahran suggested as he lit a match.

Sure enough there was a plastic box with a lid and in it was a pillow, a sheet and a couple of blankets. I took them out and shook them. They smelt a bit stale, but they were dry. I set about making up our bed for the night. When I had finished, it looked much more inviting and a hundred times better than the straw bed I had imagined we might be spending the night on.

Ahran had got the fire going and the hut was feeling much cosier.

"That's better," I said, moving over to the fire and holding my hands out.

Ahran began to rummage through the wall cupboard above a table and chairs that were pushed against the wall. "Sometimes they leave some basic supplies of food. It depends how long ago it was last used or how soon they intend on using it again," he said distractedly.

"It looks like we might be in luck." He took a tin out of the cupboard and opened the lid.

I peered into it. There were some sachets of some kind of powdered hot drink and a packet of unopened biscuits. It was an unexpected, but most welcome little cache. It had been hours since we had eaten. I dared to think that we were having a well-deserved run of luck after the day we'd just had.

Ahran found a tin kettle and went outside to fill it from the tap by the door. I rooted around the cupboards and found a couple of mugs. Ahran had been right. The hut was surprisingly well-equipped, it had everything a shepherd might need for a night. A five-star hotel didn't seem any more appealing at that moment.

I sat down in front of the fire and hugged my knees whilst Ahran put the kettle on top of the wood burner and emptied the sachets into two mugs.

"Is anyone likely to find us here?" I asked.

"I doubt it. The reason they have these huts is because we are a long way away from the farmhouse, or indeed any house. The chances of anyone coming here tonight are slim," he said as he put another log on the fire. "Anyway, it's unlikely that the sheep would have started lambing yet. But now that the fire's got going, I'll switch the lamp off, just as a precaution." He turned off the lamp and the light from the fire was enough to cast a flickering glow around the hut.

He handed me a steaming mug and sat next to me.

I took a sip of what turned out to be a creamy tasting hot chocolate and stared into the fire, my thoughts turning to Toby. Would he be tucked up in bed or alone in a cold and draughty prison cell? I hated the thought of him having to suffer for one second. *If that bitch Bazeera touched one hair on his head I would kill her myself!* I reached around to the waistband at the small of my back and my fingertips brushed over the handle of the gun that I had tucked in there just before we had jumped off the train. I was relieved to find it still there, at least I had the means to dispatch her given half the chance. I snorted. At what point had I changed my mind about using a gun?

"What is it?" Ahran asked.

"Oh, nothing."

We continued to sip our drinks in silence and my mind wandered off in a different direction. Was there any part of him that thought we had a chance together?

Jesus! Who was I kidding? What hope was there? There were so many reasons why it could never work. I started to go around in the same old circle and it made me feel confused and miserable.

"What are you thinking Sophie?"

I laughed a humourless laugh. "You wouldn't want to know."

"Try me," he replied.

"It's nothing," I said and reached for the biscuits.

"No, it is something, you look miserable." His face was full of concern and it all very nearly came tumbling out.

"I don't know, it's just everything. I didn't ask for any of this," I said despairingly.

I put my mug down and struggled to open the biscuits, my hands were shaking and I fought the tears that were threatening to spill. Ahran took the packet from me.

"Come on he said, let's get you into bed, you are exhausted."

He scooped me up into his arms, took me over to the bed and gently laid me down.

"You need to get some rest," he said as he draped the blanket over me. "I'll sleep on the floor."

"No," I said too loudly in the quiet of the hut. "No," I

repeated, more quietly. "You can't sleep on the floor, please, sleep in the bed, you must be just as tired as I am."

He hesitated. "Are you sure?"

"Yes, I'm sure," I said softly.

I moved back towards the wall to make space for him to get in and held the blanket back. He filled the space next to me and pulled me into him so that my head lay on his chest. I closed my eyes and took in a deep breath. There was that sense of complete security again. It felt like no harm could ever come to me as long as his arms were around me. I inhaled the smell of him and nestled closer. I could hear his heart beating hard and fast under my ear. In the quiet darkness of the hut the atmosphere between us suddenly changed.

"Do you hear that Sophie? That is the effect you have on me," he said, lacing our fingers together. I stared at our hands resting on his chest.

"I don't know what has happened to me since I met you. I can't seem to think straight when I'm around you," he said quietly.

I leant up on one elbow and looked into his eyes. He looked troubled and I reached up and touched the side of his face just like I had wanted to do so many times before.

"I want to kiss you so badly." His voice was husky and it did funny things to my insides.

I hesitated. "I want you to kiss me," I said, my voice little more than a whisper. I did want him to kiss me more than I had ever wanted anything else in the world. Sleep was now the furthest thing from my mind. I wanted him to wrap his arms around me so that I could lose myself in him.

I wanted to feel his warm skin against mine, to entwine our bodies so tightly that nothing could ever come between us.

His lips found mine and I knew there was no going back. Ahran had been right on the train. What was about to happen was inevitable and I had been a fool to think I could stop it. I opened my mouth to the demand of his tongue and felt his intake of breath. The sensation of his hot demanding mouth made a burgeoning heat spread through my body and a quiet moan escape from my throat. My hand found the top button of his shirt. I hesitated and he gently caressed my throat.

"I have wanted to touch you since the first moment I saw you," he said against my lips. It was all I needed to spur me on. I started to unbutton his shirt, desperate for the feel of him. I wanted to get rid of the barrier of clothes, to feel that moment when his skin would finally touch mine unhindered. There was no voice of reason now, it had upped sticks and left, allowing my desire for him to flow freely. Talina? Talina who? My need for him was so great that any rationality had deserted me, all I knew now was how it felt to be here touching him, being touched by him, and I was hungry for more.

I fumbled with the buttons on his shirt. He helped me finish the job and shrugged it off. I tentatively touched his chest and felt the contours of his muscles beneath my fingertips. His eyes were dark pools of desire in the dim light. My fingers became sensitised by the smattering of hair over on his chest. Slowly I ran my hand down the sculpted form of his stomach and felt his muscles tense. His reaction made me feel bolder. I trailed my fingers lower to the hair that dipped down below the waistband of his jeans and I heard his sharp intake of breath.

I sat up and pulled my jumper and t-shirt over my head in one. I couldn't wait any longer. I needed to feel his skin next to mine as much as I needed to breathe. My hands went around my back to the fastening of my bra.

"Don't do that yet," he said quickly.

I looked at him uncertainly. A slow smile worked its way across his face. "I've been waiting for you all my life, let me savour this."

He started to plant slow kisses along my collar bone and I let my head drop back. Each kiss was slow and exquisite and I focused on the feel of his lips as they brushed over my skin. His mouth trailed down and I gasped as his tongue flicked over a hardened nipple through the lace of my bra. I moaned on my outward breath as the effect of what he was doing radiated throughout my body.

His hand found my other breast and his thumb mimicked the movement of his tongue.

"So beautiful," he said, his mouth hot through the lace of my bra. The heat of arousal was now throbbing in every fibre of my being and I wondered if I might expire from the sheer pleasure of it. My hands traced the hard line of muscles from his neck and down over his shoulders, he was the embodiment of male perfection and I arched my body into his shamelessly.

He paused from his devoted attention. "Oh God Sophie," he said suddenly, "I haven't got any protection with me. Have you?"

"I…no," I replied, comforted that he hadn't thought I

was a sure thing, but at the same time thinking I might go mad if we stopped now.

"We'll just have to improvise," I said suggestively. *So bold!* But this was how he made me feel when we kissed, wanton and unrestrained. Any remaining hang ups I had about not being like the Ramian women he was used to, went out the window as he resumed his reverent worship of my breasts.

"Not..." he began to say as he started to trail wet kisses over my chest and up my throat, "Being able..." He licked and nipped the side of my neck. I tilted my head to one side my breath coming in uneven gasps. I could feel my most intimate parts beginning to throb impatiently, "...To bury myself," his mouth moved up the side of my neck, his voice sounding distinctly breathless, "...In you," his licks, nips and kisses continued their trail along my jawline, "...Is going to," I turned my face my lips hungrily seeking his, "...Drive me to," and just before his mouth crushed down on mine he finally managed to finish his sentence "...Insanity."

"Then I'll go there with you," I said breathily, briefly pulling away so I could reach the waistband of his jeans to undo his belt. I undid the buckle, but struggled to undo the buttons of his fly as a result of his arousal straining forcibly against it. He helped with the buttons and pushed his jeans down over his hips. He pulled his boots and socks off and finally rid himself of his jeans. The sight of him big and bold in his form hugging boxers made the ache between my legs begin to throb painfully.

"Take your jeans off," he insisted.

I obediently did as he said. If he had told me to take a running leap off the nearest cliff, I would have flung myself off the edge with reckless abandon.

He gently lowered me down until I was lying on my back and he knelt over me. His eyes were hot and hungry as his gaze slowly ran down my body. "Sophie, you are so beautiful, how am I ever going to be able to keep my hands off you now?" He ran a hand down over my breast and splayed his fingers out over my stomach. He was touching me like I was some precious work of art to be admired and savoured. "The way you look now will stay with me forever."

I basked in his appreciation.

He straddled me and dipped his head to begin a luscious assault on my mouth. I ran my hands over the smooth skin of his back as he lowered himself onto me and then down further as I reached underneath his boxers and made contact with the hard muscles of his backside, the hot, hard, length of him, pressing into the top of my thigh. I grasped his rear and pulled him to me.

"Ah, Sophie, that's more than I can bear." His voice sounded pained and he pulled himself away, whilst his lips continued to burn a trail back down my neck. He pulled my bra straps off each shoulder as his mouth carried on with its devastating descent. A deep groan came from his throat as his tongue made contact with my left nipple. I arched my back forcing it further into his mouth. Just his gentle sucking nearly sent me over the edge.

Desperate to feel him in my hands, I pushed his boxers down. I gently held him, my fingertips not quite touching as they encircled him. His mouth momentarily stilled on my breast and I felt his exhalation on my skin. He said something in Ramian. I had no idea what it was, but the way he said it spurred me on. I began to run my hand up and down. He rocked his hips harmoniously with the movement of my hand. For a few delicious moments I pleasured him with tantalising strokes before he stilled and withdrew himself from my grip.

"I'm going to come before you if you continue like that," he warned, his voice strained.

He slipped his hand into my panties. It was like he had lit the touch paper that would cause the not so slow burn to my climax. I wriggled out of my underwear and his lips found mine. Our breath was coming hard and fast mingling in our mouths as our hands roamed over each other's bodies.

He throbbed impatiently in my palm. Knowing he was so close caused the exquisite tension that had been building within me to reach the point where it was ready to explode. My hand echoed the luxuriant strokes he was pleasuring me with and I tried to hold back so that we would reach that blissful moment together, but I couldn't hold off any longer, my flesh was so sensitised to his touch that I cascaded around him, my breath leaving my body in an intense rush as wave after wave crashed through me. My hand stilled as I became lost in my release and he thrust urgently against my grip spilling himself in response and groaning out his own pleasure.

18

I'm not sure how long we lay side by side, not speaking, just languishing in the delicious aftermath of what we had just shared. I wondered how it could possibly feel any better. None of my previous sexual experiences even came close.

We lay there until our breathing had evened out. Eventually, Ahran got up and I wondered where he was going until he returned with some tissue. I was touched by his attentiveness.

"Are you getting cold?" he asked.

"Yes, a little now."

He reached down and pulled the sheet and blankets over us both as he climbed back in. I welcomed the return of his warmth as I daringly slid my leg between his. He leant up on one elbow and kissed my nose. By the glow of the log burner, I could just about make out his beautiful features; his strong brow and mesmirising eyes, the straight masculine nose and those devastating lips. I didn't know what to say, all the things I wanted to say just sounded so trite in my head. His jaw was stubbly and I could still feel the tingle of his mouth on my body. I gazed at him in the subdued light, and marvelled at how it was even possible that I was here lying with him.

"You need to get some sleep," he said softly as he stroked the side of my cheek with the back of his hand.

I nodded, not quite trusting my voice. Whether it was the emotion I felt from what we had just done or whether it was the feelings I had hitherto dammed up finally breaking free, I wasn't sure, but I was scared to go to sleep in case I woke up in the morning to find the spell had broken.

He pulled me towards him so that I was in the crook of his arm and it felt the most perfect place to be.

"You never cease to surprise and amaze me," he said, his voice quietly rumbling through his chest.

"In a good way?" I asked.

He chuckled. "Yes, in a good way."

He was stroking my hair and for now I was content as I watched the dying embers of the fire. Whatever happened in the morning, I would deal with it. *Such brave thoughts.*

BEHIND MY CLOSED EYELIDS, I could tell the morning light was streaming through the windows of the hut. I was lying on my side and Ahran's body was moulded to mine, his breath warm on the back of my neck as he slept. His arm was draped over my waist and I welcomed the weight of it. I was worried that if I moved or even opened my eyes the languid contentment I felt would disappear. I lay there thinking about our night together and waited for guilt to rear its ugly head, but it didn't even show a whisker. How could I feel guilty when what we had done had felt so right? We were drawn to one another like iron filings to a magnet and I knew I would be lying if I said I wasn't falling for him.

It was a bittersweet relief to admit it. I had tried to prevent it from happening, but I had lost what was an increasingly futile battle. Did he feel the same? Or was I just a warm body substitute for Talina? There was a heavy, uncomfortable sensation in my chest. I had allowed myself to get in too deep. *So much for getting him out of my system!* What we had shared last night had only served to make me fall even further. How did Bennie manage to have her fun and walk away unscathed? When it came to Ahran it was becoming clear that I would struggle to take even one step away from him.

Did he still feel the same about me in the cold light of day? His kisses and touch had been so tender and it had been my name he had whispered in the dark. Had he wished he had been here with anyone else *but* me?

So many insecurities.

It was difficult not to feel them knowing my fragile heart was now at his mercy. The realisation made me feel exposed and vulnerable. Maybe if I looked at his face, I would find the answers I was looking for. I gently turned over trying not to wake him. As I moved, his arm tightened around my waist preventing me from moving any further.

"Sophie, are you okay?" he asked sleepily.

"Yes, I'm fine but I've got to move, I've been lying in one position for too long." If I could just look into his eyes.

He relaxed his arm and I rolled over. He raised his eyelids half-mast.

"Morning." His voice was husky with sleep. I rested my head on my hand so that I could look at him more easily.

"Morning." I was taken aback by the tenderness of his expression and the contented smile on his lips. They had to be good signs.

"You look pleased with yourself," I observed.

"I am," he replied. "I have just spent the night with *the* most beautiful woman I have ever had the good fortune to lay my eyes and *hands* on."

Better. Although I seriously doubted how that could be true.

"Oh really?" I said, feeling buoyed.

"Yes really." My heart hummed its own little merry tune.

"And I may just have to do this."

He propped himself up on his elbow and his eyes closed as he gently planted a kiss on my lips. The memory of his kisses from last night came flooding back.

"Mmm, just as good as I remembered," he said distractedly.

"You don't regret what we did last night?" I had to ask.

His mouth began to move across my jawline. "Not one bit," he replied between kisses.

He pulled away. "Do you?" he said, his eyes searching mine.

"No," I said simply. "But what about Talina?" I don't

know why I had to raise this now and spoil the moment, but I needed his reassurance.

"Talina is the last person on my mind," he replied.

"But you cheated on her last night." I sat up and pulled the sheet over my nakedness.

"Sophie, can't you see?" he said patiently. "My relationship with Talina is over. Meeting you only confirmed that."

"It's over? Does she know that?" I couldn't quite believe what I was hearing.

"She has a fair idea."

"When did you tell her?" I asked incredulously.

"When she came to the palace just before we left. I told her that when I got back we needed to talk."

"And she was happy to leave it like that?" I couldn't imagine I would have let him go so easily.

"No, she was pretty pissed, but she can't have been surprised. Things haven't exactly been going well between us recently."

"But you are engaged to be married?"

"We've known each other since we were children and I thought I would grow to love her in time, but I began to realise that I could never love her and that it would be wrong to carry on and let her think otherwise."

"But she was all over you when we were at the palace?" I was struggling to take any of this in.

"She knew things weren't right between us, but was having a hard time accepting it."

"Does anyone else know? Oh my God! Do your parents know?" The questions kept coming as the impact of what he was saying sunk in.

"I have talked to my mother about it."

"And what did she say?"

"She suspected something had been wrong for a while."

"And your father?"

"He doesn't know anything about it yet."

"How will he take you breaking off your engagement?"

"Like he does everything else, he'll lose his temper and tell me how much I'm letting my family down," he said dismissively.

"I'm sorry." I felt I was to blame.

"You have no need to apologise, if anything, I have you to thank. Talina and I would never have been happy, we want completely different things out of life."

I was unable to comprehend what implications this might have for me.

"Do you think your father will come around?"

I couldn't help thinking that I could potentially be the reason Ahran would never make amends with his father.

"Let's not talk about this now," he said, shutting me out.

I knew that by his response he wasn't completely unaffected by the thought of how his father might react. I leant forward and kissed him. I wanted to offer him my support, but didn't quite know how to verbalise it without it sounding like a cliché. I had unwittingly been the catalyst for Ahran's decision and whilst it thrilled me and sent my head into a spin, it didn't guarantee anything. In spite of this, I wanted to be there for him, be someone he could lean on and share his troubles with, but judging by his reaction to the subject of his father, we were some way off of this.

He kissed me back and pulled me into his arms. I put my

arms around him and lay my head on his chest. I listened to the slow, steady beat of his heart.

My mind was whirring with all this new information. Ahran, for all intents and purposes was no longer engaged, a free agent and he had just admitted that after meeting me he knew he didn't want to be with Talina. Suddenly, a relationship with him didn't seem quite so impossible and for the first time I felt that maybe, just maybe we had a chance of being together.

Ahran kissed my forehead.

"Even though I would like us to spend the morning getting to know each other a little better," he said, his words heavily laden with innuendo, "It's getting late and we need to move on."

"What time is it?" I asked

"It's time the shepherd is likely to be doing his daily check on his sheep."

"Really?!" I said, scrambling out of bed in a panic. I couldn't face the embarrassment of someone finding us here like this.

I picked my clothes up off the floor and hurriedly put my panties and jeans on, but my bra was nowhere to be seen. I realised Ahran hadn't moved.

"Aren't you going to get dressed?" I asked, looking over at him.

"Just admiring the view," he said, my bra casually hooked over his finger.

I snatched it off him and turned around feeling a flush of embarrassment as I put it on. I wasn't entirely comfortable standing half naked in front of him in broad daylight.

He laughed a deep rumbling laugh. It was a sound I hadn't heard nearly enough of.

I turned around just in time to see him getting out of bed. I tried not to stare at his magnificent body. Sensing his eyes on me, I made a fumbling effort at putting my t-shirt and sweater back on.

"Now that is a real shame," he said as he pulled his jeans up over his hips.

"What?" I asked feeling a little more comfortable now that I was dressed.

"Covering up that delectable body."

He stood behind me and encased me in his arms before kissing my neck. I leant back into him. If I didn't pull away now, I doubted whether either of us would be able to show the restraint we had exercised last night, especially now we both knew the promise of what our bodies were capable of together. It had been mind-blowing and I was seriously beginning to doubt whether I would be able to cope with sex with Ahran without dissolving into an ecstatic mess. He had become like a drug to me and now that I'd had a taste of him, weaning myself off was going to take my own super-human effort. I doubted whether my poor, ordinary self was up to it.

I stepped away from his kisses in an attempt to demonstrate to myself that I did still have some willpower left.

"Ah Sophie, you are killing me," he said with a pained expression on his face.

I laughed, but my smiled faded as I thought of the search ahead of us. "We've still got a little boy to find."

Ahran gave an understanding nod.

"Is it likely that I might find a toothbrush anywhere?" I asked crouching down and looking into a cupboard. Other than a couple of plates and some dusty glasses, it looked like I was about to be disappointed.

"I doubt it," Ahran said, confirming my suspicions. He reached into his jean pocket and for a moment I thought he was about to miraculously produce a toothbrush. "This is the best I can do," he said, offering me a piece of gum. He looked genuinely upset that he couldn't offer me what I had asked for.

"Thanks," I said and popped it in my mouth, pleased that if he kissed me again, my mouth would be a little more minty fresh.

He finished dressing. I folded up the bed clothes and put them back in the box. I tried to put everything back as it was. "Whoever uses this place is going to know someone has been here," I said, feeling a smidgen of guilt.

"Maybe, but after last night I don't regret us stumbling across it, do you?" he said with a sinful look in his eyes.

Do I regret spending the night here with Ahran and all but making love with him? Not one bit and whilst I had no idea where we would go from here, I would relive those precious moments for as long as I lived.

He made the three strides to where I was standing and took my face in his hands. His lips found mine. I went up onto tiptoe and arched into his body. The attraction we felt for one another was hard to resist now that we had crossed the line into the realm of lovers.

Suddenly there was a clatter outside. The noise brought us to an abrupt halt and we pulled apart.

"What was that?" I said, my heart hammering in my chest and not just because I was worried that someone might have found us out.

Ahran picked up one of the laser guns lying on the floor by the bed and grabbed hold of my hand, pulling me behind him. I was reminded that we were still very much in danger and complacency could get us killed. He threw open the door and aimed the gun outside.

A pair of black beady eyes looked back at us in surprise. I let out the breath I had been holding. They belonged to an unsuspecting ewe who scooted off as fast as her legs and pregnant belly could carry her.

"I think that's our cue to leave," he announced.

"You're right," I sighed. For about six glorious hours we had been untouchable, and as I had lain in Ahran's arms my fears and worries had drifted to the background, but the intrusion of the outside world, even if it had only been by a sheep, had brought them all back. And to add to my not inconsiderable worries, I was now terrified that as we left this little hut in the middle of nowhere the little piece of heaven I had just experienced would shatter into a million tiny pieces.

I clung to what Ahran and I had shared last night, but I was also acutely aware that we couldn't allow ourselves to become distracted. Our priority was Toby and we couldn't waste any time in finding him, he shouldn't have to spend any longer in the grasp of Bazeera than he had to. I was trying my hardest to remain optimistic and concentrated on the *when* rather than the *if*. Toby had been away from me for two nights now. We hadn't spent a night apart since Katie had died.

After one last look over the hut to make sure that everything was back in its place, it was with a heavy heart that I followed Ahran down the steps and headed out into the warm morning sun. We began to make our way around the perimeter of the vast field we found ourselves in and walked for a good hour in silence. Ahran set the pace in front and I trailed a few paces behind. I tried to keep up, but I knew I was holding him back. He could have carried out this search much faster without me. I cursed my selfishness and pigheadedness. To make matters worse, I could feel him withdrawing with each step we took. I dragged in a deep, shaky breath and scanned the landscape to see if there was a sign of a road or anything that signalled we were nearing civilisation. All I could do was trust Ahran to get us out of here and back on our way to Toby. I also hoped that I hadn't just made the biggest mistake of my life.

Every now and again Ahran looked back and asked if I was alright. Each time I nodded and smiled, but as the minutes turned into hours he barely said a word. I felt my optimism fading and the vindictive little voice in my head reminded me of all the reasons why a relationship with Ahran could never work. I was also starving. Hunger always put me in a bad mood. We'd had a breakfast of biscuits and a mug of water, but my stomach was starting to ache uncomfortably. There was something about this place. Whether it was the greater concentration of oxygen in the air or the lack of pollution, I couldn't be sure, but just being outside made you feel hungry. Just as I thought I might pass out from hunger pains I noticed a moving speck in the distance. I squinted to try and make out what it was.

"Is that a car I can see?" It was the first time either of us had spoken for some time and my voice sounded hoarse.

"It's a livestock truck."

To me it just looked like a blurry moving dot on the horizon. This news buoyed my flagging spirits.

"We might be able to catch a lift into the town," Ahran speculated.

This thought made me uneasy. I had never hitchhiked in my life. Wasn't it common knowledge that you had to have a death wish to hitchhike? I'd seen *The Hitcher*, it had scared me half to death. I may have had a laser gun tucked in my waistband, but it comforted me no end to know I also had Ahran who was a lethal weapon in his own right.

It took us another twenty minutes to get to the road and I spent most of that time trying to block out images of slashed throats and dumped bodies in my mind. Ahran took my hand in his and gave it a gentle squeeze; he must have sensed my apprehension. It was the first contact we'd had since leaving the lambing hut and I can't say it calmed my nerves, it just changed my focus.

"Do you think this road goes to the town we would have stopped at on the train last night?" I asked.

"I'm pretty sure it does."

"What are we going to do when we get there?"

"Hire a car or get the train again if we have to."

Neither option thrilled me.

"You haven't heard any more from the King I take it?"

"No, the battery on my phone died."

I felt disappointed that we had nothing more to go on and surprised and frustrated that for all their technological advances Ramians hadn't come up with a phone that had a better battery life than the ones on Earth.

We must have walked at least a mile and no vehicles passed us in that time until Ahran suddenly stopped and looked back down the road.

"I can hear something."

I strained my ears, not able to hear anything other than the odd cricket and the long grass on the verge jostling in the breeze. It was some time before a vehicle came into view. As it came closer, it turned out to be another livestock truck, a huge hovering double trailer that was virtually silent except for its bleating cargo.

Ahran flagged it down and my anxiety increased. The door slid open and Ahran leaned in to speak to the driver. A moment or two later he beckoned me towards him and I walked up to the cab expecting to see an overweight truck driver with a girly calendar pinned to the cab wall behind him, but instead the driver was a slightly built, middle-aged woman dressed in spotless, navy blue overalls.

"Hello," I said. Ahran lifted me into the cab. The woman replied in Ramian with a bright smile. She didn't seem like a likely throat slasher. I breathed a small sigh of relief. Ahran jumped up beside me and the door slid shut behind him. The huge vehicle travelled with the ease and grace of a sleek limousine rather than a fifty-tonne livestock truck. We made our way along the highway and I listened to Ahran and our unexpected animal haulier making conversation. It was good to be making faster progress, even if the prospect of getting on another train or spending endless hours on the road filled me with dread. I concentrated on the scenery and tried to clear my mind. The landscape was flat and pretty uninteresting with fields upon fields of sheep or cattle with the odd isolated homestead dotted around.

"The town is only about twenty minutes away," Ahran said, breaking my reverie. "Orlena doesn't seem to think that there are any car hire places, we might just have to risk taking the train again."

My heart sunk. Jumping off a train once was one time too many as far as I was concerned.

The landscape became more built up as we neared the town. We hit the main street and the lorry slowed up and pulled over. We said our thank yous to the obliging Orlena and jumped down onto the pavement.

It was a bustling place and not as modern looking as the larger towns I'd seen in Ramia. It was neat and spotlessly clean and there was an abundance of hanging baskets, each with a profusion of brightly coloured flowers cascading down either side of most doorways. The place had a welcome feel about it, but the thought of Bazeera's people lying in wait dampened the welcoming vibe for me.

"Let's get some food first, you must be starving."

"Yes, aren't you?" I said, surprised that his own hunger pains hadn't driven him to distraction.

"I am, but I'm kind of focussed when I'm on a trail. Will that do?" Ahran said, nodding towards a bakery a few doors down.

"Perfect!" My mouth began to water as I fantasised about Cornish pasties. Would Cornwall's most famous food export have made it to Ramia? As this trip progressed, it was becoming harder and harder to surprise me.

Ahran enveloped my hand in his and we headed for the bakers. We were accosted by the most delicious smell of warm bread and coffee as we entered the bakery. Two of the tables were occupied, one by an elderly couple and the other by a mother and two small children. Neither party looked remotely like Bazeera's agents. I relaxed a little. We went to the counter and I plumped for something that looked a bit like a round Cornish pasty. Ahran spoke to the woman whilst she served us.

"Shall we sit down and eat?" he suggested, once he had paid. "I've ordered us some coffee."

"Great." All I could think about was sinking my teeth into the pie. We chose a table towards the back of the shop, away from the window. I felt a pang as I thought of my little coffee shop at home and all the regular customers who had become an extended family of sorts. I had taken it all so much for granted. I thought about Audrey who was lying broken in a hospital bed because of me and I felt deeply guilty for not getting in touch since I had left Earth. She hadn't deserved to get caught up in this tragic mess. I vowed to phone her at the very next opportunity.

The woman who had served us at the counter brought our coffees over. She put the cups down and hesitated before addressing Ahran. They exchanged a few words and he nodded in response. The woman seemed pleased and returned to her position behind the counter.

I looked at him with raised eyebrows.

"We might not have to get the train after all," he said.

"Go on," I encouraged.

"That woman's son is selling his car and she wondered whether we would be interested in buying it," he reported.

"Are we?" The thought of travelling by road was marginally more appealing than the train.

"Maybe," he said after finishing his mouthful. "Her son is bringing it here so we can have a look at it."

When we had finished, the woman took us out through the back to where her son was waiting. The car was old and the autopilot no longer worked, but apart from that Ahran seemed satisfied it was in good working order and he bought it.

19

We stopped at a convenience store on the edge of town and bought some supplies for our journey. Ahran seemed to think it might take us a couple of days to get to where the potential sighting of Toby had been. I was thankful to be moving forward once again. He drove and we settled into a comfortable silence.

I couldn't help wondering where his thoughts were taking him. Was he thinking about the night we had spent together? Or was he thinking about the trail we were following? Was he putting his own needs and feelings to the side to focus on the job in hand? I wished I could be more detached, but there was too much at stake no matter which direction I looked in.

I had a flashback of last night. Had it been the same for him? Our hearts had sung in that remote shepherd's hut. What I was less certain about was whether he felt the same. Since we had left the hut this morning, there had been little indication that he did. Sure, he had held my hand a few times, but then he had done that on a number of occasions before. Maybe he was beginning to regret our night together. It was a painful thought.

How had I allowed this to happen? *You stupid, stupid idiot Sophie!* The now familiar insecurity began to plague me. Why had I not let Ahran get on and do his job whilst I stayed a safe distance away?

"Are you okay?" Ahran asked.

How did he do it? It was like he was tuned into my own personal frequency of emotion.

"I shouldn't have come," I said quietly.

"Sophie, not this again," he said, a hint of exasperation in his voice.

"I'm of absolutely no use at all, if anything I'm holding you back," I said, pleading my case.

He was silent for a moment and I couldn't help thinking he was trying to think of something tactful to say whilst not disagreeing with me.

"There is nothing I would have done differently if you hadn't been here, I would still be in this same situation."

I looked at him disbelievingly. "You're just saying that."

"I am just being honest," he said in his own defence.

It would have been easier if he had just agreed with me. I wanted to wrap myself in a cloak of self-deprecation. I wanted to punish myself for making Toby's rescue more difficult than it needed to be and for falling for a man so out of my league it was ridiculous.

I didn't respond and stared out the window.

"Sophie, Toby needs you. When we find him the only person he will want to see is *you*."

I broodily kept my silence. He had changed his tune since the King had used a similar line back at the palace.

"*I* want you here," he said softly.

I turned to face him and the look in his eyes began to dissolve my doubts. Maybe last night had meant something to him after all.

"How can you want me here? I have none of your *talents*. I'm an inferior human being in every way."

"Inferior?" He chuckled as if genuinely amused. "I admit there was a time when I thought your race was inferior, you were inferior."

That hurt a bit.

"But you've changed my opinion. The rest of your race may be average, but there is nothing average about you Sophie, you seem to forget that if it wasn't for you in that motel room we would probably both be dead. You're brave Sophie and an enemy with courage is a formidable opponent, you could give any of Bazeera's agents a run for their money," he said with a chuckle. I flushed at his compliment. "And…" he continued his voice lowering an octave, "There was nothing inferior about the way you behaved last night."

I felt my blush spread at his words. His smile indicated that it hadn't gone unnoticed.

"I think we both got carried away last night," I said, folding my arms across my chest. Was it an act of defiance or a feeble attempt to physically protect my heart from any further injury?

His eyes searched mine. "Do you regret what we did last night?" he challenged.

Do I wish it had never happened? At the time, it had felt

so right, it had felt like our whole life's purpose was to be together for those precious hours. But in the cold light of day, the enormity of my feelings frightened me and the chasm that was between us felt like it could never be breached. I was struggling to articulate how I felt as a myriad of emotions bore down on me.

"*Sophie.* Do you regret last night?" It seemed very important he know the answer.

"No, I don't regret what happened last night," I said quickly, I couldn't lie to him. "All I'm saying is that it shouldn't have gone as far as it did, it's not the first time we've let ourselves get carried away and we need to put a stop to it," I answered wearily. I was trying to protect myself, to rebuild the barriers that I had so foolishly allowed to crumble.

"You are not making any sense," he said and ran his fingers through his hair in frustration.

"Do you want us to stop?" His voice sounded strained as he kept his eyes on the road.

"I think we should just get on with finding Toby," I finished.

"You haven't answered my question," he pushed.

I didn't feel strong enough to cope with the feelings he was stirring in me.

"Yes, I want us to stop," I said angrily, knowing that this was my chance to stop the rail crash that had become my life.

"I don't believe you," he said harshly.

"What do you want from me Ahran?" I turned towards him, suddenly feeling very tired.

"I want *you*," he said his voice softening. "I can't carry on as if last night didn't happen and I don't want to go back to a life without you in it."

My heart stopped at his words, but my head was struggling to compute.

"Ahran, we can't possibly have a future together. We live in two completely different worlds. We aren't even the same species!" I said with a humourless laugh.

He looked at me as if to say, 'You *are* kidding.'

"Ahran, don't act as if it doesn't matter, it does," I said, trying to be rational. "How can we possibly make a relationship work? Maybe you should reconsider a life with Talina." I paused. "At least you share the same genetic make-up." Never did I think that I would be using *that* as a reason to break up with a guy.

"You might still have a chance of patching things up with her, you could put it down to a moment of pre-marital nerves." Everything I was saying went against everything I felt, but at least one of us had a chance of coming out of this with a shot at happiness.

Ahran sighed in frustration. "Talina and I *do not* have a future together, we would end up making each other miserable. How can I make you understand that?"

"I don't want to be held responsible for breaking up your relationship. What happened last night was a moment of weakness, it doesn't have to mean anything, people do it all the time and still manage to return to their lives, no harm done." If only I felt the conviction of my words.

"Sophie, I may not have known you long, but I know that

what happened last night meant something." He tried to catch my eye. I stubbornly kept my eyes trained on the road. "And I certainly don't hold you responsible for the breakup of my relationship," he continued. "There were major problems even before I met you. I had been so focussed on buying the farm I ignored them thinking that maybe our love would grow. It was a classic case of denial. I am just thankful that meeting you made me realise what a mistake I was making." He paused as if he was searching for the right words. "And as for last night being a moment of *weakness*, I knew exactly what I was doing and I wouldn't change a second of it."

I turned to face him feeling so utterly torn by what he was saying.

"I want to be with you Sophie," he confessed. "And I want to do what we did last night and more again and again." There was a hint of desperation in his voice I hadn't heard before and it was ruining me. He was saying exactly what I wanted to hear, but at the same time exactly what I didn't want to hear. This gorgeous, superhuman man was declaring his feelings for me.

"How can we possibly have a future Ahran? I don't belong here and you couldn't live in Hatherley. You've got the farm and your future is all mapped out, I couldn't expect you to give that up, you've worked so hard for it."

"We could work it out together."

"Oh God Ahran, you are making it so difficult for me to do the right thing."

"It isn't a matter of doing the right thing Sophie, it's a matter of letting fate take its course."

"You believe in fate?" I said. This surprised me, he had seemed so pragmatic.

"There are worse things to believe in when you are faced with problems to overcome."

Suddenly the phone in the charging dock rang.

Ahran cleared his throat and answered it.

I listened to him speaking to whoever it was, desperately trying to understand what he was saying.

When Ahran hit the hang up button I was none the wiser.

"Is it Toby?" I asked hopefully.

"Yes, it has been reported that Toby may well have spent the night he was kidnapped at a tavern in a small town in the heart of Bazeera's territory."

"Really? Does he know where he went from there?"

"Nobody has been able to contact the agent since. The tracking device in his phone shows that either he or his phone has not moved in the last 24 hours."

"Either way not a good sign?"

He shook his head ominously.

I grimaced. "So, what are we going to do?"

"We'll head to this tavern and see if we can find out if it was them and where they were headed."

"Is it far?"

"It should take about 12 hours by road."

I glanced at the clock. We should get there in the early hours of the morning. I felt a glimmer of hope, but it was a frustratingly long drive. Everywhere was so far away here. Maybe it was what I needed, it would at least give me time to think about what Ahran had just said. He had made it sound so easy, but I had my safe life, the cafe and Toby to think about. Did being with him mean I would have to give all that up? My head ached, and I shut my eyes and rubbed my temples. "I suppose it's good that we have a more concrete lead, it just takes so long to get anywhere," I said, unable to hide my impatience.

"Ramia is much bigger than the world you are used to, we could still catch the train if you wanted to, but you know the risks."

"No let's just get there as fast as we can by road," I said with a sigh. It would take longer, but it felt like we had a better chance of survival.

I was thankful that Ahran didn't push me any further about how I felt and we settled into what was a more highly charged silence, there was so much more to say, but neither of us broached the subject over the next 12 hours.

Ahran's phone had charged and after several attempts of trying to connect I was able to get through to the hospital back home to find out how Audrey was doing. She had gained consciousness and was on morphine to help her cope with the pain. She was asleep when I phoned and was unable to speak to her. I would have done anything to have heard her calm reassuring voice. Her doctor told me that her stroke hadn't been too serious, but she would require some fairly intensive physio to help her overcome the reduced mobility on her left side. I was overwhelmed with relief that there had been no lasting damage.

We stopped twice en route and as we traversed the Ramian landscape, Ahran and I talked about things on more neutral territory. From time to time, I couldn't help but notice the tension in his jaw. He had laid his cards out on the table, shouldn't I be thrilled? If only I could allow myself the luxury of what I wanted to feel. What chance of happiness did we have when one of us would have to sacrifice everything we held dear? And yet an even more terrifying prospect was allowing Ahran any closer than he already was. As things stood, the chances of my heart coming out of this unscathed were poor.

I laid my head back on the seat and closed my eyes to give my brain a rest. I really needed some time away from him to think, but the situation made that impossible. Eventually, I fell asleep. This time I dreamt Ahran, Toby and Audrey were walking away with their arms linked and laughing over their shoulders at me. I was trying to run towards them with huge superhuman leaps, but the bigger the leap the further they seemed to move away. My heart was pounding and I opened my mouth to scream in desperation, but nothing came out. Perspiration ran down my back from the exertion of jumping and I finally fell into a heap on the floor utterly exhausted and no longer able to see them, all I could hear was Ahran calling my name from a distance.

"Sophie? Sophie!"

I woke with a jolt and opened my eyes to find Ahran leaning towards me gently shaking my shoulder. "You were dreaming."

I rubbed my eyes in an attempt to make them focus. I took a deep breath and stopped myself from flinging my arms around his neck and never letting go.

"Please tell me I have slept for two days and that you

have found Toby," I said, sitting on my hands as an insurance against any impulsiveness on my part.

"I'm sorry, you've only been a sleep a couple of hours and we've arrived at the tavern."

It was late and we were parked outside a pub that wouldn't have looked out of place in the East End of London. It was three stories high at the end of a row of shops and had a rather British-looking pub sign showing a yard of ale swinging above the door.

"This is some kind of joke, right?" I glanced over at Ahran.

He looked slightly apologetic. "There are some people in Ramia who like to try and create a piece of the old world."

"It's like a scene out of Oliver Twist," I snorted.

"I am sure the landlord would be very pleased to hear that he has successfully created an authentic piece of Dickensian London," Ahran added.

"You've heard of Dickens?" I asked in surprise.

Ahran nodded. "We are encouraged to read other-world literature at school. Don't forget we spend much longer at school than you do, we have to fill our time somehow," he explained.

I chuckled. "It just seems so morbidly appropriate. Besides I thought Ramians thought Sapiens were inferior, why would they want to try and emulate them and their world?"

"Earth holds a certain enchantment among Ramians. We know that somehow we are descended from Earth and even though there are many things that are better about Ramia, there are many here who regard Earth as exotic. Especially those who have never visited it."

I had come across this mentality before when I had travelled around Australia on my year out. Some people still considered Britain as home even though they had lived in the southern hemisphere most, if not all, of their lives. It seemed very strange to learn that the same phenomena existed among an alien race in a completely different universe.

"So Ramians are descended from humans on Earth?" I struggled to understand how this could be.

"Yes, but we don't know how or when. It is our world's biggest mystery."

"Blimey!" The origins of the Ramian race hadn't even crossed my mind.

Ahran nodded as if to say, *Strange but true*.

"Come on let's see if Fagin can shed any light on Toby's whereabouts," he said with a wry smile.

20

Inside, the place was lit by an inadequate number of wall lights and most heads turned in our direction as we walked in. I took a cursory glance around. Apart from me, the girl serving behind the bar, and a scantily clad girl half-heartedly winding herself around a pole on a podium at the other end of the bar, the rest of the clientele were male. It was all rather seedy and I felt decidedly self-conscious as at least fifteen pairs of eyes watched us approach the bar. Ahran held my hand and gently pulled me towards him as he addressed the barmaid.

He spoke to her in Ramian. She didn't answer, but nodded her head in the direction of a short and slight, for Ramian standards, middle aged man, with a bushy moustache and shifty eyes at the other end of the bar. Our arrival had not gone unnoticed by him and he made his way over to us. Much to my surprise he spoke in heavily accented English.

"We don't see a human for three years and then two come along in as many days."

Oh my god! Had he seen Toby? My heart began to beat harder. The place was uninviting and hostile and by the way the landlord was eyeing us he wasn't particularly happy to welcome two more newcomers. It was hard to imagine a smile lighting up his face in any situation, but the thought that maybe Toby had been here filled me with hope *and* horror in equal measures.

"Can you describe the human you saw two days ago?" Ahran asked, towering over the man who leant nonchalantly against the bar. He didn't appear in the least bit intimidated by Ahran's size.

"Now why would I do that?" The landlord replied with a sneer. There was something about him that oozed menace.

"Because I am asking you nicely," Ahran said with forced patience.

The landlord snarled something at Ahran in Ramian and started to walk away from us. Before I knew what had happened, Ahran had slammed the man backwards over the bar. He gripped his throat, the tips of his thumb and fingers disappearing into the soft tissue below the man's jaw. Ahran's body was coiled with barely contained violence and he was speaking to the landlord in a low, threatening voice. It turned out that Ahran was more than a match in the menace stakes as he held the disagreeable little pit-bull against the bar. The landlord struggled for breath, his face getting redder and redder. I nervously looked around to see if anyone was about to leap to his rescue, but everyone had suddenly begun to mind their own business, carrying on with their conversations as if Ahran and the landlord were invisible. The barmaid glanced over disinterestedly as she dried a glass and I gave her a weak apologetic smile. She didn't respond and just carried on with what she was doing. How often had she witnessed something like this? Come to think of it, how often had anyone here witnessed a scene like this? I marvelled at how Ramians could think that humans were primitive and inferior. This place was unsophisticated and intimidating and they were clearly used to violence. They were no more evolved than some of the low-lifes on Earth.

Just as I was beginning to think that Ahran's hand had been around the landlord's neck for just a bit too long, he straightened and released him. The landlord made an attempt to look unruffled, but he was visibly shaken, his shifty eyes scanning the bar to see if anyone had noticed the humiliating exchange. He eyed Ahran with thinly veiled contempt although there was a hint of wary deference that hadn't been there before.

He snapped at the barmaid and she disappeared out the back.

Ahran took my elbow and steered me towards an empty table in the corner.

Once we were sat down, I leant towards him. "What did you say to him?" I whispered.

"I explained that we wanted to find out where Toby's kidnappers may have taken him and made it clear that if he prevented us from making our enquiries then I would make sure he'd be in no condition to run a business."

I got the impression that Ahran was being less graphic

than he had been with the landlord. I'd had glimpses of this side of Ahran and they were so at odds with what I knew of him.

"Why are we sitting here?"

"He has sent for one of the girls who spent the evening with Bazeera's men whilst they stayed here."

"This place is a *brothel*?" I squeaked

"Not strictly, but if any of the clientele require *female company*," he said delicately, "Then the landlord can arrange it."

"Bloody hell! Toby spent the night in a *brothel?*" I hissed. "Jesus Ahran! I thought Ramia was supposed to be some kind of Utopia, but not only are your people capable of kidnapping an innocent child, they don't think twice about bringing him to a place like *this*." The thought of Toby spending the night here made my blood run cold.

"I didn't say all Ramians were perfect, some are just as open to criminal activity and depravity as Sapiens are."

"Huh!" I looked away in disgust. The thought that Toby, through no fault of his own, was tangled up in this mess made me feel sick to my stomach.

A tired looking brunette, who looked to be in her late thirties, dressed in a short denim skirt and tight fitting t-shirt approached our table. Ahran stood up and pulled out a chair. The woman looked at him in surprise. Was she so unused to a man showing her any manners? She gave him a genuine smile which made her look ten years younger. She sat down and folded her hands in her lap. I immediately felt sorry for her. What kind of life did she have here?

Ahran spoke to her in Ramian and she nodded.

"Please speak in English then so that this lady can understand what you are saying."

"Did you see the human boy that was with the two men you…" he paused, trying not to offend her, "*Entertained* the other night?" Ahran asked.

"Yes, he sit over there," she said in broken English and pointed to a table that was at the opposite end of the bar to the dancing podium. I was thankful for small mercies.

"Did he look okay?" I interjected, wanting to feel some shred of hope that he was alright.

She shrugged. She said something to Ahran in Ramian and he translated for me.

Ahran hesitated. "She said he looked pale and tired."

I put my hand to my mouth to stifle a sob.

"Did he go with her and the men upstairs?" I asked falteringly.

"No!" The woman spat, clearly offended.

She leant towards me. "I do not *choose* this," she said gesturing around her, "But my children, they have to eat." Her eyes bored into me.

I regretted questioning her judgement. "I'm sorry. It's just that little boy you saw is the only family I have," I said.

"*This* is no place for children," she said, as if it was my fault Toby had been here.

"Did either of the men mention where they were going?" Ahran asked, breaking the tension.

Her eyes darted over to the landlord who was now behind the bar serving somebody, before bringing her attention back to Ahran. She sat back and folded her arms across her chest. Whatever she knew she wasn't telling us anymore.

Ahran reached into his pocket and pulled out his wallet. He laid a token, Ramian money, on the table in front of her and she quickly picked it up, but not before darting another look to her boss to check he wasn't watching. He was talking to one of the punters sitting at the bar and had seemingly forgotten we were still here. I didn't blame her; this poor woman was trapped in this dreadful place and she clearly needed all the money she could get.

She spoke quickly and quietly in Ramian.

"She says that they didn't say much, one of the men used his cell phone a couple of times and she heard him mention, 'the Island'," Ahran said, acting as interpreter.

"Do you know what island they were talking about?" I asked the woman.

She shook her head.

"Thank you, you have been very helpful." Ahran surreptitiously handed her another token.

"I hope you find the boy," she said, standing up and looking at me with pity in her eyes.

I gave her a shaky smile. She made her way back to the bar and sat on a stool. The landlord spoke to her and she nodded at whatever he had said. They both turned in our direction.

"Come on, let's get out of here," Ahran said, standing up.

I was more than happy to do as he suggested and he guided me back through the bar with his hand at the small of my back. Out of the corner of my eye I could see the landlord scowling at us. I half expected a mob of thugs waiting for us outside, but the street was quiet.

"Do you think they've taken Toby to this island she mentioned?" I asked as soon as we were inside the car.

"It would seem likely."

"Do you know where it is?"

To my dismay, Ahran shook his head. "No, but I know someone who might," he said. "I have a friend who lives not too far from here. We used to work together. If anyone knows anything about a mysterious island belonging to Bazeera, he will."

"Can we go there tonight?" I asked hopefully.

"It's late, I think we should find somewhere to stay and go there tomorrow," he replied.

I couldn't help feeling disappointed that I would have to wait until the morning before we could follow our latest lead.

"Did you see anywhere where we could stay?" I asked.

"We passed a large hotel about four kilometres back, we might be able to get a room there," he replied.

"That's good," I said, stifling a yawn.

We drove to the hotel and parked in the car park out the back. It must have been one or two in the morning and I was doubtful we would get a room at this time of night, but the young, and remarkably cheerful, lad at the night desk informed us that they had one double left. We checked in and headed up to our room which turned out to be a little tired looking, but comfortable and clean. My heart skipped a beat as I eyed the double bed. In spite of my tiredness, I knew I wouldn't be able to resist Ahran if he came near me. I yearned for the quiet and calm reassurance of his arms.

I quickly showered and cleaned my teeth and in under ten minutes I was crawling into bed. The sheets smelt fresh and homely. I closed my eyes, my heart pounding as I waited for Ahran to shower, but when he came out of the bathroom, he didn't get into bed. Instead, he went to the wardrobe and pulled out some bedding. It was clear he was about to make a bed up on the floor.

I couldn't let him give up a night in a comfortable bed especially after having driven almost non-stop since this morning. "You don't have to sleep on the floor," I said, sitting up and feeling not a little bit rejected.

"I think it's better for both of us if I do," he said as he laid the blanket and pillow on the floor at the bottom of the bed. His hair was wet and he was just wearing his boxers. My hands itched to touch him.

"We are both exhausted and need a good night's sleep," I argued, suddenly panicked by the thought that I wouldn't be spending the night in his arms.

"I'll get more sleep on the floor."

His words stung.

"Oh, okay," I said, trying to keep the hurt from my voice. I knew he needed to rest, but the thought that he didn't actually *want* to share a bed hadn't occurred to me. He'd had a day to reconsider his feelings, maybe he'd realised that not only did he not want to be with Talina, but I wasn't what he wanted either.

"Try and get some sleep," he said as he settled down into his makeshift bed.

I could feel tears stinging my eyes. He had obviously realised that our situation was hopeless. I reached over and switched off the lamp.

"Night Ahran," I said in a small voice.

"Night Sophie."

I lay on my back staring into the darkness as tears slid silently down my cheeks. I missed Toby so much and after this evening feared for his safety even more, but I was also terrified that as a result of my stupid insecurities I had lost Ahran for good.

I CAME TO WITH A JOLT. One minute I had been fast asleep on the floor wrapped in Ahran's warm arms and the next minute I was lying there cold and alone, squinting in the darkened room wondering where he had gone.

"Ahran?" I sat up my eyes searching for him.

I struggled to make sense of the situation. At what point had I got into bed with him? And why was he aiming a gun at the door? He turned towards me and put a forefinger to his lips, silently warning me to keep quiet.

A tap came from the other side. In the blink of an eye he pulled the door open and pointed the gun at the head of the person standing in the doorway. I squeezed my eyes tight shut expecting to hear the dull thud of the stun gun.

"Elaya!" he exclaimed.

My eyes sprang open.

"Hello brother, do you always greet your guests looking like that?" Elaya's husky voice drifted through the open door. All I could see was Ahran's semi-naked body silhou-etted by the light coming from the hall.

"I, er...come in," he said grabbing his jeans. Elaya came into the room and shut the door behind her. Once he was more decent he hugged his sister.

My relief at seeing Elaya and not one of Bazeera's trained killers turned to acute embarrassment when I real-ized what it must have looked like to her. I was also scantily dressed, sitting on the floor in a makeshift bed. I pulled the blanket up to my chin self-consciously. "It's not what it looks like," I blurted out in my embarrassment.

Elaya arched an eyebrow and looked at her brother. Why did I have to go and say something like that? I not only looked guilty, I sounded guilty. If I had kept my mouth shut we could have got away with it looking like I had slept on the floor and Ahran had slept in the bed. "Excuse me a minute," I said, fumbling for my clothes before dashing into the bathroom.

I couldn't remember getting into bed with Ahran. I had obviously gone to him in my sleep when my conscience couldn't argue. And now Elaya had all but walked in on us. It was just too embarrassing for words. I quickly got dressed and wondered how she had found us. I hesitated before re-joining them, it was no good hiding out in the bathroom. I took a deep breath and went back into the bedroom.

Ahran had opened the curtains and was sat on the bed with his long legs stretched out in front of him, crossed at the ankles. He was fully dressed now in jeans and a t-shirt. Elaya looked incredible even after her ordeal at Toby's school. She wore a skin tight black roll neck sweater and a pair of tight fitting black jeans that clung to her angular yet womanly figure, she reminded me of a spiky haired Catwoman. Ahran and his family really were spectacular looking.

She came towards me and gave me a brief hug. "Ahran tells me you've had a difficult time."

"Yes, it's not been easy," I replied.

"I'm just pleased you are both okay." She turned back to Ahran. "I knew you were still on the move because of the tracking device in your phone, but for some reason I couldn't get through to you." She seemed to be ignoring the fact that she had just found me and her brother in bed together. I silently thanked her for not saying anything.

"My phone seems to be working intermittently. It was in my back pocket when we jumped off the train."

Elaya raised her eyebrows, but didn't question us as to why we had jumped off a train. Clearly this sort of thing didn't come as much of a surprise to her.

"Shouldn't you still be at home recovering?" I asked.

"What and miss all the fun?"

Now that I was over my initial awkwardness I was pleased to see her, it was good to see a friendly face. "I can't tell you how sorry I am about what happened to you." I felt the need to apologise, she had already suffered enough for me and Toby.

"I've faced worse."

She emanated a vitality that didn't make me doubt her resilience.

"Has there been any further intelligence on the kidnapper's movements?" she asked, directing her question to

Ahran. She had switched from caring sister to professional agent in the blink of an eye.

"We found out last night that Bazeera's men may have taken Toby to some island."

Elaya nodded absorbing this information. "Do you know where that might be?" she asked.

Ahran shook his head. "No, but I think Galius Vanhallen might?"

Elaya sat down on the chair in the corner of the room and I sat on the bed a few feet away from Ahran.

"Have you spoken to him?" she asked.

"I've left a message, but he doesn't live far from here," Ahran replied.

"Galius lives in Morana?" she asked, her voice full of surprise.

"Yes, he married a Moranian girl."

Elaya's eyebrows shot up. "Galius is *married?!*"

Ahran smiled. "Married, has a child, runs his own horse stud."

Elaya laughed. "The mighty Galius tamed by a woman, I never thought I'd see the day," she said, shaking her head in disbelief.

It was a breath of normalcy to watch the easy exchange between Ahran and his sister.

"How did you get here so quickly?" I asked. "It has taken us forever to get to this place."

"I flew and then got the train," she replied.

"You weren't followed?" I asked thinking back to our scrapes with Bazeera's men and *woman* on our way here.

"No, it's easier to blend in on your own." I struggled to

believe that Elaya *blended in* anywhere, however she had just confirmed my fears that Ahran would have been much better off without me.

"Is there any chance of getting some breakfast? I am starving," Elaya said, looking at her watch. "I've been travelling all night."

"Yes, let's get some breakfast here before we set off, they start serving at six thirty, it must be nearly that now," Ahran said.

"Its six forty and breakfast is served," Elaya said, standing up.

Ahran put his boots on and I stole a look at him as I bent down to put mine on. He caught my eye and winked. It was an insanely intimate gesture and my heart lurched hopefully.

We walked along the corridor and down into the reception area. Ahran slipped his arm around me possessively which didn't go unnoticed by Elaya. My self-preservation button had failed and it was all I could do to stop myself from melting into his side. I hadn't a clue where we stood, but I was relieved to feel the warmth of his arm against my back. I was done fighting my feelings for him, even if they were about to lead me into a lifetime of misery. All I could do now was take what I could get and deal with the fallout when this was all over.

We entered the restaurant and were ushered to our table by a young girl who bore a striking resemblance to the boy on reception last night. A couple of the other tables were occupied and there were hushed conversations as people ate their breakfast.

We sat down and the girl brought us some coffee before

taking our breakfast order. I was desperate for a proper cup of tea, but settled for the coffee, I didn't fancy the spicy, sickly offering I'd had at the palace. Ahran's phone rang, it rang off and then rang again. He looked at the caller display. "I am just going to take this outside," he said, answering the call.

He spoke in Ramian as he walked away from us. I wondered why he felt the need to take it outside and then felt a stab of jealousy at the prospect of it being Talina. I watched him leave the restaurant.

"I see that you and my brother have become …*close*," Elaya said, not wasting any time.

I knew I wouldn't be able to avoid this conversation for much longer and it was pointless lying to her.

"Um, sort of." I found it difficult to meet her eyes. I wasn't sure how to answer her because I wasn't sure of the answer myself.

"I can see that he cares for you by the way he looks at you."

Her words were dangerously reassuring.

"I care about him too," I admitted.

She looked at me suspiciously, the way a protective sister would. She hesitated before she said what she was about to say. "I've never thought Talina was a good match."

This was music to my ears.

"But I'm going to warn you for my brother's sake," she said, all signs of female solidarity vanishing.

21

"As much as I believe Talina and my brother are wrong for one another it would bring great dishonour to our family if Ahran was to break his engagement," Elaya warned. "He is a first born male with great status in our society and my parents would have thought long and hard about making the right match for him."

"But he doesn't love her," I said, sounding like a sulky child.

Elaya gave a humourless laugh. "Unfortunately for him, due to his sex and birth order, marriage for love doesn't come into it."

I could feel hot tears beginning to form. Elaya had confirmed what I already feared, Ahran and I were doomed.

"It is firmly believed in our culture that once the right match has been made, a strong, loving relationship will develop in time. It could happen between Talina and Ahran," Elaya said.

I baulked at the thought of Ahran and Talina being in love.

"What would happen if Ahran broke his engagement?" I didn't let on that he had already pretty much done this.

"He would lose his inheritance, his title and bring shame on our family."

Ahran had been economical with the truth. If he chose to be with me he would lose everything.

Elaya put her hand over mine and gave it a squeeze. "I am sorry to upset you. I like you Sophie, and I wish that our society worked differently, but I love my brother and I want you to understand that the cost to him would be great if he chose to have a future with you."

I didn't blame Elaya for telling me this. I understood what it was like to feel fiercely protective of your sibling. I would have done the same for my sister.

Suddenly, something occurred to me. "Surely Tagan was betrothed to a woman, has he not brought shame on his family for having an illegitimate child?"

Elaya slowly shook her head. "It's amazing what is forgiven when your beloved son and heir dies," she said with a wry smile. "I'm afraid that if Toby had been a girl there would be little interest in the child and Halsan's throne would pass to the next in line."

"Who would that be?"

"Technically, our uncle, but he has shown little appetite for the throne, so it would be Ahran."

Jeez, if it wasn't for Toby, Ahran could become king one day. Ahran had never shown any bitterness towards Toby, in fact quite the opposite, he was putting his life on the line to find him.

"But Toby is not a full-blooded Ramian, so can't the throne be passed to Ahran anyway?" I was clutching at straws. I thought I had found a flaw in Halsan's plan that would provide me with the loophole I needed to get Toby and me out of this madness and allow us to get on with our normal, earthly lives no matter what the collateral damage to my own heart was.

"Toby is still Tagan's son and a male heir to continue the Halsan bloodline," Elaya explained.

"I thought your people were so advanced, but the more I find out about your society the more archaic it sounds," I said angrily. "I wish I'd never heard of Ramia."

"I understand your anger," Elaya said sympathetically. "Your world has been turned upside down, but Halsan is a powerful and determined man and now that he has a direct heir, he won't give up."

I looked across at her, my tears spilling onto my cheeks at the hopelessness of it all.

"My advice to you is to accept the situation with your nephew and walk away from Ahran." Her words made my chest feel tight. "If it is any consolation I understand what it's like to love a man you shouldn't love," she said.

I hadn't said I was in love with Ahran. Was it that obvious? "What am I going to do?" I said, feeling a renewed sense of hopelessness.

"I'm sorry. I just want you to know what is at stake."

"Would Ahran lose his farm if he chose to be with me?"

Maybe if he was able to keep his farm I might still have a chance.

"If my father has helped him financially, then yes."

Ahran was making his way back to our table and Elaya and I brought our conversation to an abrupt halt.

"I am sorry to have taken so long. I've spoken to the King and given him an update." His voice trailed off.

"What's wrong?" Ahran looked from me to Elaya.

"Nothing, we were just talking girl talk," I said, quickly rearranging my expression.

As if I didn't already know that Ahran and I were doomed, Elaya's bombshell had thrown cold water over any burning embers of hope. It hadn't even occurred to me that Ahran's father might have a stake in his farm. After everything I had heard about him I was beginning to detest the man. I also felt angry at Ahran for not being totally honest with me. I couldn't stand by and allow him to make the sacrifices he would have to make if he wanted to be with me. I should have stuck to my original plan to bury my feelings, find Toby, and get the hell out of here.

Ahran sat down. "Is there any news?" I asked, changing the subject and quietly congratulating myself for walling up my feelings so quickly.

"No, nothing about Toby, but I've spoken to Galius and he's happy for us to visit."

I smiled the most genuine smile I could muster. At least we were a step closer to finding Toby.

Ahran took hold of my hand. Little did I know that whilst I had been sitting there I had gathered a handful of the tablecloth in my fist.

"Are you sure you are okay?" he asked, his eyes searching mine.

"I'm fine, just feeling a bit anxious." I wasn't going to tell him about the conversation with Elaya. It was better that I made a clean break.

Our breakfasts arrived and both Elaya and Ahran devoured theirs. I struggled to eat mine. It was as much as I could do to swallow a couple of mouthfuls. I sipped the strong coffee which just made me feel sicker than I already felt. I barely heard the conversation Ahran and Elaya had.

When we finished Ahran paid the bill.

"You've hardly eaten anything Sophie." Ahran pointed to the breakfast I had barely touched.

"I'm not hungry," I said, brushing it off.

He failed to look convinced and pulled me close to him as we left the restaurant.

Ahran and Elaya took it in turns to drive. They conversed in Ramian and English, but I wasn't really listening. From time to time, I rubbed my temples in an attempt to soothe my pounding headache. Where was this island? When I tried to imagine where they might be holding Toby all I could come up with was an Indiana Jones-style fortress surrounded by a crocodile infested swamp. I closed my eyes hoping that the journey might pass more quickly if I was asleep. But as soon as I closed my eyes my mind flooded with images of Ahran and Toby being shot at. Getting onto the island was one thing, but getting out alive was another. Waves of nausea started to wash over me. I tried to take some deep breaths in the hope that it would subside, but the waves were getting stronger and I was struggling to breathe.

"Elaya could you please pull over?" I asked shakily.

Ahran turned around. "Sophie, are you alright?

"Can you please just stop the car?"

As soon as the car came to a halt, I scrambled out and brought up my coffee and what I had eaten of my breakfast onto the side of the road.

Ahran stood by my side and stroked my hair.

I wretched and coughed until my stomach was empty. Finally, I was able to take a couple of steadying breaths.

"I'm sorry, I think I'm just a bit car sick," I croaked.

Elaya handed me a bottle of water and I took a few sips. Ahran stooped down to pick me up, worry etched into his face, but I put my hand on his chest to stop him.

"No, it's fine. I'm okay, really."

I no longer felt sick, but my head was throbbing.

"You hardly ate anything at breakfast, you need some food inside you," Ahran said disapprovingly. "We'll stop somewhere and get you something to eat."

The thought of food made my stomach churn, but I had to pull myself together, Ahran would know something was wrong and I had to make him believe that I was okay. I didn't want him to worry about me as well as finding Toby.

We drove for another twenty minutes before we came across a village. Ahran went into one of the shops and came out with some warm pastries. I managed to force half of one down under his watchful eye. He drove the remaining leg and I eventually got some sleep. We arrived at Galius's by early evening.

The approach to the house was down a long gravel drive flanked by white fenced paddocks. We pulled up outside an impressive farmhouse with shutters at the windows. I assumed it was Galius waiting at the front door for us and he took the wide front steps, two at a time down to us.

The man was huge.

Not only was he tall, but he was broad and muscular. His black hair was shoulder length and wavy. His forehead, cheeks and chin were well-defined, and he had a long noble nose. He reminded me of a Roman gladiator, but instead of leather combat gear, he wore a faded pair of jeans, a wide leather belt and a blue checked shirt with the sleeves rolled up to the elbows showing forearms that would have made a champion body builder weep.

Ahran got out of the car and he and Galius embraced, giving each other a firm clap on the back. Elaya and I joined the two men on the drive. Ahran was almost as tall as Galius, but he wasn't quite the man mountain that Galius was, he was much more athletic in comparison.

"You know my sister of course," Ahran said, switching to English as he introduced Elaya.

"As beautiful as ever, Elaya," Galius said, complimenting her and kissing her hand with an exaggerated flourish just like an other world d'Artagnan.

"Galius, good to see you," she replied, batting his compliment to the side. In spite of her measured greeting her face lit up. She was obviously pleased to see him.

"Married yet?"

She shook her head.

"What's wrong with the men in Dinara? I'd marry you tomorrow if Salara hadn't already made an honest man out of me."

"That's the problem, I've not met anyone who measures up to you Galius," Elaya said playfully.

Galius threw his head back and laughed loudly. "When you've met the best, forget the rest," he said with an arrogant arch of his eyebrow, the humour evident on his face.

"Galius, this is Sophie, Toby's aunt," Ahran said, introducing me. "Sophie, Lieutenant Galius Vanhallen."

I could feel myself blush as he gave me the once over before dipping his head in a reverent bow that was more respectful than his initial appraisal of me.

"It's nice to meet you Sophie. I trust Ahran has been looking after you during your time in Ramia?" I wasn't sure if there was a double meaning to his words, but his expression was innocent when he straightened. I wondered whether Ahran had said anything to him about me. Just at that moment Ahran snaked his arm around my waist as if he wanted there to be little doubt about the status of our relationship.

"It's good to meet you too," I said politely with my hand outstretched, seizing the opportunity to move away from Ahran's encircling arm. It was so much easier to resist him when we weren't touching.

Galius shook my hand firmly in his large, work-roughened hand.

"It's a beautiful place you have here," I remarked, my gaze sweeping over the surrounding landscape. To add to the idyllic picture before me a mare and foal grazed idly in the paddock next to the house.

His face shone with pride.

"Thanks. Us army boys don't make bad farmers do we Ahran?" he said, giving him a wink.

At that moment, a little dark haired boy, who couldn't have been more than three, came running out of the house in his pyjamas shrieking and babbling. We all turned to watch him running down the steps with his mother following closely behind. Galius bent down and swept the boy up onto his shoulders. It was a long way up.

"This is my son Raffy," he said proudly.

"He's the image of you," Elaya remarked. She was absolutely right, the little boy had dark wavy hair and big brown eyes to die for. He was a miniature Galius.

Raffy chirped something at us and everyone laughed. Galius's wife came and stood by her husband. She was tall and bigger built than Elaya with long dark hair cascading in waves down her back. She was very striking. She gave us all a warm smile and kissed Ahran and Elaya on both cheeks.

"This is my wife Salara, I am afraid she doesn't speak English," Galius said.

She leant forward and kissed me too.

"Hello," she said in a heavy accent.

"Graatcha," I replied, using the equivalent word in Ramian.

Both Ahran and Elaya raised their eyebrows at me.

I grinned at them both. "Don't get too excited. It's one of the only words I've picked up since I've been here. Your language is impossible!"

They both smiled.

"Graatcha," Salara replied, beaming at me. When she

smiled like that I could see how she had attracted the mighty Galius.

"Let us go inside. Salara has made dinner, she is an excellent cook." Galius looked at his wife adoringly and I could tell that in spite of his flirty behaviour he was smitten with his wife. I couldn't help feel a pang of jealousy. Some people had all the luck.

ONCE SALARA HAD PUT little Raffy to bed she joined us in the kitchen and Galius poured us all a glass of wine.

The conversation was a mixture of Ramian and English so neither myself nor Salara felt left out. When they were all speaking Ramian, I took the opportunity to take in my surroundings. It was a huge rectangular kitchen with a modern looking range at one end. The oak table we were sitting at dominated the room. The wall down one side was lined with units below a window with a view out onto the drive. The opposite wall was made of glass and looked out onto a large patio area, swimming pool and the fields beyond, most of which had grazing horses in them.

Galius caught me looking out the window. "It will be too dark to show you all around once we've eaten. Perhaps Salara can give you the grand tour tomorrow Sophie?" he suggested. "I'll have to show you folks around another time," he said, turning to Elaya and Ahran.

"I'd really like to see what you've got here," Ahran said with genuine enthusiasm.

"You and Elaya are going to the Island?" I asked,

directing my question at Ahran. What Galius had said surprised me. For some reason I had assumed Ahran would be going alone.

"Yes, and Galius is coming too."

I glanced at Salara and caught her uneasy expression. I had been oblivious to their conversation, but she of course had understood every word. As much as I could have thrown my arms around them all for joining in the search for Toby, my heart sank at the thought of all their lives being at risk. "When will you be leaving?"

"We'll set off later tonight," Ahran replied quietly.

I knew there was little point in trying to persuade him to take me with them. Toby couldn't have had a better rescue party, but I felt decidedly uncomfortable that Galius was about to put himself in great danger without even knowing who Toby was. I couldn't look Salara in the eye.

"You'll be safe Sophie, nobody knows you are here and Salara will take good care of you," Galius said.

He had misunderstood my troubled expression. He must have thought a great deal of Ahran to leave his family on such a dangerous mission and it gave me a renewed respect for Salara. She had been warm and welcoming and yet had every reason to blame me for her husband risking his life. "Is it necessary that Galius goes?" I asked, hoping they might reconsider. I already had enough people to worry about.

"I know the jungle well. I spent a long time staking out the area once," Galius answered. "I can lead Elaya and Ahran there quicker than they would be able to find it on their own."

It was obviously a done deal. "I don't know how to thank you," I said, my expression of gratitude sounding woefully inadequate.

"I just know how I would feel if someone had taken Raffy." An uncomfortable expression flickered across Galius' face. "I can't stand by and let Bazeera get away with what she has done. She is feared by many here and is capable of great cruelty. It would be a satisfying victory if we are successful."

I understood his motivation even though I didn't like his use of the word *if*. "And you have to leave tonight?" The thought of them traipsing through a dark jungle did not sit comfortably with me.

"It is better that we make our way to the island during the night," Ahran replied.

"The edge of the jungle is only about half an hour's drive from here and we need to make the most of the cover of darkness," Galius explained. Any further enquiries on my part were cut short by Salara, who was ready to serve our meal.

The conversation over dinner was about Galius' business, but it wasn't long before Elaya and Ahran started to discuss tactics. I helped Salara do the washing up. Once we had finished she quickly made her excuses to leave and went outside to tend to the horses for the night. I got the distinct impression she didn't want to hang around to hear the finer details of their rescue mission. I stayed, sipping my wine, ignorant of their plan.

When we had finished our drinks, Galius showed me to a homely living room with enormous soft cushioned sofas.

"We need to go and see to a few things, will you be alright here?" Ahran asked. He touched my cheek and I briefly closed my eyes in response. My chest constricted. The more he touched me the more I craved his touch.

"I'll be fine," I said unconvincingly. He tenderly kissed my forehead and hesitated before turning around to join the others.

I slumped on the sofa, closed my eyes and laid my head back on the cushions. I felt a dizzying tangle of emotions; relief and terror for Toby's sake; fear for the safety of Ahran, Elaya and Galius; guilt for bringing this to Salara and her family; hatred for Bazeera who was responsible for putting us all in this situation and at complete loss as to how I was going to get through the rest of my life without Ahran.

So much had happened in the last week. My life was no longer safe and familiar. I was no longer sure of anything and my old anxieties about what the future might hold returned with a vengeance. Now there was even more reason to fear what lay ahead, I was *in love*. It was a bitter-sweet realisation. I turned my head into one of the cushions on the sofa and sobbed.

I don't know how long I had sat there crying, but my tears had mostly subsided when I heard someone enter the room.

It was Salara.

She looked at me sympathetically. I could tell by the puffiness of her eyes she had been crying too and I wanted to put my arms around her and comfort her. Would she blame me for her husband risking his life and push me away? She had every right to. I gave her a weak smile instead. She beckoned me to follow her and took me upstairs to where I would be spending the night.

The room was prettily decorated with a delicately embroidered bedspread. She had laid out a nightdress and a change of clothes for me and there were two neatly folded towels on the chair in the corner of the room. She pointed to the en-suite and turned to leave. I gently grabbed her hand and gave it a squeeze, she looked at me with tears in her eyes. She had been trying to put on a brave face, but my small gesture of sympathy clearly dissolved her fragile composure.

"I am so sorry about all of this," I said, even though I knew she couldn't understand me.

She nodded and smiled and seemed to appreciate my concern. She gave my hand a gentle squeeze back and then left me standing in the middle of the room.

Ahran, Elaya and Galius had been gone for some time and I wondered whether they had left already to avoid a difficult goodbye. I let out a shaky breath and picked up one of the towels before making my way into the bathroom, my tears spilling over once more. I heard the bedroom door open.

I turned around to find Ahran standing there, the expression on his face stopping me in my tracks. He closed the door behind him and I wiped the tears from my eyes. He hesitated, fighting some internal battle that he either won or lost because within four strides his arms were around me, his mouth crushing mine. I responded without thinking. My hands reached up around his neck as I took his mouth as hungrily as he was taking mine. He lifted me up and we fell onto the bed together.

Neither of us said a word as we stripped our clothes off as quickly as we could with our mouths barely parting. I couldn't think. I didn't want to think. All I wanted was Ahran on me, inside me, taking me to a place without fear or pain or misery.

My hands roamed his back, feeling every hard, beautiful muscle. I pressed him to me as I wrapped my legs around him again. I was so desperate for the moment when I would feel him against me, sliding into me, that I thought I might die if I had to wait any longer. I felt his fingers glide between my legs and I arched my back in response pushing myself down onto his hand. Suddenly, he pulled away and I whimpered my disappointment. He couldn't leave me now, my body screamed for him. I opened my eyes and was rewarded by the sight of him rolling protection down his long, hard length. Never had he looked more beautiful.

I parted my legs ready to receive him and our eyes met as he hovered over me. I was so overwhelmed by what I saw there. It was a look of unbridled passion, but tinged with pain and regret and it made my heart ache. He gently touched his mouth to mine and he slowly entered me. For a heart shattering moment, we lay there neither of us moving, joined in the most intimate way, our hearts beating hard against each other's.

We began to move as one, each stroke becoming more urgent than the last. We were both driven by the desperate need to reach the point where our bodies would become one, and yet I knew that once we got there it would be the end for us. We drove each other to the edge, neither of us able to stop, our breath coming hard and fast.

We climaxed together, crying out simultaneously. Wave after wave pulsed through me, my tears a steady stream soaking into the covers beneath my head. I welcomed the weight of him as he lay on me, his chest heaving with exertion. I imprinted the feel of him into every cell of my body, my hands splaying out on his back, attempting to create maximum surface area through which to absorb him. Every second that passed was a second closer to the moment he would have to leave. It was a soul crushing irony to know that the sooner he was gone, the sooner Toby could be rescued, and the sooner Toby was rescued, the sooner Ahran would be lost to me.

"I will find him and I will bring him back to you and then we can be together," he whispered against my lips.

I kissed him for the last time, my lips saying goodbye and a part of me dying as he pulled away. I rolled over and buried my head in the pillow. I knew if I watched him walk out the door my heart would tear right out of my chest.

I'm not sure how long I laid there. The most incredible physical experience I had ever known with a man was completely overshadowed by the pain and sense of loss I was feeling knowing that we didn't stand a chance together. I knew that as powerful as my feelings were for him and the connection we undoubtedly had were not enough to span the thousands of light years that were between our two worlds. It wasn't the first time I had almost laughed at myself. Only *I* could fall in a love with a superhuman alien who lived a million miles away. But putting aside all the characteristics of Ahran that set him apart from ordinary men, there was nothing about our situation that gave us a chance of any kind of future together. If we chose each other, it would mean losing everything and everyone we knew and everything we had worked for. I couldn't ask him to make that sacrifice and I couldn't give up what I had struggled to achieve particularly in the year since Katie's death. I had come so far.

So, as the sharp knife of hopelessness edged closer to my heart, I knew we were over before we had really begun. It had been a careless fantasy. All I could do now was focus on Toby. He had the best rescue party and I could only hope that I hadn't lost him too.

TAGAN'S CHANGE
Book 2

1

I woke with a start, my heart pounding in my ears. "Ahran," I whispered, struggling to make sense of where I was. Had something woken me or had I been dreaming? I strained my ears, feeling sure that I'd heard something, but the house was quiet. Taking a deep breath, I laid back down. It must have been a dream. Feeling edgy I turned over and pulled the bedspread up under my chin. I felt a wave of misery, followed by hopelessness riding on a tide of loss. It was the middle of the night and I was lying in bed in Galius and Salara's guest room, the same bed Ahran and I had made urgent and soul-crushing love in. The same bed in which I realised Ahran and I could never be together. It had been a whirlwind love affair that had never really gathered any momentum, like a novel half written with an ending that was never to be. I felt desperately sorry for myself as my tears began to swell and run down my cheeks.

Why did my chest feel like it was under the heel of some giant torturer? How was emotion able to cause such physical hurt? I took a shaky breath disappointed with myself for getting so involved in such a short period of time. Surely life had taught me something over the twenty-six years I had lived it. Don't get too close, don't let anyone get too close, don't care too much, and most certainly do not fall in love. It was like my own little personal curse, loving something only ended in tears.

There it was again. A noise, a hollow thud. Were they back? Had they rescued Toby? Were they celebrating and had forgotten to wake me up?

This time a loud crash and the sound of glass breaking.

I sat bolt upright, adrenaline pumping furiously through my veins. These weren't the sounds of a jubilant rescue party. Something was wrong. I wiped my eyes, all self-pitying thoughts dissolving as my adrenaline increased. I felt for the nightdress Salara had given me, slipped it over my head and jumped out of bed. I frantically searched for my stun gun in the dark, if my instincts were correct, I needed something to defend myself with. I felt across the surface of the chest of drawers next to the bed, but it was nowhere to be found and then I remembered, I'd left it in the car. I cursed myself for being so careless. More crashes came from downstairs.

Not daring to switch the light on, I continued to search in the darkness for something that would serve as a weapon. I could almost taste the blood in my mouth as it surged around my body and rang in my ears. My fingers fumbled across a marble based lamp on the dressing table. I picked it up and wrenched it from the wall holding it upside down like a club. I turned the handle of the bedroom door. I hadn't forged a plan, who knew what I faced? But there was no way I was staying up here waiting to find out. If Salara was in trouble, she needed help.

I gingerly stepped out of my room. The light from the kitchen was shining up the stairs, but the house was silent once again. I started to tiptoe across the landing when a hand whipped out of nowhere and clamped itself across my mouth stifling my scream. I struggled to break free, whilst another hand grabbed my waist pinning me to an unrelenting male body. He growled in my ear and I swung the lamp backwards, it barely made contact before it fell out of my hands and hit the floor with a heavy thud. Desperately trying to work out my next move, I struggled against the hands that were holding me so tightly I could barely breathe.

My captor lifted me by the waist and carried me downstairs whilst I clawed at the hand covering my mouth. I thrashed as much as I could, my bare heel even made contact with his shin a couple of times, but to little effect. His hand shifted away from my mouth to take a better hold of my writhing form. "Get off me you bastard!" I gasped as we entered the kitchen. He hitched me up his body and I managed a backward kick, this time my heel making perfect contact with his groin. He cried out, momentarily loosening his grip and I broke free. I scrambled around the table, frantically scanning the room for something I could use as a weapon.

I caught sight of Salara lying motionless on the kitchen floor and it made me feel sick. Her eyes were closed and there was blood trickling from a large cut on her forehead. I thought of Galius who was currently trying to rescue my nephew whilst his wife lay bleeding on his kitchen floor, and after what must have been a momentous struggle, judging by the state of the place. *Oh god, please let her be alright!* I could feel the rage welling up inside me. How dare someone do this to her?!

I lurched towards the knives that were in a wooden block on the kitchen surface and grabbed the handle of one of them, pulling it free from its sheath. It was a long, sharp carving knife. I swung around to my abductor who was circumnavigating the table to get to me, his heavy build and lack of athleticism playing to my advantage. I growled at him like a thing possessed. I definitely wasn't going down without a fight.

He came towards me menacingly and I lunged towards him with the knife in my hand. I took a couple of swipes and he leant back dodging the first, but I caught him with the second, the edge of the blade slicing across his cheek. Blood sprang to the surface and oozed satisfyingly down his cheek. The shock of what I had just done paralysed him for a moment and he touched the side of his face in disbelief. I seized my chance. I threw myself at him, putting my whole body weight behind the knife and plunged the eight-inch knife into his stomach.

He staggered backwards with the handle sticking out of his abdomen. A look of surprise plastered across his face.

"Die, you asshole!" I yelled, shaking with anger and fear.

Obligingly, he fell to his knees gasping for breath. I froze for a minute wondering whether adrenaline would give him enough momentum to strike again, but he crumpled to the floor.

I barely gave him another thought as I ran over to Salara and knelt down by her still form. I swept a lock of blood-soaked hair away from the wound on her head. "Salara," I called softly. I couldn't tell whether she was dead or alive as my shaking fingers tried to find a pulse in her neck. I sensed movement at the kitchen door behind me and my head snapped around in time to see another intruder in dark clothing pointing a gun at me and in that second the most excruciating jolt hit my body.

THE NEXT THING I knew I was lying on the back seat of a truck bumping along uneven ground. My arms and legs were bound and there was a thick piece of tape across my mouth. My body felt like it had been hit by a juggernaut. It was still dark, but I could just about make out a dark figure in the driver's seat. My mind raced as I tried to piece together what had happened.

Had they killed Salara? And what had happened to Raffy? Was he still asleep in his cot or had they harmed him too? I stifled a whimper. I was pretty sure I had killed one of my attackers and had been stun gunned by the other. I wasn't aware of the searing pain of a wound just an excruciating ache that was causing every muscle in my body to spasm painfully. Judging by the feel of the terrain we were travelling over, I could only guess that we were heading to Bazeera's island.

Had Toby's rescue party actually made it there? And what was my captor's intentions regarding me? Surely, if he had wanted me dead he would have killed me back at the house.

The truck slowed and I shut my eyes pretending to still be unconscious. We came to a halt and I heard the rumble of voices outside. The driver got out and I heard another engine stutter and then roar to life. It sounded like the outboard motor of a boat. We had to be near water and across from the island. The only thing that made me feel any better was that I might get to see Toby.

The door by my head opened and the man pulled me out and threw me over his shoulder. It was all I could do to stop myself from screaming out in pain as my body protested at the sudden movement. There was a nauseating stench of stagnant water and diesel fumes. He carried me onto the boat and threw me roughly onto the bench seat, my head hitting the side of the boat on landing. I let out a muffled cry. No one heard it over the sound of the engine. My vision blurred and I thought I was about to pass out again. The driver opened the throttle and the engine roared as we pulled away from the water's edge.

We moved across the water at speed, every jolt causing me more pain, and after what seemed like an eternity, we reached the other side. The engine died and the boat rocked as one of the men climbed out and secured the boat to the jetty. The other man picked me up and threw me over his shoulder again. He stepped off the boat, carried me up a bank and onto a gravel path leading to an entrance at the side of a building which was lit by spotlights from the ground. I caught a glimpse of creamy coloured sandstone walls as we passed through a doorway into a damp smelling corridor. From my limited vantage point we were inside some kind of castle. My image of an Indiana Jones-style fortress hadn't been too far off the mark. The men's voices echoed as they chatted to each other, it was as if they were carrying out little more than an ordinary shopping delivery. The aching of the aftershock from the stun gun was easing, but my head hurt and my stomach felt bruised against the man's shoulder.

We wound our way along a number of corridors and up two flights of steps until we came to a heavy wooden door. It creaked as one of the men pushed it open. I was expecting a prison cell, but much to my surprise it was a lavishly decorated bedroom. I was thrown unceremoniously onto the bed and I braced myself as my captor leant towards me, thanks to the tape around my wrists there was little I could do in my defence. Fortunately, all he did was rip the tape away from my mouth, causing my skin to burn. I eyed him warily as he pulled out a knife, not daring to move a hair as he sliced through the tape that bound my hands and ankles together. And then without saying a word he turned on his heels and left. I listened to him turning the key in the lock.

I let out a breath as my fear subsided and slowly eased up onto my elbows. My head felt like it was about to explode as I gingerly surveyed the room. It was softly lit and the air was a few degrees warmer than out in the corridor. I was lying on a huge four poster bed draped in heavy, deep red velvet. The bed was flanked by two ornately carved bedside tables with a lamp on each, their shades matching the colour of the luxurious bed covers and drapes. There was an enormous open fireplace with a fire crackling in its hearth and a deep pile rug laid out on the smooth polished stone floor in front of it. Two armchairs had been arranged invitingly around the hearth. There were a couple of large, dark wooden pieces of furniture against two of the walls and in the corner was a huge roll-top free standing bath. I half expected to see steam rising from it. The whole room looked like the honeymoon suite of an expensive Scottish castle and was the complete opposite of what I had been expecting during my uncomfortable journey here. All I hoped was that Toby had been living in similar luxury.

Ok, so now what? As lovely as the room was, it was still my prison. I got up off the bed and winced at the pain that jabbed in my head. I padded over to the windows and rattled the shutters, they were firmly locked. I'm not sure what I thought I could have done because I was pretty sure I was a few stories up. Feeling chilled, I headed over to the fireplace to warm myself and caught sight of my appearance in a large full length mirror that stood next to the dressing table. God I was a mess! My hair looked like a hastily assembled bird's nest and the pretty night dress that Salara had lent me had the rusty smear of blood all down the front. Poor Salara. The thought of Galius finding out his wife had been brutally attacked or worse, *killed* was not one I wanted to dwell on. I prayed she was going to be okay.

I stood by the fire for several minutes staring into the flames and warmed my hands. How long was I going to be kept here? And where was everyone else? Were they safe or were they locked up just like me? No matter in which direction I looked, there really was no way out of this one I thought gloomily. I strained to hear any sound, but there was only silence beyond the crackle of the fire and I could feel my rising panic. *Deep breaths Sophie! Deep breaths!*

I went to the wash basin and splashed water onto my face and washed my hands before drying them with a towel hanging on a rail next to the sink. I pulled my hair into a pony tail with the hairband on my wrist and sat in one of the armchairs, staring into the fire and waited. I tried not to play out all the possible scenarios about what might have happened to Toby's rescue party in my head and desperately hoped they already had Toby and were on their way out of here. I couldn't understand what Bazeera wanted with me, I was nothing to her, but if Toby and Ahran were safe that was all that mattered. It comforted me enormously to know that Toby had a family now who would love and care for him, if indeed, this was the beginning of my own demise.

I wasn't sure how long I had been sitting there when I heard someone unlock the door. I jumped out of the chair my heart racing. It was another of Bazeera's henchmen and I stood my ground as he came towards me. He had a roll of tape in his hand and he gestured for me to turn around. Maybe the news I had killed one of his colleagues had spread and he wasn't taking any chances. I felt a satisfied smile tug at my lips. I had no choice now though, and turned away from him with my hands behind my back. My heart's fast staccato rhythm echoed in my ears as I contemplated where he was taking me. Was this it? Was my time really up?

We walked down a number of corridors and the flagstone floor felt cold under my bare feet. The place was indeed like a large medieval castle and much older than any of the buildings I had seen in Ramia. Finally, we came to a set of large, wooden, heavily studded double doors. My guard pushed one of them open and I stumbled as he pushed me roughly into an enormous room. At one end, two large banners displaying coats of arms hung on the wall, a large banqueting table stood in the middle and to my utter horror, Ahran was bound to one of the chairs around it, his head slumped forward on his chest frighteningly still.

"Ahran!" I shrieked, and tried to break free from the hand that was restraining me. For one heart-stopping moment I thought he was dead.

At the sound of my voice, he slowly lifted his head. It was sweet relief to see him move, but I gasped when I saw his face. His left eye was purple and swollen and there was a nasty gash across his cheek which was encrusted with dried blood. The deep red of fresh bruising was beginning to show itself along his jawline and his mouth was taped. My heart twisted painfully and I pulled against the unrelenting hands holding me.

"What have they done to you?" I cried.

Tagan's Change is available on Amazon now

BOOKS BY AMELIA FORD AND THEIR ORDER:

Coming Soon

Damned and Damaged

For more information about Amelia and her books visit

www.amelia-ford.com

www.facebook.com/AmeliaFordAuthor

Note to Reader

Hopefully you've enjoyed reading Tagan's Child. Please would you take a few moments to review it on Amazon? Many thanks.